MERCILE

The berserker's back was to her. His hands gripped the bars
of the bay's stall as though he would rip them out. Is saw
the muscles standing out on his shoulders, biceps, and
forearms . . .

The berserker spun so quickly Is had no time to move — not
that it would have done her any good. His massive hand
closed on the front of her coat, and he pulled her toward him.
He laughed, revealing large, flat teeth that reminded her of
the horse's . . .

Behind him, the bay whinnied, rearing up and striking the
bars with his hooves. The berserker shoved Is away. Her
feet flew off the ground as if she weighed nothing at all. Her
back slammed against the wall across the aisle from the
stallion's stall, and her head snapped back against the bars.
She crumpled to the ground . . .

The Berserker's Horse

A STUNNING NOVEL OF SCIENCE FICTION BY
Lisa Maxwell

THE
BERSERKER'S
HORSE

LISA MAXWELL

ACE BOOKS, NEW YORK

This book is an Ace original edition,
and has never been previously published.

THE BERSERKER'S HORSE

An Ace Book/published by arrangement with
the author

PRINTING HISTORY
Ace edition/May 1995

ISBN: 0-441-00199-8

ACE®
Ace Books are published by The Berkley Publishing Group,
200 Madison Avenue, New York, NY 10016.
ACE and the "A" design are trademarks
belonging to Charter Communications, Inc.

PRINTED IN THE UNITED STATES OF AMERICA

10 9 8 7 6 5 4 3 2 1

–|–

Yesterday Is had been able to handle the stallion with just a rope attached to the ring of his halter. Today she would need to use a chain wrapped around his sensitive nose in such a way that it would cause considerable pain if the horse pulled against her. By tomorrow pain would not subdue the horse, it would enrage him.

Is watched the horse circle his stall impatiently as she prepared his feed. Suddenly he snaked his neck out, raking the wall with his teeth for no apparent reason. A grim little smile stretched Is's lips. Today she would pour the feed through the slot. Yesterday she had walked into his stall carrying the feed, and the horse had nuzzled her while she scratched his neck. But no more. From here on, her life depended on how well she read the horse. He would kill her if she made a mistake.

While Is was pouring the grain, the stallion attacked. Charging across the stall, he hit the iron bars in front of her face with enough force to rattle them. His flat, yellow teeth were inches away. Is's body jerked as she overrode the reflex to dodge. Those teeth would not rip like canines; they would bruise and crush. The horse was not really biting; he was punching, and a punch like he'd delivered to the bars would knock her to the ground, where his hooves could kill her.

Unable to reach her, the stallion attacked his grain. His hooves hit the wall as he lashed out savagely with both hind legs.

Is had seen the work other war-horses' hooves had done to those specially reinforced walls, tearing out great splinters of wood. She would probably have to replace the inside boards after this horse was gone too.

Three days, at most. Then the berserker would arrive.

She had trained the horse to be a weapon, while others had trained a man. When horse and man met, it would be as though other humans no longer existed. Even now the bond Is had had with the stallion was weakening. By tomorrow he would be a weapon without a master. The next day he would meet the man who was genetically engineered to be his master, and they would have a bond, instantly, that would overshadow the one Is had worked to develop since the horse had been a gangly legged yearling. Jealousy was not appropriate. The tie between horse and berserker was designed into their genes. Is had forged hers with hard work, patience, and talent. It had served its purpose, and now it was time to let go.

She felt the sadness that always wanted to overwhelm her when one of her horses was taken, but from now on there would be no time for emotion. Her life would be on the line every moment she was with the horse. The day the berserker arrived to claim the horse would be the worst. It would demand considerable tact to get a man, nearly as dangerous to her as the horse would have become by then, mounted on that horse and on his way.

From a distance at which she would not disturb the horse, Is watched him eating. His neck arched as he bit into the grain as though it were an enemy. His blood-bay coat rippled over well-developed muscles. His eye, which had looked so intelligent and kind yesterday, was hard and cold today. He struck the bars again, and wet grain splattered from his mouth unheeded.

Is went to feed the rest of the stock and get her own breakfast. Along with the bay stallion, she was training three younger horses. As each one matured, a berserker would come to take it.

Is was not allowed to name any of the horses; she was supposed to remember they were not hers to keep. But the only time she remembered that was when a berserker was coming. So today, while she fed "her" horses, she felt the loss of all of them, although it was only the blood-bay who was going.

She took time over her own breakfast, sitting on the porch of her small house, overlooking the paddocks where the three younger horses grazed, in front of a backdrop of mountains. Is lived alone, here at this final outpost, before the range of mountains they called the Boundary.

When she returned, the bay was more subdued. He came over to see her, ears pricked and eyes interested, and Is felt the old bond that united them, as the horse must be feeling it now. This morning would be the last time. She shoved the thought aside. It would only lead to sadness, and inattention of that sort could get her killed.

She was careful, reaching between the bars and snapping the lead to the horse's halter before she rolled the door open. His ears flicked back at the sound, and his eyes turned hard. Quickly, Is gave the lead a jerk. "Stand."

He stood, ears in neutral, eyes on her, and Is breathed relief. His training was still good this morning. No, she corrected herself. His training was still good for that moment. It could change anytime, or from moment to moment. Anything could set him off. She had not lived this long by being sloppy, but she had not stayed in this line of work by being overcautious either.

She kept well to the side as the stallion came through the door, never presenting herself as a target. His massive shoulders towered over her as she walked beside him.

In the aisle, Is cross-tied him with a rope snapped to either side of his halter, so he could not turn his head far enough to bite her. He would not allow her to groom him, twitching his skin, pinning his ears back, and stamping his hooves. He was a good seventeen hands tall, his legs like pillars and his hooves the size of dinner plates.

Is put the brushes away and brought out the saddle. The stallion stood like a rock while she tightened the girth, and put his head down, yawning his mouth wide to accept the bit, like some kid's pony. She was always thankful he had learned to do this. As big as he was, she would never be able to get his bridle on if he did not cooperate. His head alone was as big as her torso.

Before leading him from the barn, Is put the halter back on over the bridle and attached a long canvas line to it. She would exercise him around her in a circle on the lunge line before she mounted. This would warm up his muscles and get some of the freshness out of him. By tomorrow it would no longer be safe to work him this way. He would attack her if he saw her on the ground. No voice commands, whip, or use of force would stop him.

He moved off on command, trotting with his wonderful swinging gait. His dark, red-bay coat gleamed over fluidly moving muscles as he circled her. He arched his neck, tossing his head now and then with good spirits. The horse seemed to float over the ground, his black mane lifting from his neck, catching the breeze with each stride. His black tail arched from his beautifully muscled rump like a proud flag, the end of it swaying softly in the tempo of his trot, as he circled before a backdrop of autumn-colored ridges and the snowcapped giants of the Boundary.

When she asked him to canter, he bounded into the slow gallop, snorting softly to himself in rhythm with his strides, and she marveled how a creature so massive could be so light on the ground.

She would never tire of watching, and he seemed to delight in his own movement. Is had chosen to exercise him this way so she could see him one more time like this. Sadness threatened her again, but she drove it away. She would not lose these precious moments to outside thoughts.

She called him down to a halt. One moment he was bounding, the next he was standing as still as though he had been there all day, square as a small building.

He allowed her to approach and remove the lunge line, but he showed an edge of impatience, and Is knew better than to take too long or try to fraternize with him. He was the king, allowing her to mount because it suited his purposes. This day she would not delude herself into believing otherwise.

He moved off before she signaled him, but she did not dare reprimand him. His neck arched before her, and his body was like a coiled spring under her. She was aware of his incredible power, and that she directed this power only because he allowed it to be so.

She had barely to think of using the aids that would tell him to canter and he was off, bounding high and light, into that slow gallop, and suddenly Is's heart was soaring with his strides. She merely had to think what she wanted and he did it, she the mind, he the body. They went through all the preparatory exercises as though they were playing—trotting in place, turns on one spot at the canter, flying changes of lead. But this was a horse of war, and these were only the preliminary exercises Is had taught him to get him ready for his real training. Now she asked him for those movements— rearing, leaping forward, leaping into the air and lashing out with his hind hooves—movements of death.

For the first time the stallion's whole heart was in these exercises. Before, he had done them out of obedience to her. Today he seemed to understand them. Today he leapt higher, kicked harder.

Sadness struck Is like one of the horse's kicks. He was what he had been bred to be, and what she had trained him to be. He was ready.

Is reminded herself of the necessity of this. Without the berserkers to drive them back, the Marauding Blueskins would come out of the Boundary and attack the farmers. But it was not possible to send an army in to kill all the marauders, for without them, other terrible "things" would come out of the Boundary, killing the farmers, destroying the land, and disrupting the whole chain that allowed the cities to exist. And so an uneasy balance had been reached. The berserkers went into the Boundary singly and engaged the Blueskin's best warriors in battle, and if they exhibited enough of the qualities that the marauders prized, including showing no fear of death, then the Blueskins honored the truce another season.

Carefully, so as not to irritate the stallion, Is quieted him to a walk. After a moment, when he saw they were done for the day, he relaxed, stretching his neck and striding forward. He could have been a lady's hack. But Is knew what lay just beneath the surface.

When the horse was cool, she groomed him, and he leaned into her currying, enjoying the massage. She spent extra time, stroking his glistening coat with soft brushes, and soft cloths, trying not to think anything at all, living in the euphoria of the wonderful ride they had just had, letting them both down gently with the grooming.

Then she spent the day grooming the other horses, but she had no heart for working them. The two-year-old colt was frisky and pushy in the cool autumn weather, throwing his neck while she curried him, grabbing at anything that came near his mouth. Today it was beyond her to chastise him. Let him enjoy being the healthy young animal he was.

The four-year-old was more disciplined and easier to groom. Even though Is had always given him as much love and attention as she had the others, he seemed to have little use for her, remaining aloof and disdainful of her ministrations.

She left the six-year-old for last. Whenever she glanced at him, he was watching her with dark, intelligent eyes. When the bay stallion was gone, Is would concentrate her training on this horse.

For a while she lost herself in grooming his soft, liver-chestnut coat. It was the color of rich soil and shone with the warm sheen of polished leather. He was the most docile stallion Is had ever handled, and she had trouble imagining him as a fully trained war-horse, viciously attacking anything that came near him. But he would. It was programmed into his brain, to be triggered when he was fully mature and his berserker came. *You have no choice,* she told him silently. *Just like me.*

Sadness wanted to own her. She didn't dare give it an opening. The questions she had begun to ask when the third or fourth horse left were more insistent now, demanding she look at them. But she could not. Not now. The next two days she had to survive.

She heard the bay kicking during the night and incorporated the sounds into her dreams, where horse after horse left her care to be killed. Some were galloped to death. Some were slain by weapons their hooves and teeth could not match. Some were betrayed by their berserkers. All were betrayed by her.

She awoke before dawn, feeling as though she had received the kicking of the horse's hooves, and lay until light, listening to the horse attacking his stall.

He charged the bars when she came to feed him, and she did not stay to assess his temper this morning, but went back to her house and ate her own breakfast slowly, keeping her thoughts on how to exercise the horse. At this point she was always tempted to leave them in their stalls. But she couldn't. The way the stallion was acting, he would damage himself in there. She could not explain to a berserker that there was no horse to carry him. The horse *had* to be ready.

He tried to take her arm off when she reached between the bars to snap a lead on his halter. She snubbed him to the bars with one lead and got another one on the other side of his halter, effectively cross-tying him in the stall.

When she rolled the door back, he reared and struck out with his massive, iron-shod hooves. Is didn't even try to groom him. She held the saddle out before her so he could see that it was the one she used for galloping him. He tossed his head, ears still pinned against his neck, but he did not rear again. She moved into his stall, slowly, but not too slowly. If he sensed fear, he would go berserk on her. She kept her mind on the immediate moment, every movement.

He allowed her to lift the saddle onto his back. The girth fell twisted, and she had to reach farther under his belly than she liked to straighten it, but he stood. Today she put the bridle on over his halter so she did not have to untie him until she had the bit in his mouth.

The moment of truth came when she unsnapped him. She undid the far side quietly, with no fuss, so he wouldn't take notice, then slide outside the stall, around the corner of the door, before unsnapping the near side. He came forward immediately. If she had been in front of him, he might have attacked. As he came through the door, she let his head and neck pass her, then walked at his shoulder, reached up and took the reins and some mane in her left hand, and as they approached the end of the aisle, grabbed the saddle with her right hand and jumped up. He was too tall for her to vault cleanly onto his back. She had to settle for jumping high enough to put her left foot in the stirrup, then swing over. He accepted this because they had practiced the routine in preparation for today. She never allowed herself to miss that jump.

He broke into a trot as soon as they were through the door, and Is didn't try to restrain him. In a moment he was off in the canter, and in a few strides he had extended into a gallop. Is gave him the signal to slow, which he largely ignored, so she crouched over his neck, like a jockey, and let him run. She couldn't have stopped him anyway. He allowed her to suggest the direction, and she steered him into a flat bottomland along the river. She had galloped him here frequently to condition him, but this was different. Today Is had no control of him, and he ran as she had never allowed him to run before. In spite of her many years of galloping horses, Is's heart surged with adrenaline, and suddenly she was enjoying herself with a fierce kind of joy that wiped away everything else.

She had to let him run enough so he would be ready to let

her stop him, but not so much that he exhausted his best energy for tomorrow. She tried to time this so they would walk long enough to arrive at the barn cooled out, but not walk so long he became uncontrollable again.

She rode him right into the barn before slipping from his back. He was relaxed and happy after the gallop, and Is had a few minutes to untack him, but he had to be back in his stall before his mood swung.

When she let the other horses out into their paddocks, the two younger horses moved immediately off to graze, but the liver-chestnut stayed, watching her expectantly with his wide-set, expressive eyes until she went to stroke him. Then, suddenly, she leaned against him and began to cry. She had never done that before, never, and it felt awful, but she could not stop. She had no choice but to hang onto his neck while she shivered and sobbed.

Afterward she was mad at herself. She understood the necessity for berserkers as well as anyone. Without them, innocent people would die, the way her mother and father had died. It was better to sacrifice a few specially trained men, and a few horses, than to allow the slaughter of innocent people.

From time to time, as she went through the mending and repairing that she'd saved for this day, she heard the bay kick. He was no longer her beloved companion. He wanted only to fight, and he would get that wish.

That night she slept lightly, waking each time the stallion's hooves hit the walls. She could almost track the berserker's progress by the restlessness of the stallion.

Long before it was light, Is was too nervous to stay in bed any more. She got up and began to disguise herself for the berserker. A tight undershirt effectively bound her breasts. The heavy work shirt that went on over that was baggy and sexless, and hid how slight her frame was. She twisted her dark shoulder-length hair into a knot on top of her head and pulled a floppy-brimmed hat low over her eyes. Heavy-weight jeans, lace-up men's boots, and a man's thick leather jacket finished the disguise. She looked as much like a man as it was possible to make her slight body and delicate-featured face look. Her mind was full of all the other berserkers she had handled and all the things that could go wrong.

He came just after dawn. Is was alerted by the bay's whinny, and went out to watch the man approach. The horse he rode came forward at a shambling trot, his once proud head low to the ground, his toes dragging lines of dust up from the unpaved road. He was too spent even to answer the bay's challenge, which that horse trumpeted repeatedly, interspersed with the crashes of his hooves hitting the walls.

Is ignored the bay and watched the berserker. He spotted her standing on the porch of her house and kicked his horse toward her.

The poor beast picked up his head and broke into a canter, unable to disregard a command from his rider. He came to a halt in front of her house, and Is clamped harsh control on her feelings and looked at the rider. His eyes were glazed over and unreadable in some way that made her shiver inside.

He stepped down from the saddle and stood staring at her. He was at least seven feet tall, with width to match his height. The tight-fitting riding breeches he wore revealed his massive thighs. A light mail vest left his arms exposed, and Is could see his well-developed muscles. He would have had a handsome face, except for those eyes. They stared fixedly at something Is couldn't see.

Had he been another person, she might have assumed he was in a state of exhaustion. With a berserker, it was never safe to assume anything. The blood that coursed through his veins was highly augmented with hormones to forestall fatigue, pain, and fear, and strongly laced with chemicals that could be instantly tripped into rage or lust.

The man looked even bigger as Is came down off the porch.

He was standing on his horse's left, so Is went to the

animal's right side, took the reins, and started for the barn. Sometimes this worked.

Sometimes the horses refused to follow her. Even as close to death as this one looked, if his rider got mad, the horse might well attack her. Although he was a galloping horse, not a war-horse, he was linked to the berserker's brain in the same way, and easily had the strength and size to kill her.

But this one followed quietly, and Is led him toward a stall at the far end of the barn from the bay's. The bay stopped his challenging when he could see the other horse. He pressed his nostrils against the bars, sniffing deeply, arching his neck, and making a rumbling sound in his throat. The horse Is was leading didn't respond. The berserker did.

He went past her, slamming her against his old horse. The horse staggered, went to his knees, and stayed there swaying as though he were trying to decide whether to get up or just go ahead and fall down.

Is overrode her feelings for the horse. If he went down, she might not be able to get the berserker's saddle off him. Quickly, while the horse was still on his knees, she undid the girth and pulled the saddle from his back. As though that gave him more will, he tried to rise, stumbled, careened against the wall, scrambled a few more steps, and then found his footing and stood, legs wide, head low, nostrils flared, and sides heaving.

The berserker paid him no attention. He was in front of the bay's stall, and that horse had quieted and was standing, with ears pricked, looking at the man. If only the berserker didn't open the door, or do something else stupid, Is might have a minute to deal with this poor horse.

The horse's head hung at her knees. His eyes were sunken with dehydration. His coat had been soaked with sweat and had dried into a crusty mat. He was beginning to wobble on his widely placed legs. Is did not want him to go down in the aisle. She gave the reins a tug, afraid to speak a word of command to the horse because the berserker would hear and know she was a woman.

The poor horse lifted his tired head and staggered after her into the stall she had prepared for him. The clean straw rustled loudly as the horse dropped to his knees. Quickly Is slipped his bridle from his head. She always tried to do this before they went down. It was her way of telling the horse he had accomplished his mission, the final praise this horse might get. His hind legs buckled, and he fell heavily on his side.

To get to the door, Is had to step over his legs. She was careful. Sometimes the horses went into convulsions.

At the door she looked back. The horse looked so huge lying flat out, like an already bloated corpse. His flanks heaved with the effort of breathing. Mud was caked on his legs and under his belly. A thick layer of white, chalky sweat had dried between his hind legs.

He was finer of bone than her bay, more of a galloper, while the bay, with his heavier legs and bigger hooves, was designed for the rigors of rearing and kicking. Is could imagine the horse that was lying before her standing, sleek and full of himself, his bright chestnut coat gleaming—the way the trainer must have kept it before the berserker came—his eyes intelligent and trusting, instead of the way they were now, half-open and staring. She turned away before the questions could come, but her body shook with suppressed rage.

The berserker's back was to her. His hands gripped the bars of the bay's stall as though he would rip them out. Is saw the muscles standing out on his shoulders, biceps, and forearms. For a moment she was too angry to be afraid of him. A rational part of her mind knew she was in deep trouble. The augmented senses of the berserker would pick up her pheromones of aggressiveness.

The berserker spun so quickly Is had no time to move— not that it would have done her any good. His massive hand closed on the front of her coat, and he pulled her toward him. His eyes were focused now. He laughed, revealing large, flat teeth that reminded her of the horse's. His grip

constricted the coat around her torso, and she was thankful
for its thick leather. It kept him from feeling the way his
hand was twisting her breast. She wanted to cry out with the
pain, but she fought to stay silent. If he didn't realize she
was a woman, he might kill her, but he wouldn't rape her.
She tried to keep this coat heavily saturated with a man's
scent by making Brandy wear it every time he visited. Now
she prayed the berserker wouldn't smell her woman's fear.

Behind him, the bay whinnied, rearing up and striking the
bars with his hooves. The berserker shoved Is away. Her
feet flew off the ground as if she weighed nothing at all. Her
back slammed against the wall across the aisle from the
stallion's stall, and her head snapped back against the bars.
She crumpled to the ground.

. . . Nothing hurt. Not really, though it seemed as if
something should. There was a very loud ringing in her
head. If it would just stop, she could find out about the rest
of her body. There were other sounds too. Crashing, and the
ripping of wood. Like a horse kicking down a stall. But her
eyes would only see black. She better move anyway. Maybe
back into the dying horse's stall . . . Standing up seemed
out of the question. Crawl. Her body had lost the technique
of it. Fear hit her with a rush of adrenaline which took her
over the edge of dizziness into unconsciousness.

-||-

Brandy found Is two days later, curled up to the horse's stiff corpse.

Brandy was the cleanup rider who came after the berserkers. He was supposed to be a doctor, among other things, but the only medicine he seemed to know how to administer was brandy. Thus the name.

Most of the time it didn't matter. Berserkers either didn't touch others, or they destroyed them. Brandy would drink with the ones who had survived. He buried the others. He buried dead horses, repaired barns, brought new stock, and he brought news. For most of the Border Station trainers, he was the only contact with the rest of the world.

By the time Brandy found her, Is had a fever as well as a concussion. When he managed to rouse her, she was not particularly rational. The dying horse had kept her warm for a while, but now it was cold and stiff. Is had been unable to get up and tend the other horses, and that was all that was on her mind. Brandy had to see to them before Is would stop fighting him and let him put her to bed.

Brandy used his horse to pull the dead horse out of the barn. His horse was accustomed to such work. The weather had been cold, and the corpse was holding together well, so Brandy just kept dragging it all day. When it got dark, he unhooked the corpse, retrieved his rope, and headed back, relying on his horse to take him back as surely as a compass to the other horses and the feed waiting at the barn.

Usually Brandy buried the horses—didn't want too many

predators around a barn area, especially this close to the
Boundary—but there was too much work to do this time.
The barn was a wreck. The one, super-reinforced stall was
almost immune to both horse and computer-augmented
human berserker, but the rest of the barn was of ordinary
construction. Sturdy enough for other horses, it had been
like kindling to the berserker.

It took them eleven days to repair the damage. The first
two days Is was too weak to get out of bed. Brandy had to
help her to the bathroom, and she hated him for it. She was
furious at being ill, furious at the berserker, and, Brandy
suspected, furious at the system.

Whenever Brandy went out, he saw carrion birds circling
where the dead horse lay. This close to the Boundary, there
might be other "things" feeding on the horse too. It hadn't
been very smart to leave it above ground, but that was done
now.

They used up the stockpiled lumber repairing the barn.
Brandy would have to send in a wagon crew to cut more,
and Is wouldn't like that. She was one of the most solitary
trainers he dealt with.

Trainers were an odd lot anyway, living alone most of
their lives, suspicious of people and devoted to their horses,
but Brandy got on with them mostly. For some of the
women, his occasional visits were their only sexual contact.
But not Is. They said her family had been killed by
marauding Blueskins when she was little. Brandy could
guess how that had been. Marauders didn't usually harm
children, but they'd have raped her mother. Is would have
seen the whole thing.

He felt bad for Is. The Alliance could have fixed her—he
knew enough about medicine to know that—but the Alliance needed her the way she was. It took a certain kind of
hard to live the way the trainers lived. They had to stay
alone in these outposts, facing the difficult and sometimes
dangerous task of training the war-horses, and then they had
to face the berserkers' visits. But hardest of all, they had to

send the horses they loved to their deaths. They *had* to believe those deaths were necessary.

This close to the Boundary, there wasn't any way to lie to the trainers. They saw how the berserkers treated their line horses. Farther from the Boundary, it wasn't so bad. The implants hadn't caused the berserkers' brains to release their chemicals yet. But the closer they got to the Boundary, the harder they pushed their horses, and by the time they were within three days' ride of the Border Stations, their computer-augmented minds were picking up the magno electric output of the stallions' specially equipped brains. From then on rider and horse fed on each other's emotions. By the time the berserker arrived at the last stations, neither rider nor horse was entirely sane.

The rider was damn near as dangerous as the horse at that point. Brandy didn't envy the Border Station trainers their jobs. But it was too bad about Is; she would be beautiful if she'd take a care about it. When she was with her horses, she radiated such vitality and caring . . . That shouldn't be wasted on horses. Brandy sometimes fantasized about her taking his arm and turning that look on him. But it would never be.

As long as he stayed in his role, Is was willing to accept him. She'd talk about her horses and show him their progress, all animated and beautiful, and he'd want her so badly. But if he ever made any move, offered any hint that he'd like to change things, she'd retreat with a coldness he knew hid fear. While he played in his mind with how it would be to break through that fear and seduce her, he knew he would never try. She was one of the Alliance's best Border Station trainers, and his job was to keep her that way.

-|||-

Brandy watched Is work the liver-chestnut stallion. He was a beautiful animal with sloping shoulders, great, muscular hindquarters, and a lovely, arched neck. Except that his head was a little large and a little Roman-nosed, his conformation was nearly perfect, showing the best mix of the bulk of the draft horse and the refinement and speed of the racing breeds. Brandy could see the horse's training had come a long way since his last visit. There was a special communion between Is and this horse. That wasn't good. Brandy knew the danger signs.

You could lose a good trainer a lot of ways. Sometimes they got hurt one time too many by the horses and lost their nerve. Sometimes they got too scared of the berserker's visits. Sometimes they became too attached to a horse. And worst of all, sometimes they started questioning the system.

Is had at least two of the danger signs. She was too attached to this horse, and Brandy suspected that a lot of the anger she had held against the marauders who killed her parents had swung around to be focused against the system that took her horses from her and made her vulnerable to the berserkers.

Sometimes it helped to remind the trainers how important they were to the success of the entire Alliance. To the rest of the population, the trainers were heroes. Not only could they handle the much-feared war-horses, but they were the only thing standing between the people and the marauders and other evil things that came out of the Boundary, because without the trainers the berserkers would have no horses.

The horse trainers were usually picked from the children of the upper classes. It was easy for Brandy to appeal to the patriotism that was so inculcated into them. But Is was an anomaly in the system, the orphaned daughter of farm parents. She had not been of a high enough station to receive the benefits of the culture she now worked to protect.

Brandy knew it was time to bring Is in.

He also knew that short of drugging and tying her, he'd never make it. Once Is saw the way of things, she'd go rogue, and it would be ten days to a place where Brandy could count on help with her. He couldn't handle her alone for that long.

He thought about knocking her out and taking the horses. She'd be on foot then, and she'd either stay here and the Alliance would pick her up for reconditioning, or she'd trek off and hide. The important thing was that Brandy mustn't let her take the horses and run.

In the end Brandy decided on the course he usually took, the course of least resistance.

He got Is to drink with him.

She usually wouldn't drink more than a few sips, but Brandy was quite skillful. He pretended to be getting drunk and started telling Is the kind of stories she'd want to hear: rumors about how the whole berserker system might be shutting down. He wasn't supposed to tell her this, oh no. But who could she tell? And with drunken sincerity, he made her swear to secrecy anyway. Then he told her how the Alliance had found a better way to control the marauders.

As with the berserker system, it would avoid an all-out war, which would decimate the Blueskins. For, although everyone hated the Blueskins, they did serve a function. Their savagery kept all the other things that lived behind the Boundary in check, so those other dangers didn't venture out of the Boundary and become a problem for the Alliance either.

The new method would appeal to the Blueskin's primitive awe of a superior warrior, as the berserkers did. But unlike using berserkers, the new plan would not risk the lives of horses.

Brandy could not really tell Is more about it. He wasn't even supposed to tell this much, and he changed the subject to how war-horses were going to be kept in state. They had been such an important part of the Alliance for so long, they would still be bred and trained, but for show and display only. They'd be honored for all time for the role they had played in making the Alliance a safe place to live. Of course, the trainers would go with their horses. Who else could show them? Surely not the berserkers. There'd be no more berserkers made. The trainers would be glorified for the part they'd played in defending the Alliance. Brandy managed to get two drinks into Is that night.

With her armor somewhat relaxed, Brandy set the hypnotic induction field, and Is went under easily enough. It was a different Brandy who spoke to her then. His voice was cultured. His cadence was exactly fitted to the field for maximum strength. Even so he didn't try to do too much. He just told her to stay here, better days were coming soon, and he reminded her of the dangers that lurked in the Boundary.

Three days later, when Brandy was leaving, Is asked him how long it would be before he sent the lumber crew. That was the only clue she gave him.

He paused to think about his answer, then told her he had to visit the station to the east of hers before he headed back to the Alliance. It would probably be two weeks before he got to where he could *fast* the order, then maybe another two or three weeks before the wagon arrived at her place.

He headed out in the proper direction, put two ridges between them, and turned abruptly south.

Is waited until the next day. Then she took the liver chestnut for a ride, and found where Brandy's tracks turned south. She rode home slowly. In her heart she had known Brandy was lying to her. Things were not going to change, not soon. Brandy was heading back to where he could fast his order immediately. He had deliberately built more time into his plan to mislead her. It would not be a lumber wagon that came, and it would not take the four plus weeks Brandy wanted her to believe. Is didn't know exactly what was happening. She only knew she had lost her last horse to a berserker.

With that decision came a sudden upwelling of her spirit. Delighted by the unexpected feeling of freedom, Is put the stallion into a gallop. He went effortlessly, his long strides springing them over the rough ground as if it were cushioned meadowland. For a time Is let the stallion's rhythm carry her, her body working in unison with his. She loved the power and speed that were suddenly hers, the horse's body an extension of her own. She thought nothing, and immersed herself in the animal pleasure of galloping.

By the time she had walked the stallion cool, her mind was working again, frantically. It was one thing to decide to steal a war-horse and run; it was another to do it. For one thing, Is was terrified. The only direction open to her was into the Boundary. There was no doubt in her mind that the Alliance would hunt her down and punish—kill—her if she stayed in their territory. Stealing a war-horse would be considered an act of treason. Her only hope of escaping the Alliance lay in going into the Boundary.

She didn't know if the Alliance would send troopers, or even a berserker, after her. But it was the other things that lived in the Boundary that she found herself fearing most.

The Blueskins were first on her mind. She knew what they did to women, and she feared them deeply. But at least they were human. Except for the bluish cast to their skin, they looked like other men, just larger and stronger than most. But the other things that were said to live in the Boundary . . . Is had no idea how she could face them.

The great lizards could run down a horse over a short distance. She knew of their voracious appetites. Then there was something that stood on its back legs like a man, with long, hooked claws on its hands and the strength of a berserker. More frightening than that, there were forces that could manifest themselves as winds, or rock slides, voices where there shouldn't be voices, fogs that could drive you off your route and drive you crazy, rivers that were poison, eagles large enough to consider her prey, and other things, more evil and less understandable. She found her mind full of them.

She tried to tell herself that death at their hands wasn't any worse than awaiting her fate with the Alliance. She believed herself. That didn't make her fear any less.

She thought about how it would be if she got the stallion killed, and that almost stopped her. But his fate with the Alliance would be no better.

Horses didn't want to be weapons. Left on their own, horses ran away from danger. Running away would be her strategy too. This stallion wasn't as heavily built as some of the war-horses she'd trained, and he was faster than most. She'd do everything she could to protect him. Surely that was better then letting him be ridden into attack by a man who cared about nothing but attack.

Somewhere along the line Is found that she had decided not to take the other two horses. The liver chestnut was "hers" in some way the other two weren't, so it wasn't so much like stealing.

She waited six more days before leaving, needing a head start on whatever troopers Brandy had sent for her, but not wanting the other horses left alone too long. They would be safe in their paddocks for the two or three days the troopers should be behind her, and she'd leave them more than enough hay for a week, in case she'd miscalculated. They would soil and waste a lot of it, their pens would be a mess, and they would be high-spirited, but the troopers could handle them. If she were wrong about the troopers coming, the horses would die. But her guts told her she was not wrong.

She spent the intervening days getting ready, sewing her

quilts together to make a sleeping bag, and making a tent
and tarp from the waterproof grain sacks.

She packed rice, beans, and flour, but she knew she would
have to learn to live off the land even more than she did
now. She took her hunting knives, her skinning knives, rope
for snares and other purposes, and extra leather for repairing
tack.

The things that would be most irreplaceable were metal:
a bucket, the knives, a rasp for the horse's hooves, a
hammer, a bowl, spoon, and cup, the axe. It helped that she
had already lived a simple existence, close to the land, all
these years.

When she finally turned the stallion's head north, he
looked more like a pack animal than a war-horse. The two
younger stallions were in the paddock where she often left
them when she rode the liver chestnut. When they crested
the first ridge, she stopped and looked back. For some
reason both the young stallions raised their heads and
whinnied. There was no way they could know she was not
coming back. It was just coincidence she told herself.

She was more sad to leave them behind than she had
thought she would be. She took one last look at the valley
where she had lived. The grass was still showing green in
irregular splotches, but the bushes and trees were mostly
leafless. Their bare branches had a reddish cast. A few
bright yellow leaves still clung here and there in clumps,
adding dashes of color. The taller grasses, where the horses
hadn't eaten, were shades of bay and chestnut. It was not a
good time of year to be setting out across mountains.

The house, barn, and paddocks nestled in the middle of
the valley, a little village unto themselves. Is had stood
down there and looked up at this ridge, how many times?
She had watched these mountains in all their moods.
Survived their winters, celebrated the springs, cursed the
mud, hated the ice as she'd broken it from the water buckets
in the stalls, and basked in the heat of late summer
afternoons with her horses grazing all around her. Over the

years, she'd watched colts grow and change from gangly, uncoordinated yearlings to beautiful, intelligent beings as she sculpted their bodies and brought out their capacity to learn with her training. It was her life.

It called her now to return. But she knew it was already changed. Troopers were riding toward her, as she should be riding away from them.

Is turned the stallion down the ridge.

They kept to a northerly direction, letting the lay of the mountains determine their course. She had never gone more than half a day's ride in this direction and was soon in new territory, but the berserkers always went this way, so there must be a pass through which they could ride a horse. Her plan was to get through that pass as quickly as she could, then bear east or west and try to find a sheltered place to spend the winter. Maybe, if she didn't go too deep into the Boundary, nothing would bother her.

From the top of a ridge she studied the land ahead. The mountains rose like a barrier, sheer and uninviting. There was only one notch in their formidable facade. It had to be the pass.

That evening they camped near a little creek and Is let the horse loose to graze. They were too far from home for him to head back there, and he would probably stay with her for companionship. If he wouldn't, it was as well to find out now. Is ate a cold dinner. It was her plan to have no cook fires until she was sure there was no pursuit. She did not know when that would be.

In spite of being tired, she was lonely and nervous and could not bring herself to go inside a tent where she would feel cut off from the land, and could be trapped. She pitched only the tarp, unrolled her sleeping bag under it, and lay awake a long time imagining all the things, natural and supernatural, that could kill a horse. He was her only friend now.

Horses had been her only friends for a long time, but her

dreams were full of the horrors from a time before that was true.

. . . Her father had tried to defend them from the Blueskins, with an axe. He hadn't limped as he'd walked forward to meet the riders. It was the only time Is had seen him not limp on his gimped-up leg. When they had seen that he would fight, the Blueskins had dismounted, but they still towered over him. Their bare chests were painted in slashes of blood red and rock-sickle orange that made their skin look even more blue.

Her father's axe glinted in the morning sun, raised above his shoulder. Is saw it begin its forward, downward stroke . . .

The scream ripped across her dream. Her mother's scream. The harsh grunts of the men . . . the blood across her mother's bare thigh . . .

Absolute stillness.

. . . The sun not moving in the sky. The heat pressing her to the ground. The weight of the shovel. The over-loud scrape of its bite into the gravelly soil. An eternity passing, one shovel full after the next, after the next.

. . . The grave grew, until it was deeper than Is was tall. A moon lit the sky above her, but in the grave it was dark, and very still. She slept there when her body stopped moving. The earth was cold. She should be cold.

. . . When she threw a shovel full of dirt out, it fell back in. She had to climb out to move the dirt away from the edge so it wouldn't keep falling in. A sound drew her attention. A horse came trotting out of the mist. It was gray like the mist, with a black leather harness and blinkers on its bridle. It was pulling a flatbed wagon.

When she saw the two men, she felt relief. It didn't occur to her that they would take her away. She didn't realize she couldn't stay at her home anymore because she was only twelve years old and they couldn't leave her there alone. She was only relieved they had come, because they would know how to get her mother into the grave. She had been dreading that. The thought of having to touch her mother's stiff and violated body was terrible enough. But the thought of having to drag her across the ground, which was the only way Is could move her, and to watch her fall into the hole, had made Is feel panicky.

And then there was her father. The Blueskins had cut his head off with his own axe, and Is was afraid to pick it up with her hands. Even though it was just her father, now she was afraid of it, afraid of him . . . but these men wouldn't be afraid to pick up a man's head and put it in a grave.

She was relieved when they told her to get in the wagon. When the wagon started to move away, Is knew it wasn't right to leave, but the man told her to stay right where she was, and she was confused, and then she looked back and saw the smoke. They had not buried her parents, they had burned them, and maybe the house and everything.

. . . She heard the man running behind her and ran as hard as she could, but he grabbed her. She fought as her mother had fought, but he was too strong. He carried her back to the wagon and tied her to it.

The other man was angry when he caught up to them. The two men argued. The second man asked her to promise she wouldn't run away again, so he could untie her. She wouldn't promise anything to a man who'd burned her home.

. . . Is stirred, crossing from dream into wakefulness without leaving the dream behind. It had happened half her lifetime ago, but the dreams kept it as clear as yesterday.

She shifted her position, trying to shift her thoughts, and another memory took her into sleep.

. . . The man's footsteps echoed in the stone hallway as he walked in front of her. She had to hurry to keep up with him in this strange, cold place.

He stopped at one in the endless row of doors they had been passing. "Go in." They were the first words he had said to her except "Follow me."

There were probably ten kids in the room. They were sitting on a bench, and they all stared at Is as she walked in.

The door closed behind her, and she stood, uncertain what to do.

Finally one of the boys got up and sauntered over to her. He was a lot taller than she. He had a haughty, belligerent air about him as he walked around her. Suddenly he reached out and jerked her shirt, ripping it.

"What kind of clothing is that?" he asked scornfully.

"It's rags," a girl answered. She unfolded gracefully from the bench, and she was tall and beautiful and at least three or four years older than Is. But her tone and posture were insulting. "It's what peasants wear. Ain't you never seen a peasant?" she said to the boy.

It was a shirt Is's mother had made for her. It was the same woven fiber that everyone wore where Is came from. But these kids were dressed in some materials Is had never seen before. They were neat and clean, and their hair was done in fancy ways, not the braids Is wore. She knew she didn't belong there, and she wanted to leave as much as the other children seemed to want her to leave, but the man had said, "Your parents are dead, do you understand that? They are dead. Gone. Your home is gone."

They had been in a room with a high ceiling, and wood panels covering the perfectly good stone walls, because they were so rich here they could have both. "You have nowhere to go except where we tell you to go. You don't own anything. You don't have any rights. You're a ward of the Alliance. That means we're going to feed and house you, and you're going to learn to do something useful to earn your keep. You understand that? Earn your keep?" He was a very stern man, with downturned lines at the corners of his mouth. He seemed to be angry at her for being there, although Is didn't want to be there any more than he wanted her there. "You can make this easy on yourself, or hard," he said. "Your folks would have wanted you to do what you're told, learn to earn your keep."

. . . Is stirred, breaking free of the dream, and waking to

the utter blackness of a foggy night, which reflected the bleak despair she had felt at the school.

Everyone had earned their keep on her family's farm. But on the farm there had been love, and happiness, and sharing. In the government school it had been so different. She'd decided pretty quickly to follow the man's advice. She'd learn whatever she had to learn to get out of there as quickly as she could.

After six horrible months in the school, Is had been picked to go to the equestrian school, and the contact with the horses had come as a great relief. Although her poor farm parents had not been allowed to own a horse, Is had been around plenty of other animals. She knew their basic natures, and she knew they would always be true to those drives. If you understood that, an animal would never betray you. It couldn't betray its nature.

To Is, horses were the most beautiful of all animals. The way the government restricted their use and breeding made them even more thrilling because they were unobtainable. On horseback, one would be taller, faster, more beautiful, and surely smarter, more pure, and more courageous than ordinary mortals. But beneath all the romanticisms in her heart, Is knew horses were animals. She applied herself to learning their true natures while she worked at cleaning their stalls, grooming them, feeding them, and learning to care for their medical problems, but she never missed a chance to watch the riders being trained.

Lowly apprentices, like Is, had to work for years before they were allowed to train as riders. Her dreams were now full of the horrors of those years, when her only relief had been the quiet moments spent grooming the horses.

Is broke out of her memories to the song of a bird, a meadowlark.

A mist had formed a few feet above the ground, like a blanket across the dirt. When Is stood, her head was above the fog, and the morning was outrageously beautiful. The sky was deep blue, not a cloud anywhere. The peaks rose all around, snowcapped against the sky. A creek gurgled, unseen. As Is walked, the mist swirled about her legs. Then she saw the stallion and her heart leapt. He had stayed. Is had not allowed herself to know how important that was to her. Suddenly the whole thing seemed possible. They might get somewhere and find a place to live, and it wouldn't be much different from life at the station, except the horse would never be taken from her. She could be happy.

She waded through the mist to him. He was resting one hind leg, sleeping in the way horses do, aware of her approach but not truly awake. She spoke to him and touched his neck. His hair felt damp, and she could see how the moisture had collected in little beads on the tips of the long hair he was growing for winter, until her hand stroked it and left a wet swath where she had touched. He turned his face to her. His eyes were so gentle and trusting, Is was suddenly overcome with the feeling that she had done the right thing trying to rescue him from becoming a war-horse. He towered over her. His head, alone, was nearly as big as her torso, but he was all gentleness. She stroked his ears the way he liked and let herself feel her love for him. The meadowlark called again, clear, and achingly beautiful, and the stallion turned his head, his ears pointed to listen.

"Lark," she said softly, explaining to him that it was just a bird, nothing to fear. Then a funny feeling passed through her. "Lark," she said again, and it was his name. She had never named a horse before. It was against the law. But suddenly the law had no hold over her.

With the name she confirmed herself. Outlaw. It was as simple as that.

-IV-

The trail into the pass was beginning to seem like a highway to Is. She had to rethink her strategy. Not only would the troopers know this route, but anything coming out of the other side of the Boundary would probably take this path. Is thought about meeting a party of marauders and turned aside.

The only other place that looked slightly passable was a high saddle between two snow-covered peaks, so she set a new course of landmarks to steer her toward it.

Halfway through the morning it began to rain, just a drizzle, and the mist that came with it obscured the mountains around her. In time the plodding through the gray, featureless landscape had a stupefying effect on Is. Huddled into herself, she may have missed some warning signs. The first she knew of trouble was when Lark's head came up and he stopped in his tracks. From his body posture, Is guessed he was hearing other horses. Any moment he would whinny and give them away. Abruptly Is turned him back the way they had come and set off in a trot.

It might have worked . . . if the other horse hadn't whinnied first.

Is heard it, distant and questioning, the high tones dampened by the fog. Before she could do anything, Lark's neigh rang out, impossibly loud in the hushed, damp land. For long seconds it rolled away into the distance, like thunder, reverberating off the hillsides.

Is kicked Lark into a gallop. If he were galloping, maybe

he wouldn't whinny. Maybe the echoes would confuse pursuit. Things were moving too fast for any real planning, but they would have to get off the ridge they were on, and down into the forest, soon, to hide. Is was looking for the right spot when riders burst from the trees below and slightly ahead on the left. They were traveling at a quick trot in the same direction Is was galloping. Her body was asking Lark for a sliding halt before her mind registered that the riders hadn't seen her.

They were not government men. She could see the telltale blueish cast of marauder's skin. There were five of them.

Lark's hooves clattered on the rocky ground as he tried to obey Is's command to check his speed and turn. If even one of the Blueskins looked up, they'd be on her in heartbeats. In the interminable seconds it took Lark to sit back on his hindquarters and turn, none of them heard him. None of them looked up. As Is sent Lark plunging down the slope to her right, her last impression was of the blue-skinned riders, bare from their waists up, on weedy, thin horses, hardly bigger than ponies, looking straight ahead and trotting as though they had somewhere to go. But those small, un-pretty horses would be quicker and more maneuverable than her massive war-horse on this steep, rocky terrain.

Her mind had registered all that in a flash, while her body dealt with trying to slow Lark before they plunged into the trees. But he could not obey her. He was skidding, hock-deep in a landslide of mud, rocks, and loose debris. The rocks hit the trees first. One fist-sized stone got airborne and bit a hunk out of a pine, with a sound like a dull explosion. Then the rest of the rocks and the mud arrived, rattling the trees like a hurricane and making a noise Is couldn't have screamed over. No way would the marauders on the other side of the ridge not hear it. But she had more immediate problems. At the speed they were going, if they hit a tree . . . Lark could break his neck. There was no time for her imagination to carry her further. The first branch hit her—just a little, offhand slap across her ribs—which nearly knocked her off Lark, and reminded her that she could get hurt too.

She felt something snag Lark's hind leg, just for a moment. But it was long enough to reorient him sideways on the slide. If he lost his footing now, he'd roll.

Is didn't really make a decision to drop from his side; she just did it.

. . . The mud was cold and wet, and full of hard rocks, and moving very fast. For a little piece of eternity, Is had enough of her own problems not to worry about Lark. Then her hands caught hold of a root, and she anchored herself against the worst of the slide in time to see Lark lose his footing and roll. For a moment his legs thrashed wildly in the air, before he flipped all the way over and got his feet under him just in time to broadside a tree. He hung there a moment, while the worst of the slide went on by, and the tree leaned over, real slow, until it stopped at about forty-five degrees.

By then Is was slide-skittering down to him, starting a little spill of her own. But the slope was wiped bare of anything large and loose, and she was mostly skiing on raw mud. Lark gave himself a shake and steeped free of the tree. Is had time to note that he seemed willing to stand equally on all his legs, then she had to put some real attention into stopping before she slid under him.

Most horses would have been spooked out of their wits. He greeted her like a long-lost friend, snuffling all over her, as though reassuring himself of something. His pupils were big, and Is could see the muscle in his left hind leg trembling. She put her arms around his neck, and suddenly she was shaking so badly she couldn't stand without his support. She clung there a moment, trying to get control of herself. This was no time to go to pieces—marauders behind them, more ahead, and Lark might be hurt. That thought galvanized her into action.

She went over Lark with her hands. He was covered with mud, and she couldn't see anything. If he was scraped or

cut, at least it wasn't bad enough to bleed through the mud.
He seemed OK, although he might have some pretty sore
muscles.

Her own knuckles were scraped raw, and she didn't doubt
she would be sore too, as soon as the adrenaline settled out
of her system.

Lark's saddle was probably all scraped up under the mud
that was covering it, but she'd have to find out about that
later. The packs she kept her gear in seemed intact. The
reins had broken, and the headstall had been pulled off one
ear. Is righted that and led Lark by the little piece of rein that
was still dangling from one side of the bit. He seemed
willing enough to move. She'd have to get him on level
ground to be sure he was really OK . . . get him to a
stream . . . wash him down . . . check out the tack. The
thought she was trying not to think finally surfaced. *Why
hadn't the marauders come?*

They *had* to have heard all that noise.

But they'd have been here by now if they had.

Had they thought it was a landslide, and not wanted to be
anywhere near it? Had they not heard it? Mountains *could*
play tricks with sound.

Suddenly Is had to stop. Her legs just wouldn't go any
farther.

It could have all been over—as quick as that!

Lark could have been terribly hurt, and she'd have no
way to help him. Was it really worth risking breaking his
neck trying to save him from the Alliance?

What if the marauders caught her? They'd rape her and
beat her and stab her—like her mother. She could see the
blood. She would never forget the smell of it, or her
mother's cries and the harsh grunts of the men. Never! Any
sort of death was preferable to that.

She could go back. Turn herself in. She didn't know what
the Alliance would do. Punish her? Retrain her? The horror
of her years in the government schools filled her, and she

knew she could never go back to that. Death was better. Any sort of death.

It was then that she saw that she might run Lark to death trying to escape, the same way the berserkers ran their line horses to death.

She had not understood this before. She had never really understood what it would be like to be pursued. Somewhere, deep inside, she had believed that since she was saving Lark's life she would be lucky. Everything would work out because she was doing the right thing for the horse.

She leaned against Lark's neck and thought about turning back. The government would take good care of Lark—until they sent him out to die.

If the Blueskins caught them, they might even take good care of Lark. But their much smaller horses had been thin and weedy. Lark would not do well on the harsh, sparse diets on which those mountain ponies survived. Is had no idea how the marauders felt about their animals. Were they just creatures of utility, to be abandoned when they were sick or hurt? She had no guarantee they wouldn't kill Lark and eat him.

She started to walk again. The Blueskins must be well gone by now. But the initial whinny had come from the other direction. It couldn't have been one of the ponies in the band she had seen. There must be more marauders up there.

The first, most important thing was to make sure Lark was all right. Somewhere there'd be a stream to wash him down, and she'd repair the bridle. It was some minutes before Is realized that she had decided. She would not be captured, even at the risk of both of their lives.

It began raining again when evening came. The mud sloughed off her and Lark and ran down their legs in brown rivulets. As much as Is feared stopping, it was impossible to go on in the dark. The ground was slippery, and the rocks were beginning to ice, and if she stopped guiding Lark, he would turn back the way they had come, looking for the other horses. Is pitched her tent, but sitting around in the miserable damp was worse than riding, soaked through, had been.

The cold made Is hungry, and once the reins had been mended, she had nothing to think about but her hunger and how hopeless her situation really was. She ate sparingly from her dry rations, longing for hot food and a warm, dry place to be. It was a long, miserable night, and her mind couldn't seem to find any happy thoughts to think. It kept taking her back to her first days in the government school.

. . . She was following the boy with red hair. She had never seen hair that color, and his skin was mottled with red spots too, like a hound her father had kept. She had tried not to stare when he'd been introduced to her. Even his eyelashes were red.

He was fifteen, and he was in charge of her. Someone had to be in charge of her. She had no idea how to get around in the world in which she found herself. She was used to a rough cabin, meals that were cooked in a stove that was heated by burning wood, and quiet.

The cafeteria was bigger then the inside of their house and barn put together. And the noise! So many people, making so much noise, just to eat. She followed the boy in. Jacob was his name. She could even remember that.

People stared at her and stopped talking.

The food tasted bad, soft and overcooked. The noise and hostility and strangeness kept Is from being able to eat anyway. Where she came from, you didn't take what you couldn't finish. But some angry-looking women had shoveled the food onto her plate, plop, plop, and she'd been afraid to protest.

Anyway, after Jacob saw she wasn't going to eat it, he reached over and switched his empty plate for hers and ate her food too. She'd thought he was doing her a favor. Later she learned he was breaking the rules, having two lunches. And that day she'd been too dumb to know she could have sold it to him for something: protection, information, something. Instead, she'd just let him take it, and people had seen and known she was stupid.

Jacob was supposed to show her around, so she'd know where the rooms were when someone told her to go to one of them. Is followed him and tried to remember, but mostly she was lost. The buildings were so big, and most of the rooms didn't have windows. There was no way to find her direction from the sun and the plants and the wind. She felt intimidated, but the atmosphere was so hostile she could not allow herself to show it.

One of the rooms Jacob took her to was the library.

Is was suddenly confronted by books from wall to wall. Books from ceiling to floor. Books so high up there were ladders and walkways to reach them. Books like the ones her parents had told her about, but that she had never gotten to see. Books that a farmer would never get to read, because farmers couldn't read. Farmers weren't allowed to learn to read.

But Is's parents had secretly wished that Is could have a better station in life than theirs. Is hadn't cared. She'd been completely content. But she'd understood how much her parents revered books and education. Now, suddenly, their dreams for her were possible.

A whole world opened up before her. She walked slowly into the room, not even aware of having done so, but drawn by something too strong to name. It was the first thing that had meant anything to her since the death of her parents.

"Isadora! Isadora, pssst." She didn't hear Jacob's urgent whisper before the two men who were seated in the room, reading, raised their heads and stared at her. She would never forget the look of cold contempt they gave her. Even in the cafeteria the hostility had been minor compared to this. She froze.

"What *dare* you in here, Student?" It wasn't a question. It was a denouncement.

Is could not answer. What had drawn her in was the antithesis of what she faced now. She could not explain the

fascination she had felt. She had wanted to understand how
it felt to look inside a book and learn something just by
seeing with your eyes. How it could be to not have to put
your hands into it, or lift with your back, or get covered in
its smell, or feel it through your whole body. How did it feel
to learn just through your eyes? Just sitting still?

After long seconds, the man turned his gaze on Jacob,
who had stayed at the door behind her.

"Explain."

No one had ever used that tone of voice to Is before. Her
father at his angriest, at some thoughtless or harmful
mistake, might demand an explanation from her. But he
would listen to it. She knew these men would not. They
were not asking why she had come into a room she had not
known she should not enter; they were showing her how
stupid and ugly and worthless she was. Evidently Jacob
understood this too, because he did not answer either.

"Your name, Student."

"Jacob Onry, sir."

Is heard the fear in Jacob's voice. But there was something else there too, something conniving, something dis-
honest, and wrong. The man turned his gaze on her.

"Your name, Student."

Is understood with all her heart the injustice of what this
man was trying to do to her. She understood how reprehen-
sible it was of Jacob to allow this man to do that to him. For
one blinding instant she understood the wickedness of the
whole place.

"Isadora Drey," she answered, and it came out like a
challenge. *I am my parent's child. They were better people
than you, and I am better than you.*

. . . But that was before, before they'd had her long
enough.

She rubbed her face, as though she could scrub away the
memory. Why should she think about that small act of
defiance now? She had never been able to reconcile what
she had seemed to know inside—something she seemed to

have learned from her parents—with what was expected of her at the school.

There was something terribly wrong going on. But her child's sense of correctness had been pitted against all the people at the school. All the adults Is should have trusted and honored, and all the older, wiser students, couldn't all be wrong, so Is had come to doubt herself. She had tried to do what she thought her parents would want her to do, to behave by the rules of her new home. When that had proven impossible, she had learned to do what she had to to survive, in order to get out of the school.

Eventually she dozed, but her sleep was filled with strange dreams, inspired by the ceaseless wind, and her old confusion was with her more relentlessly than it had been in years.

By morning it had stopped raining. The sky had been washed to the palest of pale blues, as though color had bled from it with the rain. Everything had a washed-clean feeling to it. After its rain bath Lark's coat was soft as a newborn foal's, soft as Is's own hair. In spite of their situation, her spirits rose. It suddenly seemed that things might work out.

She draped yesterday's wet clothes over Lark's rump and shoulders, tucking the ends under the saddle so they wouldn't blow off as they walked. It was the only way the clothes were ever going to get dry. He looked like a peasant's clothesline, her proud war-horse, but there wasn't anyone to see him. Is hoped.

The wind continued all morning. Wispy clouds scudded overhead, and by afternoon the mountaintops were shrouded again.

So far they had seen nothing unnatural, and not even any of the larger natural predators had appeared. Is hoped it would stay that way. Whenever she heard a meadowlark call, she thought it was good luck.

It was hard to guess how much land they covered. The saddle, which had seemed to be only over the next ridge,

now seemed to get farther away as the land between it and
Is came into view.

Each day, they gained altitude. There was very little
grazing, and Lark was loosing weight noticeably. Is prom-
ised him a rest in the first good pastureland they came to
once they'd crossed the saddle.

The day they finally crested the ridge was hot and sunny.
The sky was bleached almost to white and offered no
shielding from the sun. There was a silence and a stillness
to the air, as though it were too tired from the heat and
altitude to carry any sound. Even Lark's hooves on the
rocky ground, and the saddle leather's soft squeaking,
seemed distant.

Is found herself staring into space, thinking nothing,
immersed in each plodding step of the toiling horse. They
were almost in the midst of the riders before Is saw them.

Blueskins. A dozen of them, with their backs to her, in a
rough half circle. And facing them, four government riders,
their sleek, proud animals dominating the Blueskins' scruffy
ponies.

Is should have already whirled Lark around and been
galloping away as fast as she could, but her mind was taking
in all sorts of conflicting observations. All she managed was
to jerk Lark to a halt. And even that was odd. He should
have seen the horses first. His head should have come up.
He should have whinnied.

They were close enough that one of the other horses
should have seen him. No doubt they would at any moment.
I should be galloping away. Why were Alliance troopers
talking to Blueskins? *I should be galloping away.* The riders
were so much at ease even their horses were dozing. Several
of the Blueskins' ponies had their hind legs cocked, resting.
Their tails swished leisurely. The government horses were
every bit as relaxed. One rider had swung a leg over the
front of his saddle and was leaning his elbow on his knee.
He must have felt very much at ease with these Blueskin
"enemies" to sit that way.

All of this information went into Is's mind in an instant. What she did next made no more sense to her wildly yammering nerves, which were screaming at her to turn and run, than the scene in front of her did. She turned Lark right and walked him forward. Her course would take her in a big circle around the riders, but she would be out in the open all the time. There was no cover.

Lark went without the slightest hesitation. He didn't even try to turn his head to look at the other horses. Is didn't look at the riders again either, pretending that if she didn't see them, they couldn't see her. It was a child's game, totally irrational, and going to get her killed. She was so tense with listening for the first shout of discovery, her head ached. When she finally did look back, she had gone farther than she'd realized. There were no riders in sight.

For a moment Is was relieved. Then she began to question if she had really seen them. The whole thing seemed so impossible. But each horse and each rider was etched in her mind's eye. Details she had not been conscious of seeing came back to her: the long, cruel-looking shanks on the Blueskins' bits, their animal-skin saddle pads, their long, braided hair, the paint pony with the scraggly tail. Then the visions of her mother came, as real and detailed as the riders. Is was suddenly in no mood to question anything. She sent Lark into a trot, the fastest pace she dared on the steep, shaley slope.

When darkness came, Is could not bring herself to stop. It was not just the riders behind her that kept her going. She could not face being still with herself, trapped in a tent, cut off from her horse and from movement. The questions she was trying desperately not to ask herself would corner her. They'd ask themselves if her mind were not busy with riding.

The horse could see well enough in the dark, and there was no grazing, or water, here to rest him anyway. It would be better also to get down to cover before daylight came.

She let Lark pick the way. As long as they kept going downhill, they couldn't go too wrong.

Eventually, Lark brought them to a little stream. Is took his bridle off, lay flat out on the ground, and fell asleep while he grazed. When she woke, he was standing nearby with his head hanging above her. Smiling, she turned over and slept some more.

Later, the birds woke her. Lark had moved away to graze. Is could hear him tearing the grass, and hear the occasional swish of his tail or stomp of his foot as the insects found him. She could have stayed there, in that dream place where there was only the horse she loved, and the land, and no great need to do anything; but there were also Blueskins, and government men, and winter coming. She stretched and picked up Lark's bridle.

-V-

Is called the valley Safehome, hoping it was going to be
both of those things.

The day after crossing the saddle, she had spotted a wide
swath of trees that were greener than the mostly pine,
old-growth forests everywhere else. The lighter-colored
trees were immature—which meant their branches were
low to the ground and their boles close together—possibly
because those acres had burned.

It was exactly the kind of place *not* to ride a horse. But Is
had gone down there anyway, because surrounded by those
impenetrable trees there was a meadow that the forest hadn't
reclaimed yet. Lark had had to squeeze between trees and
duck under branches, but they had made it, and it was worth
it.

Is felt safe in their little hidden valley. No other horseman
would come here. The meadow was an elongated, egg-
shaped bowl, surrounded on three sides by steep land and
miles of the sort of trees that would turn horsemen away. On
the fourth side, the bowl was shallow, but opened to a
forbidding, snow-covered range that was too steep for
horses.

With the days getting shorter and colder, Is hurried to
build a shed for Lark, cutting trees with the axe she had
brought, and having Lark drag them like a common plow
horse. She had not really kept track of the days, but the
moon had been waxing when she left her home, and it had
been full and waxing again before they found the valley.

It was full again before Is had the shed finished. Above
Lark's stall, she had built a half loft. They would be
protected there from the worst of the wind and snow, and
Lark would be a good source of heat.

The peaks around them had already assumed their winter
mantle of snow, and the wind was often strong in the
surrounding trees, sounding like a rushing river, or fiercely
driven rain, but the valley seemed to be protected from the
worst of it.

The day the first snow fell in the valley, Is took time off
from her winter preparations. She had started the tradition of
celebrating the first snowfall of each winter when she had
lived at the Border Station.

It had made no sense to keep the usual holidays. Either
she felt sad remembering good times with her parents, or
sad remembering the horrible times at the school, where
holidays had become just one more chance to be humiliated
and embarrassed.

So Is had invented her own special occasions. First Snow
was one of her favorites. She could entertain herself for
weeks looking forward to it and trying to guess what day it
would come. It certainly kept her from dreading it, which
she might otherwise have done.

She'd had different ways of celebrating, but they always
included a ride, just to enjoy the changed landscape, and
usually she would dive into her stores of winter food and
find something special to eat.

This year she had no stash of powdered chocolate or
carefully rationed sugar to make herself a holiday treat, but
she didn't let that bother her. She saddled Lark, and then set
off for the far end of the valley, enjoying the large, powdery
flakes that settled on Lark's mane like jewels.

Winter turned out to be a delight. On the coldest or
stormiest days they stayed indoors and Is listened to Lark
chewing the dried grass she doled out to him while she
repaired leaks in the roof or worked the hides of the small
animals she'd killed. Sometimes, when the snow was too

deep for Lark, Is would leave him in the stall and go hunting on snowshoes she'd made herself. She hunted rabbits mostly, as they were numerous and Is identified with the other small predators that hunted them.

So the winter passed and spring came.

They celebrated the thawing of the ground with progressively harder workouts. Although they were alone, Is had decided not to give up Lark's training. Lark was too good, and too much fun to train. Besides, Is needed the riding to keep her spirits high.

She discovered a wide place in the stream that ran near their shed and took her first bath of the year. It was very cold, and invigorated from it, she took Lark for a long gallop.

So spring passed. Summer took hold of the land, and everything slowed. The land dreamed its summer dream, and Is dreamed with it, living one day at a time, moment by moment, slowly, in pace with the land.

-VI-

It was mid-summer, and they were hacking lazily back from a ride that had taken them out of the shallow end of the valley, when they came upon the mare so suddenly neither of them had any warning. They were just cresting a rise when Lark's head snapped up and he stopped so quickly that even though he had only been walking, Is was jarred.

Not twenty feet away the mare's head also snapped up. Both animals stood frozen at the unexpected sight of each other, while Is sat equally immobilized. In an instant she took in the mare's refined head, her expressive eyes, her fine bones. She was a dark bay, with black mane and tail, and no white markings, and she was much too fine to be a marauder's horse. This mare did not belong here, in a way that sent Is's heart racing.

The mare wore no bridle, and the saddle had been pulled off to her left side.

Lark lowered and raised his head several times, trying to focus the mare better. Perhaps he thought it was odd, the way she seemed unwilling or unable to move.

The mare broke the deadlock by nickering.

To Is it sounded like a plea for help.

Lark lowered his head, and Is felt him relax. He made a soft, wuffling sound of reassurance as he walked forward. Is had not imagined the plea in the mare's call.

They were only a horse's length from the mare, and Lark was reaching out his neck to sniff her nose, when Is saw the man. She wanted to jerk the stallion's head away, turn, and flee, but already it was too late. But even while she was overriding her reflexes, it registered that not only was the man not lying in ambush, he was probably dead. He was sprawled on his face, one arm thrown out and the other under him. His body was turned at the hips, and his foot was twisted in the stirrup. He must have resisted falling, clutching to the saddle so hard he nearly dragged it off with him. Wherever the mare had come from, and whoever had trained her, they had instilled in her a trust so deep that all she could do with this terrifying situation was wait for help. Is's heart went out to her. She was gallant, and beautiful, and in trouble.

Is had to step over the man to position herself where she would have enough leverage to get the girth undone. The mare stood like a statue while Is struggled with it. But the moment the saddle was off, she stepped carefully away from the man and began to graze. By then Is had taken in enough clues to realize the horse had stood like that for hours, maybe a day or more. Everything within reach of her head had been eaten, and yet she was starving rather than take the chance of dragging the man.

It took an incredibly talented trainer, and a special horse, to get that kind of trust. The man who was lying at her feet could be that trainer, but such a horseman wasn't likely to have a fall like this. More likely this man had stolen the mare from some very expensive stud. She was certainly a quality animal.

On the other hand, the mare was wearing no bridle, and there were no broken pieces lying around. The inescapable conclusion was the man had been riding without one. That was no rookie horsemanship.

Is had been so caught up in the mare's plight she had ignored the man. It wouldn't matter. If he was not dead, he was probably so badly hurt she couldn't help him anyway. She hadn't really had any intention of trying. Whoever he was, he was dangerous to her. But now that she thought he might be the horseman who had trained this incredible mare, Is was more interested in him.

She knelt by him and very gingerly touched his cheek. It was warm.

She freed his foot from the stirrup and rolled him over. If his back was broken, he would die anyway. She wasn't concerned about doing further harm.

He had cut the side of his face, and it was caked with dried blood and mud, so that Is couldn't tell if it was a deep cut. His skin was very light, and his hair blond, almost to the point of being colorless. Behind their closed lids, his eyes looked sunken, like the eyes of a dehydrated horse. The skin around them was dark, almost bluish, and bruised-looking.

Is watched his chest rise and fall. His breathing was shallow compared to hers, but regular. She started to feel for broken ribs and then stopped. She had to decide whether to try to help him, or not. She *could* just ride away.

If he hadn't stolen the mare, he had to be some sort of government official to have such a quality animal. He wasn't wearing a trooper's uniform, and Is had never heard of a bridle-less school within the government, but that didn't mean there wasn't one. If he had found her, she should be getting away before others followed him. Is glanced around nervously, and her eyes came to rest on the mare. If she tried to leave, the mare would probably follow. Is would have to tie her. But if the man didn't recover, the mare would starve to death. She *could* take the horse and leave the man to his fate. But if this was the horseman who had trained the mare, she belonged to him in some way that made taking her stealing in a way that taking Lark had not been. *If* he was the man who had trained her.

If he had been some slimy thief?

He had been riding without a bridle.

He'd be trouble for her. If he recovered, he'd try to take her in, or report her at the very least. Or if he was a criminal himself? He might try to steal Lark. Rape her.

Nothing good could possibly come of helping him.

While her mind ran through all that, and her body begged her to run, her eyes watched the horses. They were grazing side by side. The mare was hungrily pulling the grass as fast as she could. Is stared at her a long time, but she already knew what she would do. Somehow, it was for the mare.

Maybe the man would have the good grace to die.

Is finally rigged up a travois, using pieces of her tack and pieces of the man's tack, and two small trees.

The mare accepted the harness and the strange contraption of poles quietly, and Is got the man onto the rope hammock she'd tied between the poles. There was a chance the mare would take off galloping and kick the whole thing to splinters, the man included. Is didn't have any idea how to control her without a bridle except to walk at her head and expect her to follow. To Is's relief, that arrangement seemed fine to the mare.

The man didn't have the good grace to die on the trip. He didn't have good graces at all.

Is dragged him to the back of the stall because she couldn't have gotten him up to the loft if she'd wanted to. She felt funny going through his stuff, so as soon as she found his sleeping bag, she stopped. It was a marvelous bag. It had been packed down to such a small bundle Is hadn't been sure what it was until she'd pulled it out of its bag. Then it expanded magically until it was thicker and warmer than her own makeshift one, but not a third the weight. Only a very important man, high in the government, would have something like that.

The man was terribly dehydrated, so Is rigged up a stomach tube to get water into him. He choked and gagged but didn't vomit, and she guessed she'd gotten it into his stomach, not his lungs, when she blew into it and he didn't cough. She dribbled a little water down it, and that didn't kill him either.

That wasn't the worst of it. The worst was when his bladder started working again. Is gave up on modesty and wrestled all his clothes off him, then rigged up a tube to that end of him too. Getting the tube on, and getting it to stay on, were no easy tasks. She was thoroughly disgusted with the whole thing until the next time his bladder let go and it ran down the tube, and out of the stall, and she didn't have to clean it up. Then she was sort of proud of herself.

Other than the fluid, and a general cleanup of the man's cuts—none of which were serious—Is didn't know what to do for him. She wasn't going to try to feed him. If he was that far gone, let him die. She'd done her part.

The mare settled happily in with the stallion. Over the next few days, Is spent a lot of time watching them. She imagined the colt they would produce, and thought about where the mare could be from, and about where to bury the man, who must be in some sort of a coma. But she didn't let herself think about what she'd do if he lived, took the mare, and left.

On the fourth day the man started having convulsions. They terrified Is. She was sorry she'd ever gotten involved. She hadn't done him any favor. He would be dead of exposure by now if she'd left him. That night she had nightmares about him suddenly rising up out of the bed and attacking her, or the horses. She planned ways to defend herself, and them, while she knew it was all quite illogical.

The next morning, she decided it was time to go through the man's saddlebags for clues to his identity. The clothes she found were high quality, Alliance material. There were packets of dehydrated food, and then she found the tools.

She couldn't even guess their uses. Common people had axes, shovels, picks, things like that. His tools were sophisticated, smooth things whose purpose wasn't apparent. If he had stolen them as well as the horse, he must be a very wanted criminal.

The convulsions lasted, on and off, for two days. Then the man seemed to sleep differently. If he'd been in a coma before, now he was just sleeping regular sleep, except it went on and on. Three days later, he woke up.

Is had come into the stall to get Lark's bridle. She was

halfway across the room when she felt the man's eyes on her and froze, suddenly afraid to meet those eyes. Every berserker she'd ever dealt with flashed before her vision, all their eyes cold, deadly, unreachable. She knew this man wasn't a berserker. He wasn't built like one. But it didn't matter. She was afraid his eyes would be like that.

She had to force herself to turn and face the man.

He wasn't what she expected at all. His face looked much kinder with his eyes open. His expression was soft. "Beatific" was the word Is thought. He looked as if he'd opened his eyes on heaven. His mind must have been keeping him chock-full of painkillers for him to look at her like that. She couldn't quite look away. If that was what dying was like, she'd never fear it again.

His eyes closed, and the breath went out of him like a sigh. Is stood frozen, watching for the sleeping bag to move, to tell her he was still breathing. She was hoping very hard, but she didn't know what she was hoping. After a moment the man's chest began to rise and fall again, and Is started breathing too. Her legs felt rubbery as she walked the rest of the way across the stall. Her hand shook as she reached for Lark's bridle.

Whoever the man was, if he lived, Is would have to leave her safe little valley. She was mad at herself for having helped him, mad at him, mad at fate. She hadn't been doing anyone any harm. She'd stolen the horse, but damn it, she'd saved his life. The Alliance had lots of other horses. She'd been happy enough living with just Lark. Maybe that couldn't have lasted. Maybe because she'd known that one way or another it couldn't go on forever, she'd cherished every moment carefully. But there was nothing else for her.

The man woke again in the night. Is heard him trying to get up. She listened, holding her breath, almost holding her heart still. He didn't make it far. She heard him fall, then silence. She knew she should go down and see if he was all right, but she couldn't. For once fear won over discipline. She wasn't going down until it was light. She knew he

couldn't make it up the ladder, and yet she couldn't sleep,
fearing him, and being angry at herself in turn.

The man had made it to the middle of the stall. He looked
like a little boy curled up on the floor. His skin was even
whiter than Is remembered, and his face was innocent in
sleep, and gentle enough to be the man who had trained the
mare. He'd gotten the tubes off. Is went by him and he
didn't wake.

The horses were not far away, and Is went to them and
touched Lark, and then the mare. She had come to love this
mare, for her overpowering loyalty and manners that were
as delicate as her conformation. The mare raised her head
and regarded Is with large, expressive eyes. Is tried to
imagine how leaving her behind would feel. But she
couldn't go just yet. The man might still die, and the mare
would not survive alone once summer ended. Is put her head
against the mare's withers and began to shake. She knew she
was giving up her own best chance to survive.

If she wasn't going to let the man die, she should help
him. It was nonsense to be afraid to go back in and cover
him with the sleeping bag. She turned and marched herself
into the stall.

The man was gone.

Adrenaline flooded Is while she fought for rational
control. He was only a very sick, very weak man; he
couldn't *do* anything. But her body had taken her out the
door to check on the horses before she could convince
herself.

They were grazing as placidly as they had been when she
left them.

She saw the man's footprints in the wet grass. He had
gone around the side of the shed. Is forced herself to stand
and take several deep breaths before she sauntered after
him.

The man was sitting with his back against the shed, legs
sprawled in front of him, eyes closed. The morning sun was
on his face, lighting his blond hair to white. Dark circles

showed like bruises under his eyes. His cheeks were sunken and his ribs stood out. He looked frail and very much in need of her help. It had been so much foolishness to be afraid of him.

He heard her and opened his eyes. They were gray, like the mist on the mountains. Soft.

He tried to smile, expressing his gratitude and apologizing for his continued need more perfectly than any words could have. He reached his arm out toward her, asking for help to rise, and Is put his arm around her shoulder and helped him up, surprised at how natural and easy it was to touch him like this. They began to walk back around the shed. He was as thin as a skeleton, and as light. He had to stop every few steps to rest, but he seemed completely unashamed of his nakedness, and so Is ignored it too. When they got inside, he collapsed into the sleeping bag and fell asleep instantly.

Is heard him get up again in the night and listened to his slow, staggery steps as he chuffed through the dried grass with which she bedded the stall. His steps stopped near the door, and after a while she heard him making water. Then he had to rest awhile before he could make it back to bed.

In the morning, with the forked stick she used for cleaning up after the horses, Is pitched out the straw he'd soiled. He watched her from his bed and smiled with a little embarrassed, apologetic smile when she looked at him.

"Don't worry about it," she said. They were the first words she had said out loud in a very long time. She realized that the man had not spoken to her at all, and she wondered if he couldn't speak.

Over the next several days, Is fed him broth, and then the cereal gruel she made for herself. By the third day he was strong enough to sit up at her fire outside.

Then Is remembered the food concentrates in the man's pack and thought they might help him gain strength. She felt strange going into his things, so she brought the whole pack out to him. But he had leaned back against a rock and seemed to be dozing, so she decided she would just go ahead and have the food ready for him when he woke.

She had the water hot and was about to pour a packet of mix into it when she heard something behind her and turned just as the man lunged for her. There was no time to get away. She struck him, flat-handed against the chest, in a reflexive action all her years of handling the rude young stallions had honed, before she realized that he wasn't going for her, but for his pack.

He crouched, gripping the pack with both hands, and started to say something. But the sound that came out of his throat was like the cry of a hunting hawk. Startling enough from a bird, it was terrifyingly inappropriate from the man.

He turned away with a harsh movement, and his fist slammed into the pack with a sound like a fist hitting flesh.

Is jerked in reaction to his sudden violence. She moved away from him, and her hand closed over a rock. She had left her knife by the fire and was afraid to try for it now.

The man upended the pack and shook everything out with harsh, angry movements. Then he scrabbled through his belongings, flinging the food packets into the fire. The flame sputtered under the onslaught and turned green. A foul smell reached Is. Poison? Had he been poisoned? Was that why he'd had the fall? Why he'd been sick? Is wanted to ask, but she was too afraid of him now.

Even as sick and weak as the man was, he would be stronger than she. And he was not rational. His hands shook, and his eyes were wild with a haunting pain that Is did not dare look into, lest it become her own pain. He started to restuff his pack, but his movements were jerky and unco-ordinated, as though he were losing control of his body. After a moment, he gave up and sank back on his heels, gripping his head with clawlike hands as though he were in terrible pain. Is was torn between fear and pity. She had to break the tension of the silence.

"It was poisoned, wasn't it?"

He met her eyes, just for a moment, and Is had to look away from the craziness she saw there.

Maybe the people from whom he had stolen the mare, or the tools, had tried to kill him. Maybe that was their right. But at that moment Is could only feel pity for the man's pain. She couldn't imagine anyone trying to poison a high government official, so he had to be a thief.

"I'm sorry," she said softly.

He gave her a small smile that was so filled with conflicting emotion it was not really a smile. He seemed to know that it failed totally to calm her, apologize, or explain anything. He reached toward her with a conciliatory motion.

Is couldn't help herself; she drew back. The man started to say something, and this time instead of the hawk scream, he began to laugh, high-pitched and hysterical. He twisted his back to her but couldn't stop the sound. It built higher, and more frenzied, while he beat on the ground with his fists and kept laughing.

The sound jerked Is's nerves tight. She couldn't stand it. She got up and moved away, but could still hear him laughing. When it finally died down, she couldn't go back to the fire.

She watched him all night, from a distance, unable to sleep. In the morning, when he was curled sleeping by the dead coals, Is slipped in and took her knife.

She walked by the stream and tried to think what to do. The man was crazy. She didn't know if the poison had done that to him, or if he had hit his head falling from the mare. But if his moods could swing like that, and he could so totally lose control, she couldn't trust him. She had to get away from him, but how? Would he try to follow? And once she left this protected valley, there might be Alliance troopers, and Blueskins, and other horrors. She was sorry to the depths of her soul that she had saved the man's life.

She wandered farther than she had intended, thinking deeply. When she finally turned her steps for home, she had decided to try to slip away when night came.

She was only halfway home when she heard Lark's whinny. Instantly she started sprinting at top speed, leaving the streambed and cutting across the open field. The shed door was closed, and she heard the thud of Lark's heels hitting the wood. Memories of war-horses gone berserk raced through her mind, adding speed to her legs. But Lark was not a trained war-horse feeling his rider approach. The only other explanation was that the man had taken the mare and left Lark behind.

Is flew down the hill without feeling her legs pounding over the uneven ground and leaping the small bushes. The man could have taken Lark too! She'd been such an idiot to leave Lark like that. She had not given enough thought to stopping, and she skidded on the gravelly ground in front of the stall, crashing into the door. With her hand on the latch, she took a deep breath.

"Lark. Stand." She put as much command and calmness into her voice as she could, out of breath as she was. Then she rolled the door open only enough to admit her, not enough to let the horse out. In his excited state he would go after the mare with no thought of Is. It was dark, even in daylight, in the shed with the door closed. Is found Lark's bridle by memory. He quieted while she tacked him. Then she ran upstairs and threw a pack together. She did not know how much head start the man had. If she couldn't find him, she might not come back. She'd have to leave here for sure now. If he couldn't talk, he could still lead the authorities back to her. Even if he was some sort of criminal himself, he might do that, if there was a reward on her. She couldn't risk it.

She heard Lark pawing as she assembled her pack. It was easier than it had been last time.

She let Lark pick the way, moving off at a fast trot and then opening into a gallop. She didn't try to rate him until they had crossed the valley and gotten onto rocky footing. The man had gone out the shallow end of the bowl, toward the mountains. Lark seemed sure of where he was going, and Is occasionally saw hoof prints to confirm his conviction.

Is began to think it might be just as well if they didn't find the man, but it was the nature of horses to want company. There was no way Is could make Lark understand that he could not have both her and the mare. He would have to choose the mare anyway. His instincts would make him. Is did not feel cheated. That was the way horses were. It was their need for companionship, and their ability to live within a herd hierarchy that made them trainable. Is's company had supplanted that of other horses, and Lark was happy with that until it was tested against the real thing. After Lark was convinced the mare was gone, he would be happy with human companionship again.

Is was thinking that as they climbed the first ridge and turned north, deeper into the Boundary. That was the wrong direction for the man to be going if he was going to report her.

Lark was moving steadily now, not panicked, but determined. From the top of the next ridge she saw the man. He and the mare were halfway down the other side, moving at a steady walk. Lark called. Is wondered if the man would try to outrun them. Instead he turned the mare around and waited for them to pick their way down to him.

Is wasn't sure what to say or do. She let Lark touch noses with the mare. Both horses made small throaty sounds of greeting. The man sat like a sack of potatoes, not a horseman of the caliber of the one who must have trained the mare. And yet the mare wore no bridle, and he had gotten her to leave the other horse behind. Is was as confused as ever about him. He sat regarding her with those soft gray eyes in a face that was still hollow and sunken, and somehow too hard to contain those eyes.

Is said, "Where are you going?" She didn't know if he could answer.

He turned and looked north, and then back at her.

"Why north?" she asked him. He grinned suddenly. It was

a harsh baring of his teeth that was not at all like the smiles he had given her before. He made some small movement with his body, and the mare turned and began to walk. Is let Lark pace them.

"Are you going to meet someone?" If he could not answer the broader question, perhaps he would answer less general ones. But he didn't look at her.

"Are you going to turn me in?" She didn't know why she asked. If he did answer, she couldn't let herself believe him. The mare came to an abrupt stop. The man twisted around in his saddle, reached into his saddlebag, and came up with one of the shiny, metal "tools" Is had wondered about before. He twisted the end of it, pointed it at a piece of deadwood lying several meters away, and suddenly the wood was smoking. A moment later it burst into flame.

Is stared at it. She had heard of wonderful tools like that. She had seen the cutters the lumbermen used to fell and split trees to make lumber for her barn. This was something like that.

Suddenly the man turned and pointed the tool directly at her chest. For a moment Is was too shocked to believe the threat, but one look at the man's eyes convinced her. They were wild. His lips were parted in a tight grimace that wasn't a smile. His hand shook with the emotion he was feeling, but it didn't shake enough to make Is think he would miss. If he meant to kill her, he could.

Instead, he turned the tool away from her, gave it a twist, and put it back in his pack. Is sat, stunned, while the mare started to walk again. When Lark began to follow, Is let him. Her mind reeled about like a drunk. The man could have killed her. But then he'd put the tool away. Was he trying to say he meant her no harm? Was he trying to tell her not to follow him? But he had done nothing when Lark started following again. Maybe he was just crazy. Is had never seen eyes look the way his had looked, tortured and frightened and angry all at once. They couldn't be the eyes of the same man who had smiled his appreciation for her help, or an apology for his needs. They did not look like the eyes of the man who had sat stroking his mare's ears, even though the effort of lifting his hand that high had made his whole arm shake. Suddenly Is had to know what she was dealing with.

She gave Lark a short pressure with her legs that sent him in front of the mare, and wheeled him about to block the man's path. The mare halted patiently. Is had the man's attention. His eyes questioned her, sane and rational, nothing of the man who had held the weapon in them at all.

"Look, I don't know who you are. I don't know where you're going. But if you take this mare into those mountains, she'll die this winter." He took in her outburst without expression and just sat until Is felt foolish, then he gently steered the mare around her.

"There won't be enough grass," Is called after him. "She'll starve." He kept riding.

"There will be too much snow. She won't grow enough coat. She'll freeze." But he kept going.

"Damn you! She's too nice of a mare. Don't do that to her." Is sent Lark in front of the mare again and blocked her. The man met her eyes. He tried to turn the mare aside, but Is made Lark block him again. The man's mouth worked as though he were trying to speak. The crazy look was coming into his eyes again. Suddenly Is remembered his weapon. But he didn't reach for it.

His voice was high, and strained.

"Of dread thou knowest not./Ah, but where life leads thee, follow. Steady. Steady as the mare's tread." His voice broke into a high, hysterical giggle. His face worked as if he were trying to say something. He seemed almost to conquer himself. His eyes were desperate with some emotion Is couldn't understand.

Suddenly he threw his head back and shrieked laughter to the sky. Lark pinned his ears back and fidgeted nervously. Even the mare reacted, tossing her head in an uncharacteristic way.

Lark's prancing moved him out of the way, and the mare began to walk again. Is let them go. The man was insane and dangerous in some way she could not comprehend. Lark pulled at the reins to follow, but Is held him back. He fretted and whinnied as they watched the mare out of sight.

-VII-

At first Is was just going to follow the man for a couple of days. She wanted to know if he changed direction or met anyone. Then she'd turn aside and find another place to live. It was late summer; there would still be time to get ready for winter. There had to be.

But Lark wasn't happy with following. He pulled impatiently to catch up to the mare, and that evening Is had to tie him for the first time.

Partly to calm herself, and partly because she needed the food, she took her knife and went hunting. Hunting had become a ritual for her. It had not been easy for her to learn to take the lives of small animals, but that first winter she had become desperate. At first she had tried snares. But sometimes the animals were trapped but not killed, and suffered horribly until she came. So she had taught herself to kill with the small, slim knife she had brought with her.

The knife was a clean death, very quick. The most wary, most intelligent animals probably escaped. She liked to believe that.

She had learned a lot about the rabbits she hunted, and had come to love their quick, frightened temperaments. They could sense a predator with senses Is wished she had. The best way to hunt them was to wait, in a sort of not-waiting mode, for them to come to her. It was like a meditation. She had to keep her mind still, not wanting, or expecting, or hoping. The animal would come, or not.

Is found a little trail and settled herself comfortably,

dismissing all thoughts and worries. Lying in the grass, waiting in her special way, Is found the peace the land always brought her. The problems the man had introduced into her life receded. She was enveloped by the smells of the ground and the grass. She heard the birds begin their evening songs, and the rustling of insects, and finally the movement of a small animal. The rabbit came grazing his way along the little trail. A few steps, a hop, raise his ears a moment, graze a few mouthfuls, step, hop. His nose twitched constantly, but he could not smell Is in her clothes patched with rabbit skins and well saturated with the smells of the ground. Besides, he was watching for foxes, weasels, or owls, not a being he had probably never seen the likes of before.

Is always felt a kinship with these small, hunted animals. But that kinship contained the knowledge of their role as prey animals, just as she was prey to larger animals, and her own kind. The killing was not just for food, it was part of the chain. It connected her into the chain, and it made her own death more acceptable somehow.

She carried the small, warm corpse back to where Lark was tied. He had pawed a deep hole in a thwarted attempt to go to the mare. His neck and chest were wet with sweat. Is felt sorry for him. She did not mean to hurt him, but he couldn't understand.

She stroked his ears, trying to comfort, but he had little attention to spare for her, and she began to question herself. Maybe she should go with the man and take her chances. At least he was not going back to the Alliance. But he was crazy and probably an outlaw. Still, he hadn't stolen Lark when he could have, and he hadn't hurt her, only frightened her with his odd behavior. Lark finally decided the matter for her, pulling on the rope and neighing.

It was almost dark by the time Is caught up to the man. He had pitched his tent and was standing by it, alerted to her approach by the mare. He didn't seem surprised to see her, but didn't do anything to invite her to stay, or to suggest he wanted her to leave. She dismounted and untacked Lark, who went immediately to grazing with the mare.

The man had chosen his campsite well. There was water nearby, and grazing for the horses. His tent was pitched on high ground, but sheltered from any unexpected storm by the lay of the land. He was sane enough to have good camping skills.

A fire was going, and some water was warming. He watched Is skinning the rabbit, but she had entered her own world again, giving thanks to the rabbit and to the chain of which the rabbit was a part, communing in this way with her own life and death. No matter how many times she had done this, she was always reverent, always amazed at the intricacy of the small being.

The man intruded into her moment by taking the guts Is had set aside. He slit them open, and began sorting through the grasses and leaves the rabbit had eaten, very meticulously attempting to unfold and piece together each leaf and blade. Occasionally he held something up to the fire to see it better.

Is was frightened by his behavior. When he began to eat the contents of the rabbit's stomach, it was too much for her.

The cooking of the rabbit, which was usually something of a ritual for her, was ruined by the man's presence. When she offered him half, he waved it away.

Is pitched her fly and spent a restless, wary night wondering what the man might do next. It was a relief to hit the trail the next morning. She now thought of herself as the man's guard. She had to see him out of her territory and then turn back and find a place to live. She was still worried about the mare—the man was crazy enough to get her killed in the mountains—but Is didn't know how to save her.

The man's camp breaking was efficient and thorough. He took considerable care with dismantling the fire, soaking the coals and scattering them so that not only could they not start a fire, but also they would sink quickly into the ground, replenishing it. And there would be no trace of their camp. Is wasn't sure which consideration motivated him.

Is spent considerable time watching him ride, trying to figure out if he could be the horseman who had trained this mare. She could not decide. He slouched in the saddle in a way good horsemen did not. But he might have been too weak to sit up, or he could have been in some kind of pain.

Suddenly the man slipped from the mare's back and scrambled up the rocks they had been passing. Is's first thought was of ambush. She twisted around in her saddle but saw nothing. Meanwhile, the man had crouched like some wild animal, scraping frantically at the rocks with his knife. When he lifted the knife, it was covered with bright, yellow-green fungus. The man ran a finger along the side of the blade and slid all of the poisonous-looking glop into his mouth.

He started to scrape again, but his hand shook, and a moment later the knife clattered on the rocks as he pitched forward onto his hands and knees, vomiting like a dog. Is sat on Lark and watched dispassionately. Perhaps he had poisoned himself and would die.

He didn't die. When he'd finished being sick, he slid down the rock and remounted the mare. He gave Is a wan little smile and started the mare walking.

The ground continued to get steeper and more rocky all day, and the air was getting thinner. The trees had shrunk down to miniature things, the height of Lark's knees. It was a clear, still day, but the gnarled roots and twisted trunks told a story of great wind and hardship. Is could look up and see the next saddle for which they were headed outlined against the sky that was such a deep blue it was nearly purple.

As they climbed above the last of the little trees, the soil became a thin coating of pebbly rock over heartrock, and the only vegetation was a mossy, sponge-like mat.

The summit was farther away than it looked, and never seemed to get closer.

Eventually they stopped to rest, dismounting and loosening the girths to let the horses relax.

Is stretched out on the ground. The sky was a cloudless blue, and the sun pinned her to the earth. There was a silence here that was unusual in nature. Even the wind that must usually haunt these high places was still. The rocky ground was warm against her back, and the incline was just right to lie against and look over the stupendous view without having to lift her head. Ridge after ridge of tree-covered mountains faded away into the distance.

The exhausting effects of the altitude made Is lethargic. Below her an eagle circled lazily. She could see the sun glinting off the top of its wings. It was an unusual perspective to have on one of the great mountain birds, and it gave her a sensation as if she were flying. She could feel the slow wheeling around of the world under her. She began to be dizzy and concentrated on feeling the solidity of the rock under her, slipping into sleep so smoothly she didn't even realize it was coming.

. . . Horses surrounded her. Refined and delicate as the bridle-less mare, they watched her with intelligent eyes. She caught her breath at their beauty, and something else . . . less easy to name, a sort of royalty. Their presence was an honor they bestowed upon her, letting her see them, ghost silent, dream real. It was as though they wanted to tell her something. . . .

The scrunch of Lark's hooves on the gravel woke her. She sat up too fast, startled from the dream. The landscape spun and stilled, empty of a herd of horses.

The man was lying not far from her, asleep. His features were relaxed, and he looked so kind and gentle Is wished she didn't know another side of him.

Lark and the mare were standing head-to-tail, each resting a hind leg, sleeping. Their heads hung low. Their tails swished gently from time to time, swiping the flies from each other's faces. It was a scene of such contentment Is hated to disturb it. But they needed to crest the ridge and get back down to the tree line for water and grass for the horses.

Is scuffed the gravel deliberately. The man's eyes came open. He sat up and looked around, taking in the view, or, Is thought for a second, looking for her ghost herd of horses. But of course he would not have had the same dream. His eyes met hers, and he smiled that gentle, beautiful smile Is needed so much to see. He seemed to feel the same way she did; relaxed, at peace, and euphoric on the top of the world.

But he wasn't a trusted companion, and they weren't on a pleasure ride. Is stood up and went to Lark. As she was checking his hooves for rocks, the man came over and began going over the mare similarly. When he had mounted, they started up the hill again.

At the top of the saddle, the wind hit them. It was surprisingly cold, and in minutes they both had to don their coats. Now they really were on the top of the world. Behind them there were only lower ridges. Ahead the taller mountains were cut off by clouds. It was probably snowing on those peaks, although where they were, it was a bright, clear day.

As they started down, the clouds began to move toward them. Soon they were riding in a cold mist. The temperature dropped, and kept dropping. Snow came whirling out of nowhere, stinging against Is's face, driven on the wind like hail, and even Lark faltered.

The wind grew stronger, and the snow continued to come, obscuring everything but the dark shape of the mare in front of Is. It might be better, she thought, to turn back up slope and try the descent again after the storm had passed. Or it might be snowing heavily up there now too. The storm might pass as quickly as it had come, or it might sit on them for days. There was no way to tell, with mountain weather, if it would be better to push on, or stop and wait.

Suddenly Lark's hindquarters gave way. For an instant he was falling out from under Is. Only her reflexive rebalancing kept her with him as he scrabbled on the icy rocks.

Finally, one mighty plunge brought him alongside of the mare.

"We have to stop!" Is yelled at the man. "This is too dangerous!" But it was too exposed, and too steep to stop where they were. The man made a hand motion, down and to the left, as though he knew a place where they could find shelter.

It didn't turn out to be much shelter, just some sort of pocket where the ground was more level, but the worst of the wind roared by above them, like some monstrous thing bearing down on them, but never quite arriving.

Even so, there was enough wind that there was no way Is's makeshift tent was going to stay up. Instead she helped the man with his. He had some sort of tool that forced the stakes right through the snow and ice, into the rocky shelf.

When the tent was up, they dragged their gear inside, bringing snow in with them, but there was no way to keep it out—everything was covered with it. It was a struggle to get the tent flap closed against the wind, and once it was closed, it was too dark to see anything. The tent shook and shuddered with each new blast of wind. The small, bent poles that held it up bent more and snapped back into place with ominous creaking and popping sounds. But the strange, too thin fabric kept the wind out.

Is couldn't see the man and couldn't hear what he was doing. But she couldn't squat there all night, dripping snow, and getting colder by the second. She needed to get out of her wet clothes and into her bag.

The man bumped into her as she was struggling out of her jeans. He caught hold of her and she froze. She couldn't see him at all, and couldn't tell if he was on the verge of one of his crazy attacks or not. She was trapped in a tent she couldn't get out of quickly, half-undressed, half-freezing . . . He let go of her.

Shakily she rummaged in her pack and found the small, slim knife and set it where she could reach it.

By the time she had gotten into a dry shirt and crawled

into her bag, she was freezing. Her hands were so numb she
could barely feel the knife she was still gripping. There was
a real danger she would cut herself with it, so she placed it
just outside the bag, where she hoped she'd be able to find
it quickly. Her legs, from her knees down, hurt with cold.
Her feet were frozen lumps. Her hands were so cold that
trying to rub warmth into her feet and legs with them was
not working. She had to put her hands under her armpits to
warm *them*. She began to shiver and couldn't stop. Her little
homemade bag wasn't meant for this kind of cold.

She lay there feeling miserable, and worrying about the
horses. Lark was tough-skinned and hardy. If it didn't stay
this cold for too long, he would survive. But the mare had
a fine coat. She would be shivering. The horses had had no
food since mid-morning, and that made a big difference to
horses. Being grazers, they were designed to have food
passing through their systems all the time. They had not
eaten well even the day before. Between the cold and the
lack of roughage, they could colic, and that could be a
life-threatening situation with horses.

But there was nothing Is could do. She huddled in her
sleeping bag, in her own misery, and worried, far too cold to
sleep. Shivering swept through her body in waves, and
instead of getting warmer, she seemed to be getting colder.

She suffered for what seemed as if it must have been all
night, and when she was finally so cold she couldn't take
any more, she crawled out of her bag and felt her way over
to her clothes. They were stiff with frozen snow. Her pants
cracked as she got into them. At least they were too frozen
to be wet.

The cold made her have a desperate need to urinate. She
finished struggling into her clothes as quickly as she could.

Outside it was still snowing but wasn't quite as windy. Is
moved cautiously away from the horses, but she was afraid
of falling into a drift, or losing her way, so she didn't go
very far. She fumbled with her pants with fingers that were
stiff and unfeeling. Once she had them down, it was too cold

to let go. She had to stay that way quite a while before her body became convinced.

Then she made her way over to the horses. Lark seemed to be resting quietly. The mare was hunched and shivering, but there wasn't anything Is could do for her. She went to put her hands in her pockets and got a shock. She couldn't feel her pockets, or her hands. She tried to do the motion by memory. Her arms moved vaguely, as though they were asleep. There was almost no feedback. For a moment Is's heart raced with uncontrolled fear. She'd been cold before, but she'd never lost control of her hands like this.

She went back to the tent. In the dark, and with no sense of feeling in her hands, it was hard to get the flap open. She was beginning to realize that her life depended on doing it. A strange stubbornness came over her. She forced her hands to work in the way she remembered they needed to work, and somehow she got the flap open.

She thought she heard the man move in his sleeping bag. "It's me," she said to him. Her face was frozen, and her lips didn't work. The words that came out didn't sound like "It's me," but he would recognize her voice.

She had her back to him, concentrating on getting the flap sealed, when there was a sudden flicker of greenish light. She sprung around, her mind suddenly full of the horrors she had been trying to forget about this land. But it was only the man, holding a little tube in his hand. It cast a weak, greenish glow, which made his skin and hair look green and put strange, dark shadows under his eyes.

Is fought down her fear. The man's light was supposed to help her, but she had to get out of her jeans again and she wished he'd turn it off. He didn't.

Is did the only thing she could do, privacy wise. She didn't look at him. Getting her jacket off took all her concentration. Her hands refused to feel anything. The buttons on her pants nearly defeated her. By the time she had gotten down to her underwear, she was quaking all over, and her sleeping bag wasn't going to be much help.

The sound of the seals being released on the man's bag startled her. When she looked at him, he was lying back, holding the bag open to her, inviting her in.

Her body cried out for relief from the cold, but her mind screamed its fear. She couldn't move. A very long time seemed to go by. He didn't move either. He must have been getting cold, and his arm must have been getting tired, holding the bag open to her as he was. Is got up the courage to look at his eyes. They were soft, concerned, waiting. Her body was screaming at her for the offered warmth. Her mind was loosing.

She moved before she was aware of having made the decision, and slid into the bag with the man. His body was like a furnace at her back. She must have felt like ice to him. She tried to keep from touching him, but the bag was not meant for two people. There was no way to be in it and not lie against him. She tried to keep her feet at least from touching him. But he deliberately brought his body into contact with hers along its whole length and placed his feet against hers.

His arms lay across her waist, holding the bag shut. It would not seal with both of them in it.

Is lay rigid, feeling scared, feeling guilty, and more scared. It must be terrible, she thought, to curl up to someone as cold as she was. He'd expect something in return. Surely there was a price on this. He was still weak. Maybe she could fight him off. Did she have any right to take this warmth then? She lay in a turmoil. He lay still.

Eventually the warmth seeped into Is, and the tension began to fade from her body. But her mind was not ready to relax. Her thoughts took her back to the government school, and, inevitably, to Riding Master Masley.

After her experiences at the school, it had come as a relief when she was sent to the Equestrienne to be trained. She had loved the horses immediately. Of course there were still other kids, and they were all above her—she was now

Junior Apprentice Drey—and they delighted in tormenting her. But somehow it wasn't as bad because of the horses.

Until Riding Master Masley.

. . . She heard his footsteps coming up behind her and quickly tried to think if she was doing anything wrong, or could be doing something better. She was carrying a saddle and bridle to the tack room to clean them after the morning workout. She was carrying them properly, moving quickly enough. She could think of no way she could be doing this better.

She turned into the tack room and breathed a little sigh of relief. The Riding Master would go on by. Instead he came in too.

Is busied herself setting the tack up for cleaning, pretending she did not know he was in the room with her. That lasted only a moment.

"Junior Apprentice Drey," he said.

"Yes, Riding Master." He would probably send her on an errand.

Instead he came over and perched one buttock on the edge of the table where she had laid out the saddle soap, sponge, and polishing cloth. She stopped disassembling the bridle. It would be rude to continue now that he had spoken to her.

He didn't say anything else for a moment, just rested there with one buttock on the table. He was wearing the black boots that came to just below his knees, and the tight-fitting stretch pants of his profession. He had just come from riding one of the horses. One of his hands rested on the table, one on his thigh.

"I have been noticing you," he said.

Is's heart sank. It was never good to come to anyone's attention, even if it wasn't for something bad. Anyway, a Riding Master would hardly be the one to reprove her for some sloppiness in cleaning tack or mucking a stall. There were senior apprentices for that, and above them junior riders and then senior riders. The Riding Master oversaw the senior riders and trained horses. It would be years before he should take any interest in Is.

"You are eager to begin learning to ride?" he asked her.

Her eyes leapt to his before she could control herself. *Yes.* But so was everyone. Why single her out? Maybe he'd seen her watching the riders. Maybe, somehow, he knew she'd have more talent than the others. Maybe there was something about the way she handled the horses when she led them to the arena for the riders? Her heart was full of impossible hope, and her mind was quick to find ways to believe it could be so.

He began to smile. His hand reached out and settled over her hand.

"Sometimes there are ways a student might pass to the riding phase without waiting four years."

His hand felt very hot on hers. She wanted to pull away, but didn't dare. She couldn't think of anything to say. She couldn't look at him.

"Do you understand me?" he asked her.

She still couldn't answer. She wanted to ride, but she couldn't do what he was asking. She couldn't. Although she knew many kids did it, she couldn't. She didn't know what was wrong with her.

He swung his bent leg forward and wrapped the toe of his boot around the back of her thigh, hooking her with it so she couldn't move away. His other hand came up, and the fingertips touched the side of her face and ran down her neck, and for a moment his hand cupped her breast, squeezing it, not hard, but as though measuring the size of it, deciding if it was interesting enough to him, as he might size up a horse's potential. His hand felt unpleasantly hot. The lines his fingers had drawn down her body were burned into her flesh. She hated him, and desperately wanted to move away from his touch, but didn't dare.

"Come to my office after lunch," he said. Then he released her and walked away.

She couldn't do anything for a moment. She was terrified

and furious. Then she heard a small sound and looked around, frightened that what had happened had been seen.

Suzanne was standing behind the saddle racks, and she had seen the whole thing. She was a senior apprentice, and should have been the next one to move up. Her face red with hatred, she walked toward Is; Is thought Suzanne would strike her. Instead, as she went by, she spat on Is's chest.

Is wanted to scream after her. "I don't want him! You can have him! I hate him!" But she didn't. It would not matter. Suzanne would hate her anyway, maybe even more so because the Riding Master was chasing her when she wasn't trying to attract him. No matter what Is did, the other kids would hate her.

Is did not go to the Riding Master after lunch. She wondered how much trouble she was getting herself into, but she didn't go.

The next day Is was standing at the sink in the tack room washing a bit when the Riding Master came in. He walked right up to her. Pretending to reach around her for the towel, he leaned his whole body against her, pushing her hips against her backside and pinning her to the sink. She couldn't get away from him.

"Today!" His lips were practically touching her ear when he whispered that. His voice was not loud, but his breath blew her hair, and she felt the heat of the air he expelled against her cheek. Then he walked away.

Is stayed at the sink, head down, pretending to wash the bit. She couldn't look up. There were at least three other apprentices in the room. When she couldn't stay at the sink any longer, she moved to the table and began reassembling the bridle. She kept her eyes down.

This time it was Elsa, Suzanne's friend. She swaggered past Is's workstation and knocked a can of leather conditioner over so that it spilled over Is's clean tack.

"Ooops," she said.

Is was too slow to stop the catastrophe. She would have to clean up the mess and reclean the bridle. She would probably get in trouble for wasting the oil. She didn't care. Maybe it would take her all of her lunch break to get the bridle back to perfect condition.

The next day was the worst because it was the most public. Is had led one of the horses to the ring for his rider and was just turning to leave when the Riding Master came by on a horse he was training. Just as she was certain the horse was going to go on by without stopping, the Riding Master vaulted from its back, landing right beside Is. His whip came down with a whack on the rail in front of her, and his body blocked her from turning the other way. She was terrified.

"Why didn't you come to my office?" he boomed.

There was no escape.

"Why?"

"I had extra cleaning. I didn't get done," Is mumbled quickly. All the riders were looking. Even the apprentices back in the stalls would hear his voice.

He took his time, as though considering her reply, while the tension built unbearably for Is. Everyone was looking at them. The Riding Master had absolute authority in the manège, but Is had hoped that some fear of higher authority in the system would help keep him in check. Although some instructors were known for advancing students through sexual favors, it was not supposed to be done. But if he dared to humiliate her this openly, Is didn't see how she had any chance of appealing to higher authority.

"Are you slow?" he asked her.

Is didn't know what would be the best reply. He tapped the whip in front of her, bringing it down with solid whacks on the railing, waiting with exaggerated impatience for her answer.

"Well?" He was using his Riding Master's voice, which could be heard anywhere in the arena and all through the stable area.

"Do you think you can ignore what I tell you to do?" he boomed.

"No, sir," Is whispered quickly. "I hadn't finished my work. I couldn't—"

"You *are* slow," he boomed. "Don't you realize you must be very quick to be a good rider?"

"Yes, sir." Her voice was no more than a whisper. At least he was making it seem like an infraction of the rules rather than what it had been—a refusal of his sexual advances.

"If you do not like it here," he said, changing tacks suddenly, "I do not think you belong here."

Is's heart stopped. *No!* He could not throw her out of the Equestrienne. She could not survive without her horses. She had no other friends, no other reason for living. It had never occurred to her that he might have that power over her. Her eyes leapt to his, pleading. She was ready to promise him anything, just don't separate her from her horses. She saw the cruel grin lift his upper lip and knew it was too late.

"We have no use for you here." He waited long enough to see what she would do. Plead for another chance, cry, promise to do anything he wanted. But she was too stunned. None of those "proper" responses occurred to her. He turned away from her and remounted his horse. He would ride away, and her life would be over. She was furious that one man could hold such power over her. It didn't enter her mind that she could change the outcome of what was going to happen. "Pack," he said. "You will go to the Berserker's Barn."

Under any other circumstances in the world, that would have terrified Is. But at that moment it was reprieve. She didn't care about the rumors. People got killed at the Berserker's Barn. The stallions were impossible to handle. The berserkers, who were being trained to ride there, were dangerous beyond description. She didn't care. She would get to stay with horses.

. . . Escaping from her memories, Is discovered that she had warmed up enough not to shiver anymore, but she could not relax. The man's body was solid against her back. Any moment he would make some sort of move, and Is did not know what she would do. Even in his weak condition, he was stronger than her, and she had seen him when he was not in control of himself. He had not harmed her, but she knew he could. It would probably be best not to fight him. If he were a thief, he was very good at it to have gotten away with such a fine horse and equipment. If she pleased him, he might be willing to help her hide. Or, if he were some high government official . . . ? If she got in his favor, there might be all sorts of rules he could break for her. Maybe she could even return to the Alliance and not be in trouble at all.

But to her heart none of that mattered. Whatever she might think she should do to improve her position or safety, there was only one decision her body would accept. She thought carefully about where she had left her knife and how quickly she could reach it.

But the man didn't move, and finally the warmth did its work and Is relaxed too.

She woke to a feeling of peace like none she had known since she was a little girl. She had turned in her sleep and was curled into the man's chest, and his arms were wrapped around her. She lifted her head to find him looking at her. His eyes held a peace so deep . . . it could not be rational.

Suddenly Is wanted to cry. He was some sort of crazy person. The peace and security she'd felt sleeping in his arms were as false as the security of her mommy and daddy's presence had been. Worse. They had at least been stable, rational people, trying to give her a home and love. It was not their fault the events of the world were too big for them to protect her against. It was not their fault they had been raped and killed. But it had taught Is the truth of the world. No one could protect you.

She sat up quickly, before her thoughts could carry her into old grief. He didn't make any move to restrain her as she got out of the bag and struggled into her crusty clothes. When she looked back at the man, there were tears on his face. Silently, and unexpectedly, he was crying.

Is could not bear to look at him. Whatever pain he was

feeling, she would never understand it, as he would never understand her pain. She jerked her gaze away and went out before he could start doing something crazy again.

The wind had stopped. The air was very cold, crystalline. The mountains were breathtaking in fresh snow, impossibly white against the sharp, blue sky. Their stunning presence calmed Is. A winter bird trilled in the stillness, and the sound seemed to go into her very bones. Her breath momentarily fogged the scene as she let it out. She loved this land in a way she loved nothing else. It would be here always. It had a permanence that nothing else had, except death. When she died, that permanence would be hers. She was part of the chain.

The horses had moved down the slope and pawed the snow, looking for something to eat. Lark had a layer of white on his wide rump. He seemed content. The mare was hunched against the cold, her belly drawn up and her tail clamped down. She looked miserable. The best thing for her would be to get moving. She'd warm up with activity, and if they got below the snow, there would be grass and water.

The man came out of the tent, and Is went to help him pack up. She avoided meeting his eyes, and he seemed only interested in getting under way again.

-VIII-

They had crossed the valley floor and were ascending the next slope when they came upon the hoofprints of shod horses. The man dismounted to examine them. They looked recent to Is. She glanced around nervously, her heart racing. Shod horses could only be government troopers. When the man remounted and started to follow the trail, Is held Lark back. Everything she had felt she was starting to know about the man flipped over.

If the man meant to take her in, he might use the tool/weapon to keep her from running away, but he hadn't looked back yet. He didn't know she wasn't following.

She reined Lark around, hard, and drove her heels into his sides. Surprised by her sudden roughness, Lark lunged forward into the trees. Is crouched low, over his neck. Branches buffeted them as they ran, and now Lark had picked up Is's terror. He plunged down the hillside, dodging trees, ducking low branches.

Suddenly Is was nearly pitched from Lark's back as he stumbled. His neck disappeared from in front of Is as he fell, twisting. He was going down on his right shoulder. He would fall on her leg. Possibly roll over her. She kicked her feet free of the stirrups. The ground rushed at her, terrifyingly fast. In the instant before she smashed into it . . .

. . . she didn't.

The world receded into a spinning dot, and came back.

Lark stood, foursquare, under her, trembling.

She stroked his neck to reassure him, although she needed

reassurance as badly. She wasn't sure what had happened. Maybe some branch had hit her when Lark was falling, and she'd almost blacked out, but he had recovered, and she'd stayed on by reflex. OK, that made sense. She'd take good luck like that anytime it was handed to her.

Lark had recovered his composure. He stretched his head down and helped himself to the irresistibly green grass.

Funny, it almost looked like spring grass, not the tough, mature stems they'd been seeing. Maybe this little meadow was protected somehow.

She'd have loved to let him eat . . . but if the man followed her, or if he alerted the troopers, she'd be pursued. She pressed her legs to Lark's sides, and a wave of dizziness swept through her. Lark took a few steps, and the rolling movement of his walk upset Is's equilibrium as if she had never sat on a horse before. She had to clutch the saddle. When there were no further signals from her, Lark stopped to eat again.

Is slid from his back. Her knees refused to support her, and she sat on the ground. Pursuit or no pursuit, she was going to have to rest a moment. Unconsciousness overtook her in a spinning rush.

She woke to the long shadows of late afternoon. Lark grazed near her, fully tacked. His reins trailed on the ground between his feet, but he had learned not to step on them.

Funny he hadn't gone looking for the mare, but maybe the green grass held him.

There was no sign of pursuit. She'd been really lucky, but it was time to get going. Her body felt so much like dead meat as she got to her feet that she was forced to reconsider.

Maybe it wasn't such a good idea to leave this meadow. No one had found them here all day, after all.

She untacked Lark and pitched her tent. It was a lot warmer here than it had been on top of the pass.

She didn't sleep well, continually listening for Lark. Although he had not shown any desire to go after the mare, Is worried he would not be there in the morning.

Even her memories were better than worrying about the future, and she found herself thinking about her first days at the Berserker's Barn. The government rig had dropped her off at the front door to the indoor arena, armed only with a tough yellow folder, which probably told everything she had ever done wrong, and a small satchel of clothes.

She had entered the ring timidly. The inside was enormous, and quiet except for the exertions of the six horses who were working at that moment. Is closed the door quietly behind her and stood still, transfixed by the beauty of the horses. These were not the older horses—retired brood mares, and geldings who hadn't had the quality required for breeding stallions—that Is was used to handling in the Apprentice Barn. These were magnificent, highly bred, proud, powerful stallions in the peak of condition. The riders were so absorbed they hardly spared Is a glance. She stood, pressed to the wall, watching, and didn't see, or hear, the Riding Master approach.

"What are *you* doing here?" the Riding Master's rough voice demanded, stressing "you" as if she were unworthy to enter the arena with his horses and students.

Is was too startled to speak. Silently she held the folder toward him.

"Ha," he said brusquely, taking it and flipping it open. "Apprentice!" he bellowed the next second. "*Junior* apprentice!" His glance jumped from the folder to Is, and she knew he saw a weak, frightened child and forced herself to stand taller and not flinch when he bellowed. "What are those assholes thinking? An apprentice! A junior apprentice! You'll get killed." Then he paused, and suddenly his countenance softened as he thought of a possible explanation. "Are you sure they meant to send you?"

Is could only nod. She was terrified of how her voice would sound. Now she understood why Riding Master Masley had sent her here. But she wasn't going to get killed. Suddenly she was sure of that. These were horses. The most beautiful horses she had ever seen. She wasn't going to be

afraid of them, even if they did tower over her, even if their
legs were like pillars and their feet were enormous. Even if
they were stallions and she had never handled a stallion in
her life. She was going to learn how to handle them so they
didn't hurt her. They had their instincts, and they had to be
true to those instincts. She would learn their true nature,
their rules, and she'd survive—not only survive, she'd
become a rider. With new resolve she raised her eyes to
Riding Master Lowbridge's; only he wasn't looking at her
now. He was reading her file.

"Shit!" he said, summing up his disgust with her. Then he
turned and bellowed, "Arimus! Arimus!" in a voice that
could have raised the roof if it had not already been so high.

In a moment a tall young man came hustling along the
edge of the arena.

"Arimus," the Riding Master said, "this is," he had to
consult the file, "Isadora Drey. They sent us a goddamned
junior apprentice." His voice had risen again. "Assholes! I
can't believe this. You take her. You see to it she doesn't get
killed." He stalked off, grumbling loudly.

Arimus looked her over. He wore the blue of an interme-
diate, intimidating, but not as much as a senior rider or a
master. He had a very dour expression, made more dour by
his assignment.

"*Junior* apprentice?" he asked her.

Is acknowledged what was beginning to seem like a
crime.

"What do you know how to do?"

"I can groom, tack up, lead a horse, clean stalls and tack."
Her voice didn't sound as bad as she'd feared.

"You can groom, tack up, and lead a *school* horse," he
corrected with disdain, "not a real horse, not one of our
stallions, and don't forget it. This is a whole different arena
here. You can't mess around here. You've got to keep your
mind on what you're doing all the time. You *could* get
killed. Worse, you could get one of the horses hurt." He was

looking her over again, but now Is felt he wasn't trying to intimidate her. The warning was real.

He couldn't know she hadn't "messed around" in the Apprentice Barn. She had applied herself there, only she had not done what the Riding Master wanted.

"The horses aren't the only danger," Arimus continued. "They told you what we do here?" he asked and didn't wait for an answer. "We train the men who are going to be the berserkers. They've got to be damn good riders. They aren't completely berserkers yet, and some of them don't make it. Some of them don't pass the riding. Some flunk out physically, or mentally. Sometimes they go crazy." He eyed her closely. "It doesn't happen often, but when it does, it's bad. You've got to be awake. This isn't kindergarten anymore."

Is didn't say anything, but in her heart she swore to learn to handle these "real" horses, and one day to ride them. She was not afraid of the horses, and somehow she was suddenly not going to be afraid of the people either.

So she had applied herself, and she had won her way, inch by muscle-aching inch, all the way up to senior rider. Surely that had been harder than what she was facing now. At least now she was alone, and if she was alone, she could be safe.

When she finally slept, nightmarish dreams plagued her. Involved in them, she didn't wake fast enough. Lark's whinny was part of her dream. Then there was the sound of many horses milling about, and someone thrust open the tent flap.

Is came out of her sleeping bag faster than she'd ever moved in her life. She attacked—charging the man with all her might—knocked him down, and was past him, only to be tackled from behind by another man as she burst from the tent.

On her stomach, on the ground, she was very aware of the horses. Their legs were a milling forest in the moonlight, their hooves coming within inches of her prone body.

Unshod. Marauders, not government. Lark was hidden from her view.

The man who had grabbed her had his arms wrapped around her legs. She twisted around and slugged him in the face. Only he ducked, and her fist hit his shoulder rather harmlessly. Other men laughed. Someone's feet landed almost on her as he vaulted from his horse. He grabbed her by the hair and lifted. She swung at him too. She could see him well enough to see the blueish cast to his skin. Until that moment she'd been more furious than scared.

They forced her to her feet by twisting her arm behind her back. She tried to ignore the pain. Keep fighting. They were going to kill her anyway, and if they killed her before they raped her, so much the better.

Pain made her start to loose consciousness, and then adrenaline brought her to again, so that everything seemed to be happening in jerky little flashes.

Suddenly everything was quiet. She must have been out for a moment. The men had formed a circle around her. No one was moving. She got to her knees. The circle spun. She exerted her will and made the circle be still. The man she was facing was obviously the leader, exuding a severe dignity Is couldn't ignore. She stood up. The world did one complete rotation, and stopped. She ignored the places her body hurt and focused on the Blueskins. Their resemblance to berserkers struck her. They had the same wide chests and thickly muscled arms and legs, but they were shorter than berserkers.

When the leader saw that he had her attention, he beat on his bare chest with the palm of his hand, making a loud noise. Then he delivered a short, guttural speech.

He would probably be the first to rape her, but all Is could do was stare at him. She'd meant to fight as hard as she could, try to get herself killed, or at least knocked out. But now, somehow, it seemed too late. Whatever was happening here was not what she'd expected.

Chest got done with his speech, turned, and gestured, and

a man led Lark into the circle. Is came alert. She'd kill any one of them before she'd let them harm Lark. She didn't think about how.

They'd put a rope with a slip knot around Lark's neck. He'd never been led that way, and didn't know the knot could tighten, strangling him. It would be a very dangerous way to handle a fully trained war-horse, who would fight anything that hurt him, but Lark followed the man complacently into the circle, confident in the goodwill of all humans toward him.

Chest hit his chest, making the loud noises again. Then he gestured to the horse and to Is and asked something in a language Is couldn't understand. She stared defiantly at him. He gave an angry grunt.

She turned and walked toward Lark. No one made any move to stop her. She reached out and took the rope from the man who was holding Lark as though she expected him to give it to her, and he did. She slid it off Lark's neck.

Everyone fell back a few paces, making the circle bigger. For a moment Is hoped they were retreating in fear, but they weren't. Chest hit his chest again, pointed at the horse, and said something. Then he too moved back to the edge of the circle. It was obvious what they wanted.

They had not offered her bridle or saddle. She'd never ridden Lark this way before, and she wondered if he'd respond to her signals. Without the saddle they'd feel different to him, and without the bridle there would be no way to make him obey if he didn't feel like it.

She turned him downhill of her. Without stirrups she'd have to vault all the way onto his back. She experienced a moment of doubt, but threw it out harshly, jumped as high as she could, grabbed his mane, and threw her right leg over. A fairly clean vault. Now she knew for sure where her body was hurt—her left elbow, right hip and leg, left ankle. She put the pain out of her mind.

She pressed Lark's sides with her calves, asking him to

walk and steering him around the circle with her legs and
weight. He answered as though they did this all the time.

If he had been fully trained, she could have broken
through the circle in a moment. But Lark wasn't trained for
that, and neither was she. If she got out of the circle, there
would be a high-speed chase on the steep, rocky trails in the
dark. The Blueskins' weedy little animals would be faster
under these conditions. Their riders knew the country, and
they might have weapons. She gave up the idea and turned
Lark around the circle.

If Lark had been trained in the battle airs, she could have
impressed the hell out of the Blueskins. But his training had
only gotten as far as the basics that formed the groundwork
for the battle skills. The movements he knew were less
deadly and more esoteric. But it was all Is had.

She asked Lark for a canter, and he moved into that gait
with an effortless, smooth bound. Using only her seat and
legs, she brought him into a collected, high canter. They
were on a slope, on rocky ground, with only the moonlight
to see by, but Lark responded to her aids, bringing his hind
legs well under him with each slow-motion bound, balanc-
ing as though he had the best footing in the world.

Is was impressed. But what would her audience of
Blueskinned barbarians know of the hours of work that had
gone into accomplishing this seemingly simple movement,
a collected canter on the side of a mountain, with no bridle?
They would need to see something flashy.

She turned across the circle and asked Lark for a flying
change of lead. He performed it effortlessly, springing into
the air and coming down on the opposite leading leg as
though he had jumped over a small, nonexistent hurdle.
Emboldened by the ease of Lark's response, Is asked for
another change, and then another in rapid succession. Lark
sprang through the air as though he were skipping.

For Is the watchers might as well have disappeared. Lark
transported her into heaven. The perfection of his responses
made her feel her love for him overwhelmingly. Sitting his

bare back, she could feel him use every muscle, as though they were her muscles, and in a sense they were. She made a small movement, and they responded with a larger one. Hypnotized by their mutual power, she felt their coordination go beyond training and become true communication.

She asked him to halt, and he came to a standstill, setting each hoof down once and not moving it again, sitting back into his momentum in such a way that he was able to cease moving instantly.

Without thinking, Is asked for a piaffe—trot in place. She hadn't taken Lark that far in his training, but he performed it perfectly. Answering her aids to trot, halt, trot, halt, he produced the trot in place even though he had never felt her signals applied in that sequence before.

Is's heart soared. Lark was giving every bit of his heart, joyously, performing not only for her but for his audience, human and equine. Before he could tire, she asked him to trot forward, and he launched himself into the great, ground-covering strides of the extended trot with huge, high, joyous strides.

But the circle was too small for such strides, and Is brought him into a halt. She was so filled with joy she had completely forgotten her audience. She slid from Lark's back, intent only on praising him for his gallant effort . . . and remembered the Blueskins. Sophisticated horsemen would have been impressed by what they had just seen, but she didn't know what the Blueskins would think. For a moment more she didn't care. She had always known Lark had a generous heart, but this night had transcended anything in her wildest dreams. It was the ride of a lifetime, and Lark had given it to her on the rocky, steep hillside, with no bridle, surrounded by people who probably meant to harm him. She pressed against his neck, thanking him silently with all her heart until Chest spoke in harsh grunts.

Immediately a guard appeared at either of her shoulders.

They didn't touch her, and so she let them escort her. Somehow what she had just experienced had lifted her

above the Blueskins, and above fear. She had been transported into a place of incredible dignity, where any sort of
physical struggle was too out of place to be considered, and
rape was an impossible indignity.

They set off in a direction Is thought would take them
across the little meadow. But now the grass that rustled
underfoot was the dry, coarse stuff of late summer.

They walked what remained of the night, and Is's
footsteps were oddly sure. She held her head high, moving
among the rocks and roots and steep places, keeping pace
with the mounted Blueskins.

Her euphoria lasted for hours. But by morning it was
gone. She was hungry and beginning to be very tired. Her
hip and ankle hurt with each step, sucking at her attention,
draining her energy. By then it was somehow too late to
resist. She trudged on through increasing fatigue and
refused to let herself think anything. She also refused to let
herself quit. No matter how tired she got, she would keep
going. She would not ask to rest for any reason; she made
that pact with herself, and somehow it was a carryover from
Lark's gallantry last night. She was repaying him in some
way, living up to the honor of having been the one he had
allowed to train him.

Once Is had made that covenant, she never looked at it
again. Walled in by her own fortitude, she was not aware of
the changes around her. The first she knew of the approaching riders was when they came galloping, whooping, around
the group that was escorting her.

Chest and his warriors sat taller on their horses, making
them prance for benefit of the younger braves. Is caught
glimpses of Lark, neck arched, and prancing, but he didn't
try to pull away from the man who was leading him. After
a few minutes the other Blueskins departed in a clattering of
hooves and great whooping cries.

Within a few more hours of walking, they reached the
Blueskin camp. The tents were of an octagonal design Is had

never seen before. There were a lot of them. She didn't bother to count.

Is had never thought about the marauders having homes, children, and wives. They had always been the enemy— terrifying, and savage, and unreasoning.

Lark threw his head up and whinnied. He was answered from the camp by a whinny Is recognized. The man's mare was standing at the fence of a corral calling to Lark. Is's heart jumped with hope. *He* was here. As though he could help her. He was probably a captive too.

They brought her to the middle of the tents, where there was a large, clear area for gathering. The people formed a rough circle with her and Chest's group in the middle. Men and boys raced their horses around the edge of the circle, whooping and shouting. Is noticed how the women held back, peeking shyly from huddled groups near the tents.

The men who had brought her in rode tall, especially Chest. Everyone admired Lark. He was excited by being among so many horses. He pranced and arched his neck, looking huge beside the Blueskins' stunted animals.

Is was looking around at all the activity when the man to her left tripped her and threw her to her knees in the middle of the circle. Before she could get up, Chest beat on his chest, silencing everyone. His warriors went into a reenactment of capturing her and Lark. During this, Chest just stood with his chest stuck out, but Is had to admit there was a kind of dignity about him. She couldn't understand the words, but the acting was very good. She was being credited with nothing. The way the other women held back, and the way she was not even allowed to stand among the men, told her all she needed to know. The best she could hope for would be to be like the other women, a lesser citizen, maybe one of Chest's wives. That was if they didn't kill her or make her a slave. At least they would take care of Lark. They obviously admired him. They would breed him to their weedy little mares, and he would improve their herd. He'd be happy enough.

But even as tired and defeated as Is felt at that moment, she knew she would not submit to the kind of life they'd expect her to lead. She would escape, or get killed trying. She had just reached that decision when she saw the man standing among the Blueskins watching. Her heart leapt with hope. He wasn't a captive. He would help her. Then suddenly she wasn't so sure. He was crazy, and he had to be an outlaw if he consorted with the Blueskins. He might be her enemy as much as they were.

He didn't look at her, but walked into the circle, signifying that he wanted to speak. Like most of the Blueskins, he was wearing no shirt, but his skin looked pale and out of place. He was a good head shorter than most of them, and still so underweight from his illness that his ribs showed. But there was a confidence about him Is had never noticed before.

He took center stage and turned slowly around the whole circle, looking at each person in turn. Everyone became silent, watching him. Suddenly he beat on his chest the way Chest had done, making a surprisingly loud noise in the silence, startling Is. He didn't speak, but he turned and pointed at her and the stallion and beat his chest again. His meaning was clear. They belonged to him. Chest, and everyone else, stared impassively.

He turned suddenly and strode over to Is and reached out to grab her by the shoulder as if he were going to make her stand up, or something, but Is had had enough. She came to her feet, swinging at his face as hard as she could. But he deflected her punch and caught her by the wrist so effortlessly it made her feel as if she must have moved slowly. Almost before she could think of hitting him with the other hand, he grabbed that wrist too. She let him pull her toward the center of the circle. But when he moved his hand to her shoulder, as though to turn her around, she was having none of it. She meant to spin all the way around and drive her elbow into him, but the next instant she was on her knees again. She couldn't figure out how he'd done that to her.

Lark was being led into the circle. The man stood back, as though inviting everyone to look at the stallion. Is wondered if he were claiming that the horse was his too, or if he were somehow bargaining her for the horse. She got to her feet, and no one seemed to notice because at that moment *he* let out a high shriek. Is didn't just hear it with her ears. It seemed to penetrate her mind and leave her startled and momentarily helpless.

There was a commotion in the corral. His mare came out of the herd at a gallop, heading straight for the fence. She stretched her neck, eyes fixed on the fence as she judged the distance and placed her strides. On the last one, she set her hindquarters well under her and lifted over the fence in beautiful form. No one else had time to admire it, because the mare was galloping straight at the circle, and everyone had to drop their dignity and get out of her way.

Only *he* didn't move. The mare came to a sliding halt right in front of him. It was too much for Lark. He reared, thrashing the air with his front feet, landed, and reared again. Is had a flash of what Chest must be seeing: the small, white-skinned man with the stallion rearing behind him and the mare sliding to a halt in front of him, while he never even turned to see if Lark would miss him with his hooves.

Is ran forward and caught Lark's rope, and he settled.

If Chest was impressed, it didn't show. He was still standing with his perpetual frown and unassailable dignity.

Meanwhile *he* stepped back from the mare, inviting everyone to admire her the way he had the stallion. His hands shaped the slope of her shoulder, the way her neck arched out of her chest, the angle of her hindquarters, built for running. Is was struck again by what a good cross she would make with Lark. She didn't think anyone present missed the point.

Now he turned to Chest. He held his arm out and rubbed and pinched at his skin as though showing it was a different color from Chest's. Then he pointed at Is and Lark, and then

over the mountains to the northwest. Is realized he was
telling Chest that he had been taking her and Lark to his
people—people of his skin color.

Chest was having none of it. He took a step forward, hit
his chest a few times, and pointed to her and Lark.

He, in his turn, went through acting out how he was
taking Is and Lark to his people again. As soon as he was
done, Chest stepped forward. He spoke in his language, at
the same time making motions that said the man and the
mare had been going one direction, and Is and the stallion
had been going the opposite direction.

The hope drained out of Is. She looked around, wondering if there were any chance they could make a break for it.
It looked impossible to her, but if *he* tried it, she'd be ready.
Instead *he* faced Chest in a belligerent pose and hit his own
chest, uttering harsh, guttural cries. Is didn't need that
interpreted.

Chest took a step forward, and they faced off. Is noticed
how strong Chest looked. His pectoral muscles stood out as
he beat on his chest. His biceps were huge, and the muscles
of his thighs bulged as he sank into a combat stance. Chest
would kill *him.*

Is didn't want to see this. She couldn't stand to watch
someone beaten, maybe killed, in front of her. She edged
back to Lark's shoulder. When the fighting started, she
would gallop through the midst of it. Maybe she'd even
be able to pull *him* up behind her. Maybe Lark would
tolerate that. Or maybe she'd be able to create enough
disturbance that the man could get on his own mare. She
doubted they'd escape, but she couldn't do nothing. Her
body tensed with readiness to vault onto Lark's back.

Chest chose that moment to charge. Is saw that much.
Then she saw Chest flying through the air. He hit the ground
hard but was up again in an instant. A murmur of surprise
ran through the crowd.

Chest attacked again. This time Is clearly saw Chest grab
the man's shoulder. Chest's other arm was cocked back to

punch. She saw the punch go wide as *he* moved to the side. Then she saw Chest suddenly lean over and go down to one knee. She couldn't see what the man had done to make Chest do that. He seemed hardly to have moved at all. Chest tried to get up, and an instant later he was sailing through the air again.

Chest was a little slower to get up this time, more cautious in his attack. *He* seemed unready for another attack. Is wanted to scream at him. Warn him. Something.

Suddenly Chest pulled a knife from its scabbard on his thigh and slashed.

Just as the blow would have landed, Chest reversed directions so suddenly he lost his footing and sat down heavily. *He* was standing sort of nonchalantly, holding the knife delicately, as though he didn't know how to use it. Slowly, he bent over and placed the knife on the ground. Then he straightened and walked toward Is and the horses. That was all the signal Is needed. She sprang onto Lark's back with no thought of how tall he was. The man walked on by, and the mare turned obediently and followed him. Is let Lark do the same. The circle just sort of faded to let them pass through.

The man walked to one of the tents and went inside. Is was afraid to get off Lark, afraid someone else would claim her, and afraid now that *he* had undisputed right to the stallion, he wouldn't bother about her. She waited a nerve-racking eternity until the man came back out with his saddle and bags and unhurriedly tacked the mare. He didn't give Is any sign of what she should do, so she just sat and waited. They might have been invisible for all the attention anyone else paid to them.

When the man mounted the mare and started out of the village, Is let Lark follow. They rode in silence for may-be half an hour while Is debated with herself. Perhaps she should thank him. But she wasn't sure he had rescued her. Maybe he only wanted the stallion. Or maybe she now belonged to him the way she would have belonged to Chest.

She might be as much a slave among his people as she would have been among the Blueskins. She looked at him to try to determine what her relationship to him was supposed to be, and saw that his face was set in a grim expression, as though he were in pain. Is's first thought was that he had been hurt in the fight.

He realized she was looking at him and came to a halt. With a hand signal he told her to stay where she was while he dismounted and walked into the woods on the side of the trail. He moved stiffly, half bent over.

Is's instinct was to go after him. If he was hurt, he needed help. But his hand motion had definitely told her to stay here. She was torn between going after him, running away—except the Blueskins would pick her up again—and staying as he wanted. She was dithering over what to do when he returned, walking briskly and upright. She almost couldn't smother laughter when she realized what had happened. He, who had seemed so calm and invincible facing Chest, had had an attack of diarrhea now that it was over. A little sputter of laughter escaped Is. She turned her face away from him, trying to control herself. She didn't mean to laugh at him. It was just relief. She'd been in awe of him, and somewhat frightened of him. If he could handle the Blueskin like that, she had no hope of fighting him, but all of a sudden he was just her crazy man again.

She heard the creak of leather as he swung into his saddle. The horses began to walk. Is still couldn't look at him. She couldn't get the grin off her face. She was startled by a little sputtering sound which wasn't her own, quickly cut off. Surprised, she looked at the man just as he looked to see if she had heard him. That was all it took. He started to giggle, high-pitched with the stress of trying to suppress it. Is couldn't help herself. In a moment they were both out of control, laughing, bent over their horses' manes, trying not to fall off. Gale after gale swept through Is. She had never laughed like this before, and she couldn't control it at all.

Everything was funny. Every little thing set her off again. Even after her sides hurt, Is couldn't stop.

For hours, all it took was for one of them to glance at the other, and they would be off again in uncontrollable laughter.

-IX-

Since leaving the Blueskins' camp, they had followed the trails openly. The day they had laughed together had changed their relationship. The tension Is had always felt around the man had dissipated, and he seemed more relaxed too. They laughed at little things now—a horse's silly spookiness, the antics of the small animals that invaded their camps, each other's mistakes. If the man was crazy, it no longer mattered. He treated her better than any of the people at the government school had. He had not tried to claim her as his wife or slave, or dominate her in any way. He was quiet, uncomplicated company. His camping and foraging skills were excellent, and if he couldn't talk, Is didn't miss it.

Plus, if the man had learned his camping skills from his people, they must know how to live as unobtrusively with the land as he did. If he had learned his bridle-less horsemanship from them, they must be great horsemen. Is was beginning to look forward to meeting them.

Instead, one day they crested a ridge and in the valley below them was a shabby little town of about twenty wooden shacks. Even from this distance Is could see the filth and squalor of the place. Piled behind the buildings were heaps of refuse. Anything that had ever been discarded lay about on the ground.

Is brought Lark to a standstill, and her revulsion must have been evident, for the man began to explain with his hands that they had to go down there. He tapped his saddle and pointed to Lark's bare back. All of Is's possessions had become the property of the Blueskins the night they had captured her. Sitting Lark bareback for hours on end, day after day, was uncomfortable, and Lark was beginning to get rubbed places in his coat which could turn into sores.

Is was relieved that this was just a place to get supplies, but she was still leery. She was an outlaw, riding a stolen war-horse. She couldn't just ride into a town like this. There might be a reward on her. She was not going down there.

He tried to reason with her. Pointing north, he began to count off days on his fingers. They would be traveling many days. He wrapped his arms around himself and shivered, and that also was true: it had been warm enough that Is had not needed a tent or sleeping bag, but she had already had to borrow the man's jacket and he would need it himself as they got higher.

He took a wallet from his saddlebag and opened it. Is had never seen so much money. He rifled through it, selected a few bills, and put them in his pocket. Then he handed the wallet to Is, motioning that she should put it in the inside pocket of his jacket, which she was wearing. She reached out to take the money and was surprised to see her hand shaking.

She had never seen so much money. No one had money like that. He must have stolen it. She remembered how he had handled Chest. She remembered how he had shown her that a tool could be used as a weapon. What if he had killed people to steal from them? Is was unable to put the wallet inside the jacket, next to her body, if it was stolen money, if he had killed people over it . . .

He was watching her.

He couldn't miss how her hand was shaking. She thrust the wallet at him, making him take it back. He shrugged and put it in a different pocket from the one he'd put the other money in. He was still looking at her with a quizzical eyebrow cocked. She rode past him and started down the ridge in front of him, so he could only see her back.

She tried to sort out her reaction. Why should she be so upset? She was an outlaw too. She had stolen Lark. If she had stolen as much money as Lark was worth instead, it might have been more than the money he had in the wallet. She didn't know. Lark was very valuable, but she didn't know exactly how that translated into money. She didn't even know the denominations of the bills she had seen. As a trainer Is had been paid in supplies, and credits that had gone toward her retirement. She never handled money and had not been taught how to read it.

Is rode down the hill in a turmoil. She had never intended to break the law. She had been forced to it to save Lark. She wouldn't deliberately harm anyone. But that must be what the man did. He sought out people and took things from them. He hurt them, and maybe, sometimes, killed them. If she let him buy her things with his stolen money, what would that make her? She thought of her parents and wanted to weep. She had sunk so far from what they had wanted for her.

She needed to make that right. Maybe she should give herself over to the law. Maybe she should let someone in this town take her in. She tried to think about Lark. Someone would finish his training, and he would be sent out with a berserker. He would die, fighting in a way horses did not fight if left to themselves. She tried to see the government that did that to horses and people as wrong. But now she couldn't. That government was trying to protect its people. It was not its fault it had failed in her parents' case. It was trying to make something better for its people than this stinking outlaw town, or the lawlessness of people like the crazy man she was riding with. She couldn't seem to remember any of the things she had felt that had made her steal Lark.

The man caught up and rode beside her into the town. Is was in such turmoil that she hardly noticed the smell of open garbage. Everything was stained with the red mud of the streets. Nobody had bothered to pick up garbage wherever it had been dropped. They were almost to the middle of the town before Is really looked at the people who were coming out of the houses to stare at her on the war-horse and the man on the bridle-less mare. The men were all of a kind—dirty, with long, greasy hair. They all wore filthy, worn clothes and old boots. Their expressions were hard and calculating. Is's instinct for self-preservation started to resurface.

She looked around more carefully. In contrast to the men, the women wore dresses that had once been very fancy and fine but were showing signs of too much wear now. They wore elaborated hairdos like nothing Is had ever seen before, and more jewelry than she'd ever imagined. Is was reminded of the way the Imperial Guard bedecked their horses for state occasions, each service trying to outdo the others, showing off their wealth in jewel-inlaid bridles, saddle blankets of the richest cloth, and saddles so encrusted with precious stones Is had wondered how the horses could carry their weight. She had poured over pictures of such pageantry as a child, and now she saw it dimly reflected in the display these women wore. She wondered if for the men of this town, the women were not just like the guard's horses—a means to display ownership and wealth.

They passed a few dispirited-looking, half-starved horses in a corral that was ankle-deep in mud and droppings that no one had bothered to clean in what Is judged had been years. The horses eyed them listlessly. Is could see where they had chewed the wooden fence in their hunger, and she knew right then that she was not going to give herself up to anyone in this town.

They came to a building that looked a bit more kept up than the others. This one had an awning, and people were sitting under it on old, rickety chairs and ancient bales of hay they should have fed to the horses long ago.

The man dismounted, and Is followed suit, while trying to keep an eye on the people. The men sitting around watched them with cold, calculating stares. Is saw one of them get up and saunter off. She suddenly wanted to get back on Lark and leave as fast as she could. But the man didn't seem to notice anything. He was accustomed to this sort of decadence, and danger, and implied violence. He walked into the store, leaving Is in a frenzy of doubt. She didn't want to leave the horses, but she didn't know if he would be able to bargain for their supplies without an interpreter.

She heard voices inside the store, if store it was, and after a while someone came out and trotted off down the street. More people were showing up all the time. Mostly they just hung out in doorways and stared. A few came over and joined the people under the awning. A few went inside. Is wished desperately that *he* would come out and they would leave before they couldn't.

Eventually he did come out, carrying an armload of stuff. Is moved to help him store it in the mare's saddlebags. There was a sleeping bag, food concentrates, and a coat and rain slicker for her. She took them without even trying them on. They would have to do.

He turned and headed back into the store before Is could stop him. A few more people sauntered in after him, making Is very nervous for his safety, and her own. The voices she heard from inside the store seemed to be friendly enough, but she couldn't make out the words. More people kept going in. Someone came back out with a bottle in his hand and called to a man across the street. More people went in. Is fretted, while inside the store the men drank, and their voices grew louder.

Eventually she saw the man who had left the store earlier, coming back, carrying a saddle.

"Try this," he said in a heavy accent Is had never heard before.

She couldn't believe her eyes. The saddle the man was holding out to her was a berserker's saddle, built for a war-horse. She couldn't guess how this man had gotten it.

It was old, and covered with a thick layer of dust and mildew, but it had originally been made with the highest quality workmanship and the best leather. With a little cleaning, and conditioning oil, it would be like new. Other than understandable stiffness from the neglect the saddle had suffered, everything seemed in good repair. The seat would be bigger than Is needed, but the saddle would fit Lark's broad back perfectly.

In the excitement of trying the saddle on Lark, Is forgot about the hostile crowd, until one of the men who had been lounging around spoke.

"You gotta pay for the saddle, little lady," he said to her, and then to the others, "Ain't that right?"

Taking their cue from him, other men chimed in. "Yeah." "That right, Gene." "Everybody got to pay their way here." They were beginning to move around her, and their voices and actions meant her no good.

She didn't bother to reply. The man who had brought the saddle had gone into the store. He wasn't concerned about being paid. But then neither were the others, really.

Is had let herself get caught on Lark's right side and mounting from this side was something she had never seen the need to practice. To mount with the saddle, she needed to jump high enough to stick her foot in the stirrup and then swing the other leg over. It was a coordination her body knew well from the left side of the horse, but it might not translate so well to the right. She hesitated a fraction of a second, and the men closed the circle around her until it would have been foolhardy for her to turn her back on them to mount.

She thought to swing Lark around so everyone would have to move out of his way. But at that moment a man stepped forward and grabbed the lead she had thrown over Lark's neck while she had been fitting the saddle.

"Now, where would you be thinking of going without paying us?" he asked her, and others made similar comments. Is wasn't listening. If Lark had been fully trained, she could have commanded him to strike out, and the man holding the lead would have been dead. Or she could make him kick the men who were standing too close to his hindquarters. But, as it was, Lark was totally trusting. He didn't know that anyone could hurt him, and he couldn't understand what it might mean to him if someone hurt her. These men either did not recognize Lark as a war-horse, or they had figured out he was not trained. Lark would be no help to her in whatever happened next, and it never even entered her mind to call out for the man's help.

She struck the first man who reached for her, knocking his hand away with an oblique blow. They all laughed, and retreated a little, but she knew they wouldn't quit now. They were goading one another on—"Don't be afraid of the little she-lion." "Hey, Digger, did she scratch you?" "Watch out for her teeth."—still kind of good-humored among themselves, but very serious for her.

She didn't see the man come out of the store. The first she knew he was there was when one of the men said, "Ooof," and sort of sat down suddenly. The other men caught on right away, though. In a moment they had turned away from her, and *he* was the one who was surrounded.

They still weren't very serious, still razzing each other—"Now, what's this? You suppose the she-cat's his woman?" "Naw, he ain't big enough to knock her down." "Or knock her up," and laughter, and like comments.

On some signal Is missed, the whole group charged in and dove on *him*. At least she thought that was what happened; an awful lot of people hit the ground. She was going to jump on Lark and try to make him gallop into the crowd, but if *he* was on the bottom, she didn't want to trample him. Instead she raced from Lark's side, grabbed a chair, and was about to wade in swinging as hard as she could, when the mare interposed herself between Is and the men. Is looked up and *he* was sitting on the mare's back, grinning. Is was so totally dumbfounded that she stood, staring stupidly a moment, and that was all the men needed.

They'd mostly realized that the man wasn't in the heap. They turned, saw her cut off from Lark, and headed toward her. She raised the chair.

Everybody suddenly wasn't in such a hurry.

He made the next move, causing the mare to pivot out of the way so there was an opening for Is to get to Lark. She walked slowly, her muscles tight as springs. No one moved. She made it to Lark, set the chair down, and sprang into the saddle.

The mare went by them in a gallop, and Lark dug in and went too. A lesser rider than Is would have been left behind in the dust. But Is was too much a part of her horse.

Lark would never catch the mare, but he was trying. Is crouched over his shoulders and let him run. Behind her there were whoops and catcalls and whistles, but nobody chased them. For the men of the town, it had just been a little fun to break the boredom. If they had succeeded in raping her, it would have been just the same, a little entertainment for them.

They were out of the town in no time and streaking across the plains, heading for the ridge they had descended earlier. In the name of safety, Is rarely galloped her horses as fast as they could go. Even for an experienced rider, such a gallop created a rush of adrenaline that was exhilarating. Her body took over the muscular coordination of moving with the galloping horse. Her mind was suddenly free, triumphant, and as wild as the horse's mind.

When they hit the slope, the man straightened up from his crouched position and the mare slowed. Is let Lark catch her, then straightened as he slowed to stay with the other horse. The man was grinning from ear to ear, and Is realized that she was too. It felt good to be able to break and run away from that kind of harassment.

It hadn't been that way in the government school. There had been nowhere to go, and no one to go to for help. Well, that wasn't quite true. If you were "with" the right people, no one else would bother you. But Is had never been able to do the things that would have gotten her that sort of protection. She had been fair game for everyone.

They were moving along at a steady trot now. But the day had grown dark for Is. Her mind took her back to the school.

. . . "So you're the peasant?" Phil looked her over with cold appraisal.

Phil was the protector for Beth's group. For some reason Beth had befriended Is, and she wanted Phil to take Is into the group.

It was after curfew, and it was part of the test of Is's mettle to sneak out like this.

Phil walked around her, looking her over. Is glanced at Beth. Beth gave her a little encouraging smile. Beth hadn't told her it would be like this.

"So, what do you know how to do?" Phil asked.

Is knew how to milk cows, and cut hay, and weed gardens, and carry water.

"C'mon, Phil," Beth said. "She's pretty. She'll be fine. I'll watch out for her." But Is already knew enough about Beth to know that that wasn't going to reassure anyone. The next thing she knew, Phil had reached right up under her government blouse and taken hold of her breast. She felt that she had to stand there and let him, because Beth had brought her to him, and Beth's position in his gang was at stake too, over her.

"Do you know how to do it?" Phil asked in a lewd voice. "Do you know how to do it real good for a man?"

When she didn't move, Phil let go of her breast as if he were dropping it in disgust.

"She ain't no good to me," he said to Beth, as if Is weren't still standing there.

Beth was going to protest. Is could see that. Phil saw it too.

"It takes more than a hot cunt, baby," he said, sidling over to Beth. Is saw his hand go right up under Beth's skirt, as if he owned her. Beth's eyes went half-shut, and she moved her legs apart. In a moment she began to push her hips against his hand. But Phil wasn't even looking at Beth. When Is's eyes came up, startled from what she'd realized was happening, Phil was looking right into her eyes. He bared his teeth at her in a way that wasn't any kind of smile.

Is backed away, then caught herself and made herself turn and walk. Closing the door behind her, she looked back. Beth had both her hands on Phil's chest and her head was bent forward so her forehead was on his shoulder. She'd never noticed that Is had left. But Phil was watching, and his look was triumphant. He controlled both women. One he chose to keep, and the other he drove away. Somehow he had taken the initiative away from Is. She felt as conquered as Beth.

. . . Is shook herself free of the memory. Out here it was different. Surely. But the day seemed darker than it had. Maybe the only difference was that there was more room to run.

In the school she had closed the door and gone back to her own ward. But her trouble had only begun. Unprotected by any gang leader, she was harassed by everyone, blamed for anything that needed a scapegoat, and hated, fiercely, by the rest of the girls.

Early on she had tried to appeal to the authority of the adult attendants. She had quickly learned better. They had treated her as though she were a troublemaker and liar. The other students had gloated, and stepped up their harassment of her. She had learned that there would be no help. She had to cope on her own.

She glanced sideways at the man who had helped her, twice now. Unaware of her scrutiny, he reached forward and stroked the mare's neck, and in that simple act of affection, Is saw the love that bonded him to the horse.

He became aware of her looking at him, turned, and smiled, and Is saw his confidence, good spirits, and love—a mixture she could only call joy—as his eyes met hers. But she could not share that with him now, and she looked away. Twice she had been helpless and he had rescued her, facing down bigger and stronger men. Is wondered how it must feel to be able to do that.

–X–

They were making their way north and westward through mostly trackless country. The slopes were thick with forests, and the horses found it easier to travel just above the tree line. The view was stupendous.

The mountains showed all their late-summer moods, from cool mornings to hot, stultifying afternoons, broken by wind and lightning and sudden downpours.

Sometimes Is hunted in the evenings. Sometimes she hunted without killing anything, just reveling in the beauty of the animals. Sometimes she joined the man in collecting grain for cereal, because he did not eat meat. There was always time for sitting, watching the horses graze, watching the streams they camped near, watching their camp fire, or watching the stars. It was a leisurely pace, dictated by the land and the needs of the horses.

The man's company had become no more obtrusive than the horses', which was as high a compliment, to Is's way of thinking, as she could give anyone. Someone else might have wished for conversation. Is didn't miss it.

From the top of a particularly high ridge, the man pointed out landmarks. There was the saddle where they had gotten caught in the blizzard. In that valley was the Blueskins' camp. Back that direction was the town where they had gotten supplies. And there were the perpetually snowcapped mountains ahead of them, where they were going.

Is was considering how impossible it looked to get horses across those mountains, when Lark's head swung around to the left. Following his gaze, Is saw the smoke of a camp fire rising in one thin column of white, straight into the fathomless blue sky. When she pointed it out to the man, he altered their course toward it.

The next morning they saw the smoke again, and by mid-afternoon they had crested the last ridge that separated them from it. It had been smoke not from a camp fire, but from a cabin that sat just at the transition between meadow and forest, on the slope facing them.

When the man started down to it, Is followed. This looked less dangerous than the town had, and that had ended safely enough.

When they were almost to the building, Lark snorted and shied. What Is had thought was just a bare patch of ground stood up and became a dog. Lark stopped dead, snorting again. The dog was as big as a small pony, and its fur matched the soil perfectly. It stood with great dignity, eyeing them as though demanding how they dared disturb its nap. Then, with odd nobility, it stretched and yawned, arching its back high in the air. It was as thin as a snake, all legs, with a long, whip-thin tail. Having finished stretching, it moved off toward the cabin in a ground-covering trot. Lark relaxed and Is urged him forward. The mare had never hesitated, so the man was well ahead of her.

When Is looked up, a man was standing in the open doorway of the house. He had a great mane of gray hair and a thick gray beard. Is had just time to notice that much when the mare stopped. The man vaulted from her back and bowed, startling Is. Then he walked forward a few steps, stopped, and bowed again. Is was trying to understand who the old man in the cabin could be to demand this sort of respect from *him*, when, suddenly, *he* began to laugh. It was so out of keeping with what Is had just witnessed that it took her by surprise. In a moment he had completely lost control, and his laughter built into the stressed, hysterical, insane sound Is hated so much.

He threw his head back and shrieked his laughter to the

sky. Then he fell to his knees and beat the ground with his fists, still laughing. Is looked past him to the man in the doorway. That man seemed startled. The way he was standing, his right arm was hidden by the door frame, and he could have been holding a weapon in that hand. Is was suddenly tense.

At that moment the old man turned and looked at her, and she saw the wrinkles around his eyes tighten.

"So, you are ready to defend him," he said. It wasn't quite a question. His voice carried to her, surprisingly youthful. Is didn't answer.

The old man finally continued. "A crazy man, who isn't crazy. Riding a bridle-less mare. And a woman, riding a berserker's horse."

He seemed to be waiting for Is to say something. She just stared at him, hard, daring him to do anything, while *he* knelt on the ground between them, his body wracked with convulsions. It was impossible to tell which the gasping, howling sounds he was making were—laughing or sobbing.

"Life has brought me many strange things," the old man finally said, "but this is odd even by my measure." He came out of the doorway, and he was not carrying anything in his right hand. He walked over to the man. "Stand up," he said. "Stop making that noise."

To Is's surprise the man did. The silence was wonderful.

The old man turned to Is. "I wonder," he said conversationally, "what do they do to someone who steals a berserker's horse? I wonder *what* do they do with the berserker whose horse this is, eh? That should pose them a pretty problem." He grinned suddenly, as though the thought pleased him.

There was a feral quality to his smile. He regarded Is with penetrating eyes that held the quick intelligence she had seen in the wild animals she had studied. After a moment he said, "Welcome to my house," and swept an arm toward his shack. "Come in. I will feed you, and you will tell me your story." He turned and walked into the house without a backward glance.

He followed. Is hesitated. She did not trust this old man. His observations were too keen. He seemed to know too much. He was not some dumb tough like the men in the town, and not an uneducated savage, like the Blueskins. The advantage he had over her in knowledge frightened Is. She did not want to go into the house. But *he* had gone in. She dismounted and followed him in.

The first thing she saw was the books. Floor-to-ceiling bookcases covered two walls, and there were books, open, on the table. Books! Here? For an instant Is was back in the forbidden libraries of the government school, where books, and reading, and the knowledge one could have were restricted to the very highest ranks, and a person like her should not even have been in this room. For a moment it took an effort of will not to back out the door. This was *not* the government school."

She was distracted from her turmoil by the man. He had hesitated at the door, but now he ran forward.

He took a book off a shelf, hugged it, and pressed it to his lips. Is went from being appalled for him to being afraid of him in one heartbeat. He could read. He knew books. He *was* some sort of high government official, not a criminal!

He brought a book to the table, rifled through it, and found a place. He waved the old man to him and pointed to a word in the book.

For a moment Is was horror-stricken by his presumption toward the old man, who must be some high government scholar also, to have all these books. But the old man appeared more bemused than offended. He walked over and looked at the page.

"John," the old man read, sort of quizzically.

He hit his chest and tapped the page imperatively. Is would never have dared to handle a book so roughly.

"John," the old man repeated, more firmly. Then he extended his hand. "I am pleased to meet you. These days I

am known as Amil," he said. The two men clasped each
other around the wrists.

Is felt the whole room and everyone in it rushing away
from her. Everything she had thought she knew about the
man collapsed around her ears, as all she had known about
the Blueskins, the Alliance troopers, and the Boundary itself
had been collapsing. But this was too much. There shouldn't
be scholars here, and books. There suddenly wasn't enough
air for her lungs.

She must have made some sound, for the old man turned
and looked at her.

"I am intrigued," he said. "Come, sit down. I will feed
you, and you will talk, yes? Come. Wine—I have a
little—it will help you."

Is had no volition of her own. She walked over to him, sat
down at the table, and let him serve her. She was past being
appalled.

The wine did help.

Amil couldn't be a real scholar, not out here in the
wilderness like this. Even if he were, he had no power over her
here. And if John were someone even higher than a scholar?
That didn't matter here either. Here, he had to obey the rules of
the mountains, the same as anyone. But inside, Is suddenly
felt like crying. Everything had become so strange. Only
hours ago, John had been as natural a part of her life as the
horses and the land. Now he was a million miles away, gone
in some weird fashion less explicable than death.

Is didn't try to analyze the betrayal and loss she felt. She
needed to get away. She didn't realize she had risen until she
heard her chair scrape on the floor. The old man heard it too.
He had gone into the part of the room he used for a kitchen,
but now he turned and studied her.

"Don't leave us yet, I beg you," he said. "Your story has
only begun to ask its questions." He peered at her keenly.
"Besides, I am a good cook," he said, and turning away, he
added, "Why don't you just take their saddles off and let
them rest?"

Is went out without answering him. The horses were grazing a hundred meters away. The dog came out from under the shade of the house and followed her. He didn't seem unfriendly, but he didn't approach her either.

Being outdoors helped. The smell of warm horseflesh in the sun, the soft sound of the tearing of the grass as the horses grazed, the buzz of insects, the breeze, and the birdcalls—all soothed her. The mountains rose around her, steadfast and enduring. What seemed like big events to her were as nothing to them. To the mountains, scholars were just like other people, inconsequential.

It was quite warm in the sun. The horses' backs would be getting sweaty under their saddles. Is looked up the valley. She could go somewhere and live alone as she had done before, simple and uncomplicated. Or she could go back into that house where everything was different from what she had ever suspected.

In the few minutes she'd been inside, her life had changed. If she went back in there, her world would continue to change. It would never be as simple as it had been these last days. She did not want more change, and yet . . . could there be other alternatives than living the life she had run away from, or living the life of running? What were scholars, and books, doing out here, far from the government center? And a thought she didn't really dare to think—could she be allowed to learn to read? If she had reached out and touched a book, would they have let her? They had let her see the open books, and Amil had read the word "John," out loud, in front of her. What else might they allow? The kind of deep excitement that Is had learned not to feel at the government school stirred in her and would not be put down. She undid Lark's girth and put his saddle on the ground while she took the mare's off. Then she carried both saddles to the house, and the dog followed at a distance, sniffing here and there as though he were about his own business and wasn't following her at all.

"Good," Amil said, "you came back." He had stirred up

the coals in his stove, and steam was already beginning to rise from a pot on top of it. He had been busy cutting up tubers, keeping his end of the bargain.

John was standing at the bookshelf with his back to her. He didn't turn around. His forehead rested against the books on one shelf, his fingers tracing the writing on the spines of one book after another on a lower shelf. Pain emanated from him.

Is went and sat at the table where she had sat before. She didn't even try to lie. She told Amil why she had stolen Lark. John turned around and leaned his back against the bookshelves, watching her. This was the first time he'd heard any of this too. To keep from looking at him, Is watched Amil. He continued to keep himself busy in the kitchen, but she knew he was listening intently. Somehow it was easier to talk to him while he worked than it would have been if he were sitting looking at her.

When she hesitated, he asked, "How did you meet John?"

So she told him how she had found John. How sick he had been, and how she had come to believe someone had tried to poison him. When Amil glanced at John for confirmation, John nodded.

Is went on with the story, telling about the Blueskins and the outlaw town. It gave her a funny feeling to realize how differently John might tell the same tale.

Amil *was* a good cook. He knew how to use wild herbs and spices to make the simple grains and vegetables he'd prepared taste completely different from the fare on which Is had been living.

She was content to eat silently. John came to the table, but he did not touch his dinner. He pushed his plate aside and set a book in front of himself, turning the pages slowly, running his fingers lovingly over the words. Suddenly his finger stopped at a word. He tapped it imperatively. Amil, who had been watching, unhurriedly set down the odd sticks with which he was eating, wiped his mouth, and pulled a blank piece of paper and a pen to him. Then he wrote down a word that didn't look like the word John had pointed out. But John seemed happy with it. He was off again, turning pages, running his fingers down them, looking for another word.

Is was so intrigued, she forgot to eat. They managed to get a few words written down that way, but Is could see that John was struggling. He squinted hard at the words, as though it were hard for him to see them. His hand shook as he traced his finger across the page. His finger paused at a word, and Is couldn't tell if he was tapping it for Amil, or if he was just getting so out of control he couldn't proceed. She became afraid that he would tear the page if he tried to turn it.

Amil noticed too. He reached over and slid the book away.

John convulsed as if an electric current had run through him. He grabbed wildly after the book, but his movement was ill-coordinated and without aim. His face twisted. His throat worked as though he were swallowing repeatedly.

Suddenly he stood up, pushing his chair away from the table with such force it went over backward. He started to bend, as though to right it, but then he just folded up on the floor beside it. He wrapped his arms around himself and began to rock. The muscles of his arms stood out as he gripped himself. He rocked faster and began to make a sound, a high-pitched animal keening. It made the hair on Is's arms stand up. A moment later the high, hysterical laughter that Is hated so much filled the room. Suddenly John threw his head back and screamed, breaking free of the laughter for a moment, but only for a moment. It came back, wracking his body, and filling the room.

Is jerked to her feet, and then stood, undecided. Amil remained unperturbed. He continued to eat, watching John with one eyebrow raised, inquisitively, as he might watch an interesting insect crawling on the floor.

Is couldn't take any more. She went around the table and knelt by John, talking quietly as she might soothe a hurt horse. But it only seemed to make John worse. He jerked away, putting his back to her and laughing louder. Is finally exploded.

"Why don't you do something?" she shouted at Amil. "He stopped when you told him to before."

Amil set down his eating sticks, wiped his mouth, and sat looking at her for a time before he spoke.

"Perhaps he needs to laugh."

"He's not laughing. He's in pain. Can't you see that?" Is screamed. Her nerves were frayed beyond caring who Amil was.

"What else is laughter, but the release of pain?" Amil said easily, but when Is turned angrily away, he spoke more gently. "Let him release it. He has something he wants to tell us. He will return to that when he is able."

Is wavered, seeing the truth of what Amil said, but disturbed on some deep level by the uncontrolled release of pain that John's noise expressed.

"Come, sit down," Amil said, motioning to her chair. "We will talk, you and I."

So Is came back to the table and sat, answering Amil's questions as if they were having a perfectly reasonable conversation and it was not at all strange to have to shout over the noise of a man convulsing on the floor. But while her body behaved, her mind was completely unable to concentrate. She had no idea what she was telling Amil.

As abruptly as it had started, it was over. Silence filled the room. John got up, righted his chair, and sat down. Amil slid the book to him, and John began paging through it again, and Amil went back to writing down words.

Is drew her shattered nerves together. She was no longer in awe of the old man.

"You're no proper scholar," she told him. "What are you doing with all these books?"

Instead of being offended, Amil smiled. "I thought you would never ask." Meticulously he set down his eating sticks before answering her.

"You might say I have stolen them." He paused and

watched her with sparkling eyes under arched brows, smiling slightly. "Or you could say I have rescued them."

Stealing books, taking things of such power and significance, affected Is as the desecration of a holy shrine would affect someone who was deeply religious. Books, and the knowledge and power they contained, were something the government held. Citizens received the knowledge they needed in order to achieve the purposes of their lives. Her purpose had been to train war-horses. She did not need to know how to read or write, or the denominations of money. Wanting more knowledge than that was improper. Taking it was wrong in some way Is had never contemplated.

Amil's chuckle brought her whirling thoughts up sharply.

"So I have fallen from being a god, to being the worst sort of criminal," he said good-naturedly. "You might want to look at a belief system that allows that to happen." But Is didn't make any sense of his words.

"You did me the honor of telling me why you stole the war-horse. You wanted to rescue him. I wanted to rescue the books. You see, within the Alliance there are different factions. One or another gains more power, and they decide what things will be known, and what forgotten.

"Yes," he said to her expression of wonder. "It is not just the citizens who are not allowed to know things. Even within the upper levels it is sometimes better for the people holding the most power if certain things are forgotten."

"What sort of things?"

"Oh, history mostly. The way things really came to be the way they are. These," Amil waved his hand at the bookshelves, "are the old books. In many cases they are the original chronicles of an event, a discovery, or an experiment. From time to time the old books are recopied. At those times they are shortened and condensed, which I suppose *is* necessary, but they are also changed. Sometimes quite on purpose, so the next generation will believe things were different than they really were. The Alliance would have us think it is a small thing. Not all knowledge can be retained." He sighed. "I suppose they are right. A bias always creeps into history. I just hate to see it done deliberately.

"So I took the books. I couldn't see them burned. But their fate is no better. They will rot here eventually."

John had been watching the exchange keenly. He started to say something. For a moment Is believed he would succeed. Some rational sentence would come out of his mouth. Instead, at the last instant, his lips drew back and the sound he made was a scream.

He jerked to his feet, turned abruptly on his heel, and began to pace with sharp, staccato steps, punctuated by an occasional peal of high laughter. He covered the small room in three strides, spun, three more steps, a pivot, three steps—Is couldn't watch.

Amil reached out calmly, pulled John's untouched plate to him, and began to eat with the delicate, unhurried precision with which he had eaten his own supper. Is thought she would go crazy. John's unbearable tension and Amil's calm seemed equally insane to her.

Suddenly John reseated himself, opened the book, and pointed to a word. Amil put down his sticks, picked up his pen, and wrote with the same calm precision with which he had been eating. Everything was back to normal—as normal as it was going to get.

When every grain was gone, Amil took the dishes to the kitchen. He dipped hot water from a bucket sitting on the stove, poured it over the dishes, and scrubbed as meticulously as he had done everything else, interrupting his work to write down a word whenever John rapped on the table to get his attention. Is slid her hand out and touched the page. She could feel the texture of the paper and smell the slightly musty smell, almost like old leaves. She had taken too long. John had noticed. Is snatched her hand away guiltily. But John slid the book toward her. Surprised, Is raised her eyes to his, and he nodded at the book. Is lifted it, feeling the weight to it, smelling its scent, touching the texture of its binding.

The sounds from the kitchen stopped. Amil was watching her too. Defiantly Is ignored him. She took her time, and when she handed the book back to John, she did so boldly. He went back to work, and Is wondered if the message he was trying so hard to finish was going to make any sense.

Amil returned to the table with a pot of steaming water and three cups. When he poured the water into the cups, it was not clear but reddish and sweet smelling.

John suddenly pushed the book away and sat back. Amil finished taking a sip of tea, put his teacup back in its saucer, and set the whole thing away from him. Then he wiped his mouth one last time with his napkin, folded it, and set it with the cup.

"Well," he said, "shall we see what John has written?"

Is could barely believe he would decipher the writing with her sitting there. But Amil was already studying the paper.

"Ahhmm, well, this is difficult. This is an old language," he explained. "It was a root language from which were developed the languages we speak today. We all studied this as young men, but my knowledge has grown old. Well, let us see.

"'I,' and a verb that means 'to have existence,' but with the ending that denotes duty or obligation. 'I am obliged,' I suppose. Then, 'belonging to my family,' no, larger, 'my tribe or people.'" He glanced at John for confirmation.

John motioned impatiently at the paper, and Amil continued. "'I am under duty or obligation, to my people, to make information of a secret nature openly available.'"

Amil's gaze jumped from the paper to John. "You are a spy?"

John nodded quickly and vigorously as though yes, wasn't that obvious, and he was trying to hurry the old man on. But Amil sat back from the paper, and a thoughtful look came into his eyes.

"You inform on the Alliance to your people?" It was only half question. John stopped nodding. He was watching Amil with a keen alertness that made Is think John was ready to defend himself, but Amil went on calmly. "You could only do that if you had posed as a scholar. That means you would have lived at Court?" Amil paused to watch the hand signs John was making, a collecting-in motion, the center of something.

"Court Center?" The old man seemed impressed. He had named the highest seat of government research. "Who trained you? To pass as a scholar there would not be easy. That degree of knowledge is hard to come by outside the government schools, and even within them unless you are specially picked. I would have said it was impossible. But you were not trained in the government schools?"

"No," to the quick shake of John's head, "I thought not.

"So your people trained you. They have that level of knowledge? The rumors were true, then, about 'outside' spies. But I could never figure out where those spies would come from. You are not a Blueskin. And the people in the outlaw village are too uneducated. Your own people then? Whoever they are, on the far side of the Boundary. They trained you." It wasn't a question. John met Amil's gaze steadily.

Is felt the hair on her arms stir like the ruff of a frightened dog. To her the government was an all-powerful and very distant being, like a god. It was not something one could question, let alone spy on! If people were spying on it, what were they doing with what they learned? Because didn't the fact that John's people spied on the government imply they meant to do something? Not only John, but all his people were criminals of a sort Is had never imagined. She wasn't sure how she felt about that. She had hated the government school, but she had considered that her own failing. It was her inability to fit in and do what other students did that had caused the problem. Later, she had come to hate letting the government take her stallions, and she had accepted that she had to hide from the government because of what she had done, but she had not considered herself in opposition to it. It was hard to accept that there was a whole group of people who opposed the government.

Amil's voice brought her back. "Let us see." He was studying the paper again. "It is hard to get the sense of this next part. The first word means 'captured.' The ending signifies great force, or perhaps torture. This word," he pointed to it, "means 'mind,' and in its placement in the sentence it receives the force of the torture." He raised his eyes from the paper.

"You were caught and tortured?" he asked John. Their eyes met, and a depth of understanding passed between them. Sobered, Amil went back to the words.

"This word means, literally, 'divorced.' It is followed by the word for reproducing, but in an asexual form, and 'spoken language.'" He looked up, his eyes bright and serious.

"Divorced from reproducing spoken language," he repeated with dawning understanding. "They caught you. They tortured you, and then they took away your ability to speak, and turned you loose—part of your torture, and a warning to your people."

"No!" Is was surprised she'd spoken. "John can speak. He just can't do it," she hesitated, "directly. He spoke a riddle once," she said and faltered to a stop.

Amil studied her a moment before he said, "So what they did to John was even more sophisticated. They 'divorced' some sort of connection in his mind. He can speak, but he can't communicate with words. He can't even write them, or he would have written this note himself. And we saw, just trying to organize the words for me to write was almost too hard."

He turned and studied John appraisingly for a long moment. "If you were at Court Center, you would have been in Research. I was at Court South, in Records. I thought I followed the research closely. But I had no idea that what they have done to you was possible.

"More hidden knowledge. More research that didn't get recorded. Or if it did, it was kept from the general records. I can only guess how much else they have hidden from us." He turned to Is.

"That is why I took the books. They would erase so much of this research." He waved at the bookshelves. "They hide it even from the scholars, as they hide everything from the citizens." His voice trembled with rage. He took a moment to collect himself, then returned to deciphering the message.

"The next sentence begins with the imperative form of deliver, and is followed by the most respectful form of the word for lady. This message is to be delivered to a very important lady," he explained to Is. But they were interrupted as John slammed his fist against the table and gestured at Is.

"This is for you?" Amil asked. "Does he not know your name?"

Is realized she had never told it to him. She shook her head, embarrassed. It seemed so rude now, not to have told him, but she had not done it out of rudeness, or even done it on purpose. She had just fallen into the habit of not speaking to him because he did not speak to her. She was too accustomed to the horses. One doesn't tell a horse one's name. To a horse you are a certain collection of smells which the horse names in his own fashion. Besides, at first, Is had thought John might be an agent of the law. Why would she tell him her name? She missed Amil's hesitation, which was an invitation for her to tell them her name now. After a few seconds' pause Amil continued.

"The next word denotes thanks in a very heartfelt way. The whole structure of this sentence conveys gratitude in a very personal mode. It is followed by an apology, also of deep feeling." He paused, but Is made no comment. She didn't understand why John would apologize to her.

"The next paragraph begins with 'deliver' again," Amil said. "This time directed to, ahh, 'the possessive of people.' Oh, his people. This is for his people." He glanced up as though seeking John's permission to continue. John waved him on.

"'Extreme,' let me see, 'all-encompassing activities'— ahh, 'circumstances.'" He paused and tried again. "'Extreme circumstances have led me to undertake an extreme action.' " He looked to John as though for help, but John just gestured at the paper.

"This action has something to do with a, ahh, mirror." Again he glanced at John for confirmation. "The word mirror is followed by the suffix that means opposite." Amil shrugged. "A mirror that is not a mirror only, mmmm? Well, this 'mirror' has possession of . . . some sort of opening . . . oh, a key. A key to . . . ahh, 'the connection of mind and language.' And the whole thing ends with a word that means 'promise,' but is in a hopeful, almost wistful form.

"I can only conclude he thinks, or hopes, this mirror thing can help restore his ability to speak."

He studied the page a bit. "Evidently there is some risk involved. There is a sentence here about 'sudden, involuntary action of great power' in regards to this mirror. But, ahh, 'some knowledge possessed by me,' John, 'may make possible a different dialog with it.' " Amil took a moment to glance at Is.

"There is also something about a relationship that is also somehow related to the mirror's key, but has to do with a man of great strength . . ."

"Berserker," Is said.

"Yes. Also an animal of great strength." Neither of them bothered to say "horse." "And also," Amil added, "a ghost of great power."

"No?" as John thumped the table and shook his head. "Well, something amorphous but of great power." He looked at Is, but she had no idea what that could be.

"Let me see, there is also something here about 'a system of long standing'—the Alliance, I would guess. And a word for misunderstanding which implies a deliberateness and/or bad spirit in this action. This is all couched in terms of gravest warning.

"This is followed by the strongest imperative that understanding must not be lost." The old man looked at John.

"I'm sorry I can't do better with this. If I were to study it more . . ." But John shook his head. "I hope your people will translate it better than I." He studied the paper again.

"He has 'the possession of strong faith in the correctness of an action to be undertaken' by him 'concerning this mirror/non-mirror.' One sentence says something like 'imperative to attempt every road of possibility for repair of mind.' This is somehow connected to a larger purpose. This 'larger' means something very large with moral overtones, or perhaps religious.

"Then there is another imperative sentence. This time it says 'unload soul belonging' to him 'of burden of very large truth belonging to his people.'

"The next paragraph begins 'Lady,' in the most honored form—the one he used for you before. This is followed by a verb of being, in the near future tense, connected to the action of going or traveling somewhere. Then, 'people' of his 'possession,' and the word for guest in a form of highest honor. Reassurance is intended."

"He is taking me to his people," Is said. It was a relief to know her status among them would be as an honored guest, not a slave.

"So you will continue with him?" Amil said, and there was something wistful in his voice that set Is on alert. She thought for a moment that Amil might ask her to stay with him. She thought about the books. Maybe he would teach her to read! She would have knowledge. But he didn't ask, and if she had heard a longing in his voice, it was probably because he was lonely and wanted to bed with her, not teach her to read. She thought about John's people, who trained their horses to go without bridles. They would have much to teach her too, and that was the sort of thing she was suited to learn. But she felt sad and would not let herself understand why.

When she looked up, she caught John quickly looking away from her.

-XI-

The next day, as they rode away from of Amil's place, the dog appeared and followed them. Is spent the first half of the day trying to chase it back. It was probably the only company the old man had, and she did not want it to leave him. John watched her attempts with a quizzical expression and did not offer any help. Eventually Is gave up.

The going continued to get steeper and more rocky. They swung west to cross a saddle in the last ridge before they would have to cross the snowcapped giants of the range. Is no longer worried about how they were going to get the horses across those sheer, forbidding walls. A scholar would know how to do it.

They camped high in the saddle, near a little stream, and Is could feel the altitude in muscles that cramped in her legs and feet, and in her mind, which wanted to wander aimlessly from her tasks. It seemed to take forever for the water to get hot, and it never did really boil. The leaves John put into the tea sieve made the water taste bitter, and after one sip Is thought she wouldn't drink the rest. But her body craved the liquid, and making her way to the stream for more water suddenly seemed like too much effort.

She had pretty well learned to ignore the tricks her eyes liked to play when her mind was like this. So she was ignoring the man shapes she was seeing among the shadows cast by the bushes when the dog came in. He had stayed back from them all day, but now he came right up to the fire, slinking, with his skinny tail pressed under his belly. He was making a sound between growling and whining. Is snapped out of her trance.

John was already standing, facing the shadow shapes. Is suddenly remembered that there hadn't been any bushes around big enough to cast man-tall shadows. Immediately all the tales she had ever heard of the supernatural horrors of these mountains crowded her mind.

Is edged backward. The packs were behind her, and the tool in John's pack might stop the shadow men if they attacked him.

But John didn't seem afraid. In fact he got down on his knees, moving slowly, like a man trying not to scare some wild animal away. Is heard the breeze blowing through the leaves of the bushes, until she remembered that the bushes didn't exist. Then she heard voices instead. They talked rapidly and softly, one overlaying another and another. She didn't know how anyone could make sense of such speech. Sometimes there were little cracking sounds like sticks breaking. She had to keep reminding herself that there were no bushes, no breeze, no cracking sticks.

Nothing else seemed to happen for a long time. She might have dozed off, although that seemed unlikely, given how scared she was. But the next thing she knew John was surrounded by the shadow men, and she couldn't remember having seen them move.

She was determined to be more alert, but it was hard to keep the shadow men focused. Her mind kept wanting to tell her they were bushes and things, not men. They seemed to be stroking John. They weren't using hands, but gliding against him, weaving from side to side and slipping down the length of his body. He was standing again. When had that happened? Other than the *shush-shush* talking there was no sound.

The dog had stopped growl-whining sometime back. He was lying flat out on his side, not a posture a frightened dog would be in. There was some sort of darkness in the air over him, and Is knew he was dead. The shadow men had somehow sucked the life out of him.

She thought they were taking something important from John too. They might deplete him. He would lie dead like the dog when they were done with him. As afraid as Is was of the shadow men, she was more afraid to let them kill John. She stood up and moved toward them in a rush, shouting, and waving her arms, before she could loose her nerve. She had to push them back with her voice, and not just her voice, but what she was exhaling—energy, angry energy. She could almost feel it push them. Then suddenly John caught hold of her. He pulled her against him and wrapped his arms around her. Is could feel the tremors running through his body.

She stood still, making herself *be* solid, and letting him feel her solidness, because that was what he needed, but not quite allowing herself to think of it that way.

When he let her go, she saw the dog. He was curled by the coals, not flat out as she'd seen him before. She went close enough to see that he was breathing, not close enough to disturb him. The hair on her arms stood up, and goose bumps ran down her back. She felt a strong presence, but she could not say if it was benign or harmful. Her own system of superstitions made her react with fear. She desperately needed to ask John what had happened, but that was impossible.

John curled up by the fire and soon fell asleep. Is got his sleeping bag and tucked it around him. That gave her an excuse to be close to him, to touch him. After a while, she got into her own bag and sat awake the rest of the night listening to John breathing. It became a vigil, something she had to do to protect him. She didn't know from what. She kept thinking about the "ghost of great power" in Amil's translation of John's note.

John seemed fine in the morning. Is watched him for signs of strangeness and for the first time really wished she could talk to him.

Little, gusty breezes accompanied them as they rode. Whenever Is heard the wind, she turned to look, but she saw nothing unusual.

By mid-afternoon they had reached the top of the saddle. There was a light dusting of snow there. The air rising from it was cold, but the air above them was hot with the moisture-sucking stillness that only a summer afternoon at high altitude has.

Facing them was a sheer wall of mountains. The crystalline air made the mountains seem close enough to touch. Exposed rock showed in vertical stretches shining with melt water like the black bones of the earth itself. A man with a rope might make it up there; no horse would. Above them rose peaks so white the air seemed to vibrate off their color. Below them the mountains' flanks were covered with green forests, inviting and cool.

John pointed east. There the highest of the mountains ran a long, white shoulder down into the valley. John's hand motions said they would ride down into the valley, around that shoulder, and up over . . . Is supposed through a pass that was hidden from their view by the height of the long ridge of that shoulder. She calculated two days to get down to the bottom of the valley, two or three days to get around that shoulder, and perhaps another few days to get over the hidden pass. She wished it would be longer.

They camped below the tree line, sheltered from a storm that blew through. Is woke several times to the sound of low branches scraping against the tent in the wind. In the morning she knew there could have been no branches. Neither of them would pitch a tent where branches could possibly puncture its waterproof fly. Again she wished she could talk to John.

The air was cool after the rain. The horses were frisky, shying and snorting at the dark rocks like foolish youngsters instead of horses who had trekked this land for weeks already. Is laughed when John's mare refused to pass an especially big, wet rock, and then they both laughed when Is tried to ride Lark past it first and he behaved as badly as the mare.

It was dark under the tall trees as they descended, and although it had stopped raining, the branches dripped big, wet drops on them as they worked their way downward. Instead of getting lighter, the day got darker, and soon they were riding in a thick fog out of which the massive boles of the trees would appear and disappear, sinister and dark.

The gay mood of the morning slipped away. The horses shied more often and more seriously. Is could feel Lark's tension, and it increased her own mounting sense of unease.

Lark snorted, sidestepping hard, and came to a halt. The creature sat on the rock regarding them with baleful red eyes. It blinked and disappeared. Lark snorted a loud blast. His legs were braced wide. He was ready to run in any direction. Is stroked his neck. "Some trick of the light," she told him, but her voice didn't sound as reassuring as she had meant it to.

Lark continued to snort. He refused her aids to go forward, even though the mare had passed that way in front of him. Is turned him to go around the rock, since he wouldn't go by it.

Lark sidled past the rock, snorting and tense. Is didn't feel so brave herself. The back side of the rock was somehow bigger than the front of it had looked. Going around it took Is more off the track than she had thought it would. She'd been depending on Lark to pick up the mare's trail again, but he only seemed interested in shying this way and that way, from every tree and rock he saw.

Is tried to deal with Lark's foolishness, keep her sense of direction, and look for the mare's trail all at once. When she couldn't find it, and wanted to zigzag back and forth over the area looking for it, Lark wouldn't cooperate, and continually shied off the line Is would have ridden. Knowing how well the trees could muffle sound, Is decided she'd better call out before John got too far away.

Her voice sounded muted even to her own ears, as though

the fog swallowed it. She could hear no answer of any sort, but still wasn't very worried. She would keep riding downhill and find her own way around the shoulder and over the pass if she had to. Surely she'd meet up with John somewhere en route.

The fog grew thicker, and Lark more reluctant to go down into it. He snorted and shied and moved sideways. Is could feel his heart beating, and she tried to soothe him with her voice. He kept managing to turn aside from the deepest fog, which was below them. They were traversing the slope more than descending it.

Finally Is slipped from his back, took the reins, and led him into the fog. He came reluctantly, snorting and hesitating, right on her heels. With his head up, Lark towered over her, and Is hoped he wouldn't forget she was there and jump on her if he shied. She kept talking to him, and kept contact with him by means of the reins.

Suddenly Is was spun around as Lark bolted backward, dragging her with him. She couldn't hope to resist him and was forced to run after him, trying desperately not to let go of the reins. Her commands of "Whoa!" had no effect. If he got turned, he would take off at a gallop and she would not be able to hold him, or keep up. She was desperate not to let that happen, but there was nothing she could do to prevent it. He outweighed and outmuscled her many times over, and all of his training had been completely overridden by fear.

Is was jerked to the side as Lark turned. The dark bole of a tree appeared in front of her the instant before she hit it. Her hand let go of the reins without permission.

For a moment even hitting the tree didn't hurt, Is was so mad at herself. For a few seconds more she could hear Lark crashing away, then silence.

She was sitting on her backside facing the tree. The arm with which she'd held the reins had wrapped around the tree with great force, and the bark had taken her skin off. It was beginning to bleed now, stinging like crazy. As her arm had been pulled around the tree, the side of her face had smashed against the rough bark, and then her body had been slammed against the tree with enough force to fling her on her backside, three feet away. When she tried to turn her head, she felt dizzy, and the pain was suddenly so intense she had no choice but to sit still a moment. That helped. Wherever the pain had come from, it went back there and waited. Good. Let it wait. She didn't need to move just yet. She was distracted by the warm, creeping feeling of blood beginning to run down her neck. She started to put her hand up to touch her face and saw that her hand was covered with blood. She stared at it. The two outside fingers stood out at an angle that didn't look right. She tried to flex her hand. Pain came out of wherever it had been waiting and relocated itself in her hand, shooting up her arm until it made her want to be sick.

She looked away from the blood. *The pain will only get worse,* she thought. *Do it now!*

Before she could think better of it, she took hold of the two dislocated fingers with her good hand and twisted them back into place. She'd been braced for pain, but it didn't come. *Shock,* she thought. *Thank you.*

She'd better get moving before it wore off.

It felt as if something heavy were sitting on her neck. She couldn't turn her head to the right at all. If she kept her head sort of down and left, she could walk. She started to ascend, bearing off to the left all the time. Lark would go up to get out of the fog. Once he'd outrun his fear, he'd turn back. He'd want his companions, but Is doubted he'd descend into the fog again. With luck she'd find him wandering above the fog line.

She kept finding herself not ascending as steeply as she thought she should. Her arm and hand throbbed with her heartbeat, and her neck made her whole back hurt as she leaned forward to ascend the slope. She felt nauseated and weak. It was an act of major concentration to keep putting one foot above the other.

She found herself skirting the deepest patches of fog, reluctant to enter them, which was ridiculous. But every time she'd put herself up to going straight into the fog, there'd be a rock or something she'd have to go around anyway.

. . . She was not ascending enough.

Stupid to avoid the worst fog. She couldn't see farther than her own feet anyway. The ascent of the ground was her guide.

. . . She was not ascending.

No smarter than the horse to be afraid of the fog. Look at her feet. One step, the next. Keep going.

. . . She was not ascending.

The fog was a wall above her. She turned around, slowly so she wouldn't loose her balance—the lack of visual references didn't help her dizziness.

The fog was definitely thinner below her. She could make out the trunks of trees.

Maybe down was the right direction to go. Follow the original plan she'd had with Lark. When she found the pass, she'd find John. Together they'd come back looking for Lark. Or maybe Lark would find them. Yes, it made more sense to look for John than for the horse. She turned downhill.

The fog was herding her. She'd given up resisting it some time back. She'd given up thinking, and she'd never really been afraid.

She had to sit down.

The breeze came gusting over her and was gone. Seemed strange, a breeze at ground level in a forest this thick. Besides, when there was fog the air was still, usually.

The breeze came again in little fits and starts. The fog swirled and shredded when the breeze blew, only to resettle as thick as ever when it stopped. Is sat and watched this little contest. If the breeze cleared the fog away, maybe she'd have more energy. Maybe she'd be able to make her feet go where she wanted them to go.

She could hear the breeze making the leaves rustle. It was some time before she thought, *Leaves! In a pine forest?*

If she listened just right, she could hear the voices instead, one over the other in a quick *shush-shush* whisper. She couldn't begin to understand them.

She got up and moved with the breeze, downhill and left, which was the direction she'd need to go to get around the shoulder. Sometimes her mind seemed to wake up, or clear, or something. Then she'd sort of check with herself that she was still going the direction she wanted to go. The rest of the time she might as well have been sleepwalking.

When she had to stop, she lay down and slept. Let whatever was going to happen to her happen.

. . . In the dream she was riding Lark, following the mare.

Lark's left front hoof came down jarringly on a rock. The jolt traveled up Is's spine into her neck, which was sore. She put her hand up to rub her neck. The fingers were stiff. It hurt more to flex them, and squeeze her neck with them, than her neck hurt. She gave up trying to massage herself. They'd be stopping for the horses' afternoon break soon. She'd lie flat on the ground then. That would feel good. If she relaxed enough, maybe the muscles in her neck would unkink.

The mare stopped. John twisted around in his saddle and looked at her. He seemed to stare at her and past her at the same time. Is began to worry that he was going to start one of his fits. She made Lark walk past him. Then she heard John say, "Hast thou dreamed a life, or lived a dream," in a completely ordinary voice.

Shocked, Is turned to stare at him, wondering if there were some message in his riddle, or if the words were only the wanderings of a disturbed mind.

"Be thou not confused of reflections that guidest thee astray, or true. Thine own heart knowest not, lest thee be true."

"You're not real, are you?" Is challenged. "This is some

sort of dream, isn't it?" When John didn't answer, or respond to her in any way, she concluded, "Really I'm lost in the fog, and dreaming."

Then she saw what she had somehow failed to notice before: John was not sitting on his mare, but on Lark. She forgot everything else and said, "Lark," and walked toward him.

When she reached out her hand to touch him, her neck was stiff, and her hand was swollen and wouldn't open all the way, and she was surprised by that, until she stroked Lark's soft coat.

The saddle had a scrape along one side where he'd cut too close to a tree or something in his panic, but other than that everything seemed fine.

She wasn't going to fight with him about going into the fog, but now he went willingly, and she let him pick their course. Once he whinnied and broke into a trot, and she let him. In a few minutes she heard the mare's answering call.

John welcomed her with a smile, and it was that good, radiant smile that made Is feel good. Then he turned and rode on, just as if nothing had happened, and Is, following, began to doubt what *had* really happened.

-XII-

Is could tell they were getting close. John was tense with excitement, frequently turning to smile at her. His mood was infectious, and Is began to lose her apprehension.

They descended the final pass into a land of rolling meadows. The grass was thick and tall. The mare picked up her pace, either because she felt John's excitement or because she knew where they were.

Suddenly the horses threw up their heads and stopped. The mare whinnied. Four horsemen erupted into view, galloping dead at them. Is hadn't even realized there was a gully for them to come out of as they did. Lark tossed his head and began to prance. The mare whinnied and went forward at a high, springy trot. In an instant Lark was going with her, his trot thrusting him high off the ground with each extravagant stride. Is needed all her skill to keep from being bounced in the saddle.

Just as some sort of collision was imminent, the four approaching horses sat back into their haunches and slid to a stop, their hooves gouging the ground. Their riders were already vaulting off, and John threw himself from his mare's back. Lark reared, unable to contain himself, then came into a trot in place. His neck arched high in front of Is, and she could feel the suppressed power running through his body. In a moment it would erupt in some fashion. Her body informed her of that while her eyes took in the refined, bridle-less heads of the horses, their sleek coats and well-muscled bodies, and all the men, who had run together, embracing, laughing, and saying John's name.

John's mare moved to touch noses with the other horses, and Is found herself propelled forward as Lark moved to cut her off. Is knew better than to try to control him. He kept his position between his mare and the other horses, prancing and snorting, until the lead mare of that group came forward to touch noses.

The other horses started forward, and one of the men gave a shrill whistle. The horses halted as if they had become stuck to the ground. Is was impressed; then she realized that she and Lark were the center of attention. She hoped he wasn't going to do anything too disorderly. John's people were not going to think much of her horsemanship—she, who was an expert among her own people.

If Lark got the mares squealing and kicking and running around, it could be dangerous to be on his back. John motioned for her to come to him. Well, she could no more control Lark from up here than she could from down there, and it would be safer to be out of the way. Is vaulted from Lark's back, and being careful to stay out of range of the nearest mare's feet, she went to stand beside John.

Left on his own, Lark circled the mares in an exaggerated, high trot. The mares began to mill around, and there was a lot of squealing, striking, and kicking as the horses sorted one another out.

The men made no further attempt to control their mounts. They laughed good-naturedly, making short comments on their mare's behavior or admiring remarks about Lark as they withdrew a distance to let the horses have room for their displays.

They watched the horses until it seemed they were going to settle down, then everyone's attention came to focus on Is, and she was suddenly unable to ignore her fear. Every time she had been thrust into a new place, with new people, it had not gone well. They had not liked her or wanted her.

Suddenly John caught her arm, pulled her to him, and hugged her, hard.

Is was too surprised to react. When he released her, he turned her so she was facing the man who seemed to be the leader of the band.

Is found herself standing in front of him awkwardly, but knowing that John had presented her in the best way he could without words. His hands were still resting on her shoulders, and Is could feel him trembling. In a moment he would lose control.

"He can't speak," Is blurted. "The Alliance did something to him, tortured him and made it so he can't talk. And sometimes he goes crazy, but he isn't really. He can't help it. He's trying to help you. You've got to give him a chance." She stopped in embarrassment. Here she was frantically defending John to his own people, who obviously knew more about all this stuff with the Alliance than she did. They would think her some sort of imbecile and very immature. She couldn't even take refuge in her superior ability with horses here. Not with these people.

All four men were looking at her very curiously.

The leader took a step forward.

"Thank you for telling us this." He had such an aura of poise and control about him that Is settled immediately. "John is my brother." His voice was sensual in the way the sounds of nature are sensual. Compassion radiated from him. The way he pronounced "John" it sounded like "Hon."

"We are the Hluit," he said. "My name is Ondre. You would say Andrew." He looked a moment at John with his hands still resting on Is's shoulders. Then he said something in a language that sounded like birdcalls. Is heard one of the other men draw in his breath, surprised.

"I have pledged to value you as my brother values you, even should my tribe turn me aside. This I have said before warriors of my people."

Is knew she had been accorded a very high honor, but she didn't know what to do or say. Ondre rescued her again.

"Come," he said to everyone in general, "let's go home."
He turned to Is. "Then you can tell us your story, if you
will." One of the other men laughed, breaking what was left
of the tension.

"*If* the horses are ready to allow us to catch them," the
man who'd laughed said, which was the signal for the others
to comment on this man's lack of horsemanship. Is felt her
insides tighten, waiting for the cruelty behind the seemingly
easy words. Instead the man grinned and said his mare had
very good taste in stallions and he wouldn't blame her a bit
if she wasn't ready to be caught. He gave Is a big wink, and
she saw how his eyes danced and that he was not hurt at all.
But the mares were easily caught and mounted. And Is
wondered if, having seen her lack of control of Lark, they
would be willing to accept her as they would a child and
teach her their horsemanship.

As they rode, the one who had been kidded came to ride
beside her. He had a round face that looked as if it should
always be smiling, and his body was sort of soft-looking
compared to the sinewy toughness of the other men, but his
horsemanship looked excellent to Is. He introduced himself
as Petre, and the others as Don—which they pronounced
with an "h" like Dhon—and Phol. They all bantered in a
friendly manner as they rode, teasing one another about
their mares' behavior, and even teasing John about not being
able to talk and thus defend himself from their humor.

Is felt totally adrift. She had never been around people
who treated one another as these did. They seemed to
include her so naturally, but she couldn't trust it. She kept
waiting for the cruelty behind their humor.

John was grinning like a fox. He loved these people, and
was loved by them. He is home, Is thought, and tried to
understand what that meant in terms of what "home" had
been to her, the farm with her parents. But that had been a
long time ago, and she did not let herself remember too
much, because it would have hurt.

She was not allowed much time to reflect. The men were

chattering on, telling John all kinds of news he must have wanted to know, but which made no sense to Is. Under all the talk and the gaiety, Is was aware of Ondre watching her.

The teasing took a new turn as they began kidding John about the condition of his mare.

"Celeste, he's been mistreating you," one of the men addressed the mare directly. "You ought to come live with my herd." And it was true that next to the people's sleek, well-rounded animals, she did look underfed. But John just grinned even bigger and sent Celeste into a canter which quickly escalated into a gallop as everyone followed suit. Is had no choice but to let Lark run with them. Soon they were flying over the ground in a dead run, with John's mare well out in front, and Is guessed that that was his answer to the teasing.

When the village came into sight, they slowed to a respectable trot. A crowd was waiting at the outskirts of the tents. Horses grazed around the edges, and there were herds farther out on the hills. Kids came cantering out to meet them, drumming their heels on the sides of thick-bellied brood mares who obviously had no desire to gallop. Lark arched and danced but seemed willing to obey Is.

Suddenly a woman broke from the crowd and rushed to them on foot. John jumped from his mare's back and ran to her. They came together, and John lifted the woman off the ground and spun around and around with her in his arms. Then the other people rushed forward to surround him. But Is saw the way John kissed the woman before he released her, and she felt the odd, twisting sensation of pain she had come to associate with the departure of one of her horses. Then the people were on top of John, everyone hugging and talking at once. But Is saw that the way these people kissed him, and the way he kissed them, was different from the way he had kissed the one woman.

Is was angry at herself. John had never tried to tell her he was not married. In fact, she should have known he was. That would explain why he had never tried to touch her.

That, and the fact that she wasn't pretty like his tribe's women with their light hair. Nor was she cultured like the women a high Alliance official must know. She was just a rude, country seed, and John had not only other women, but great women. Of course he had not been interested in her. Is tried to put her foolishness away. These people were to be her people now; she should not start by resenting them.

She looked around and met Petre's eyes. He had stayed at her side. He leaned toward her now, so she would hear him, and said softly, "Welcome to our village. I hope your stay here will be happy, and long."

She met his eyes and found herself smiling. It was good to have someone talk to her.

-XIII-

The council was made up of men and women, some of them quite young, some very old. They all sat on the ground in an informal circle. Anyone else who wanted to hear sat outside the circle. Ondre was not among the council. He had volunteered to be responsible for Lark. His wife, Ellie, escorted Is to the circle and showed her where to sit. Everyone was sitting in the same manner, on their legs, with their buttocks resting on their heels, so Is sat that way too. It wasn't uncomfortable, and it gave her a sense of stability, which helped her find some calm.

Ellie took a place beside her. John sat directly across from her. He smiled at her, but it wasn't a real smile. He was very tense, and Is realized how important this was to him. He had given the council the note Amil had written, but there might be a lot of things Is could tell them that would help. There were also probably a million things she could do wrong without even knowing.

An old woman opened the meeting.

"We have seen you ride with John. We have heard that Ondre has extended family rites to you. On the strength of our trust in these two men, we wish also to welcome you. We have read the note John brought us, but much has happened that he cannot tell us. It would be a great help if you would tell us what you know."

Is was not sure of the protocol here. She was not sure whom she was addressing, but the woman seemed to be some sort of leader.

"I will be glad to help if I can," she said honestly, and then thought how rude her words sounded after the woman's. She glanced at John again. He gave her another tense smile and made a small go-ahead hand motion.

Is started by explaining where she'd found John, which led her to telling why she had been there, which led her to explaining why she had stolen the war-horse in the first place. Then she realized she was going backward. What they wanted to know about was John. Flustered, she took up the tale again and tried to tell it all in order and coherently.

She was very aware of John watching her acutely while she spoke. She had the feeling he was dying to say something, perhaps to disagree with some of her memories. She couldn't look at him at all. She tried to emulate Ondre's poise and calm while speaking in front of all these strangers, but she didn't know if she succeeded. They gave her virtually no feedback, their expressions remaining calm to the point of being remote and unreadable. Some of the old people especially seemed to stare into the air around her without looking directly at her. No one made any comments or asked any questions. When she was done, there was a long period of silence. Then one of the elders thanked her.

Is thought the meeting was done. She would be escorted away, and the real talking would begin. Instead a sort of free-for-all discussion began. Within the circle people spoke to their neighbors in quick, low voices that reminded Is of the almost-voices of the wind. The people beyond the circle remained silent.

One of the elders leaned over and spoke to John. Suddenly everyone was quiet again. Is had missed whatever signal had silenced them.

Everyone's attention was focused on the one man. He looked older than anyone Is had ever seen before. His head was entirely bare of hair. The flesh of his face stretched tight across his prominent cheekbones and hooked nose. His eyes were sunken in folds of wrinkles, giving his head a death skull's appearance. The top of his head was freckled with age spots. His hands, which were also spotted with age, rested on his thighs. There was no flesh left on those hands at all, just the bones and sinews, crisscrossed by protruding blue veins.

The elder dipped his head a small amount in acknowledgment, then spoke to the people in the circle.

"What they have done to John is very sophisticated." His voice creaked with age. "They have not taken away his ability to speak. As Isadora testified, he can recite poetry. These are things he has memorized, and they are other people's words. What he cannot do is form what he wants to say into words. They have disconnected that one ability without, apparently, harming anything else about his mind or body. That is extremely skillful tampering." The elder fell silent.

People began to speak quietly among themselves again.

Is found herself really trying to understand what this must be like for John. She had lived years with only her animals and no real need for speech. For John it was different. He had something very important to say to his people. But now that Is had seen his people, she suspected that even if there had been no message, John would not have been happy without speech. Speech was a part of him, of who he was, and how he related to all these people. Also, he had been some sort of scholar. Words and books, poetry and songs must be to him like her riding was to her—art, the essence of what his life was about. Unexpectedly tears welled up in her eyes. If suddenly she could not ride again, it would be more than the loss of something she liked to do. It would be the loss of who she was, and of what was important about her, and to her. It would not be like the loss of an arm or a leg; it would be the loss of what was inside her. For John, what he had lost must feel like that.

Is missed whatever signal was given to end the meeting. People were getting up. Ellie stood beside her, waiting. Is scrambled to her feet—and nearly fell over. Two men caught her as she almost careened into them. For a wild moment she couldn't understand what had happened to her. She had no control of her legs, and there was no feeling in her feet. Through her own rising panic she realized that everyone was looking at her. But their eyes were shining, and they were grinning, and a few of them laughed out loud.

"Your feet have gone to sleep," one of the men who was holding her said. He was grinning broadly.

"Happens when you're not used to sitting that way," the other man said.

"You could have sat cross-legged," a woman said. "It would have been all right." But Is had not seen anyone else sitting that way.

The feeling was coming back into her feet, with a sensation like a million hot needles being jabbed into her skin.

"You should walk," one of the men said, and he began to walk her around.

Is tried to make her legs work. Her knees wanted to buckle at odd moments, and her feet couldn't feel the ground. Without feedback from her legs, it was very hard for her to keep her balance. She didn't want to lean against this strange man, but she had to. He seemed to be enjoying himself immensely.

In just a few minutes she could walk on her own again, and Ellie took her home. The village was made up of about eighty dome-shaped tents. They were similar to John's tent, but larger. Is had lost track of John. She supposed he had gone with the woman who had kissed him earlier.

The inside of Ellie's tent was warm and glowed with a reddish cast from a small stove in the center. It smelled deliciously of a sweet tea Ondre was brewing for them. Is had not realized how tense she was until she had a moment to sit in that warm, quiet place. The tea seemed to be a mild stimulant, and Is found herself recounting her story for Ondre.

Unlike the people at the council, Ondre kept stopping her and making her back up and remember details. Somehow all the things she had not thought the council wanted to hear began to come out.

When she told Ondre about riding Lark for the Blueskins, she said, "I wanted them to think he was a dangerous war-horse and I was their only way of controlling him, but he isn't, and they must have seen that. They treated me like dirt. I guess I would have been a slave, or something, if John hadn't rescued me."

"My god, child," Ellie interrupted. "If *they* didn't rape you, they must have thought you were the next thing to a god!"

"And you kept up with them walking all night," Ondre said. "That's not easy." But his eyes said something different to his wife, and Is felt a little shudder of warning run through her as she went on with her tale.

Ondre laughed when she told him how John had beaten Chest. He made her recount every detail of that odd fight. But Is couldn't tell him much.

"It was like magic. John barely seemed to touch the Blueskin. But he must have done something I couldn't see." Her description sparked an animated discussion between Ondre and his wife, and eventually Is understood that they were discussing what "techniques" John had used to throw Chest. For the first time she realized that what she'd seen John do was not some fluke of luck.

Ondre laughed gleefully when she told him about the outlaws who had attacked John. She could see that he loved and admired his brother. Some place in her heart woke and hurt. She would never have family like this.

They were intensely interested in the old man, Amil, and the whip-thin dog who had followed them, but who must have shied away when the other men appeared, for no one had seen him.

When Is came to the part about how she'd gotten separated from John in the fog—which she had barely mentioned to the council because it seemed so confused and unlikely—Ondre was fascinated. He caught his wife's eye.

"A herd fog? In the first valley? I've never heard of one that close before."

Then Is found herself telling them about the dark figures that had come around John that one night by the fire.

"You heard them speak?" Ellie asked, implying that she believed Is *had* seen something. "You heard words?"

"Yes, but I couldn't understand them. They all talked at once, over each other."

"They touched John?" Ondre asked. "You're sure?"

"Yes. Was that bad?"

"Not necessarily. They can be frightening. But there have been times when they seem to have acted to help someone too."

"When you were lost, you said the fog was blown away. That could have been them," Ellie put in. "The fog sometimes takes travelers miles off their route. Some people have died because of it."

Is felt the stirring of a very deep fear. "I thought it was all a dream. Inside the fog I was on foot. Then, suddenly, I was with John again like nothing had happened. And he spoke, but in a riddle, and then he was gone, but Lark was there. I thought it was all a dream, but . . ." She held out her arm, showing the long, partially healed scrapes. Ondre took her hand and examined the arm carefully. Is knew what he was thinking. Those cuts were too well healed to be only three days old, the three days it had taken them to ride from what he called the first valley to the village. He exchanged a glance with Ellie. Neither one said anything.

"I don't know what really happened." It was the first time Is had confessed that, even to herself. She saw Ondre meet his wife's eye again before he answered.

"If you want to find out, we can probably help," Ellie said. But Is saw the look of alarm in Ondre's eyes.

"El . . ."

Is felt the hair stir on her arms. "Is it important to know?"

"It might be," Ellie said, "especially if you go with John."

"Why would I do that?" Is was surprised by the idea. She

had understood that John was going to look for the mirror/non-mirror thing, but that had not seemed to concern her. As far as Amil had understood the message, John seemed to expect her to stay with his people.

"You might be able to help John."

His wife rebuked him. "Ond . . ."

"No, Ellie, she needs to know."

"Yes, but Ondre, *she is Alliance trained.*" Ellie's voice sank to an urgent whisper, intensely uncomfortable talking about Is in front of Is.

"I'm sorry," Ondre said. "I do not know what her government teaches." There was a touch of surliness in his voice Is hadn't heard before. People had always been angry at her for wanting to know too much. Now he was getting mad because she didn't know enough.

They were interrupted by a girl's voice outside the tent. Ellie answered, and in a moment the tent flap lifted and a young woman entered. She smiled shyly at Is. She had the beautiful blond hair and blue eyes of many of John's people. She acknowledged Ondre with a smile and spoke to Ellie.

"Mother wanted me to tell you, we are going to have a feast. You will bring Isadora?"

Ellie laughed. "Of course," she said, as though she should have expected this. "Of course we will come."

Is felt her heart sink. She dreaded facing so many people, but she tried to tell herself it couldn't be worse than being thrown into the government school. In fact, it was bound to be better, but she was still scared as she listened to a quick discussion about food and other details. Then Ondre left with the girl and Is was alone with Ellie.

Is was suddenly aware of how dirty she was. She had only her patched-together, part-cloth, part-animal-skin clothing, and although she had washed in streams whenever she could tolerate the cold water, the dirt and smoke from the cook fires was ingrained in her clothes, skin, and hair. She probably smelled pretty strong.

Ellie chatted pleasantly while soap and shampoo appeared from nowhere. Water was heated by dropping the hot stones that lined the stove into a bucket. It made the water a degree more bearable than the snow-melt streams Is had been using.

"There is a hot spring we often use," Ellie said apologetically. "But it is a two-hour ride . . ."

Ellie's clothes fit Is well enough. The coolcloth was undoubtedly stolen. Only people high in the government wore coolcloth. It molded to Is's body, but was never binding. She could move in any direction without hinderance. It was fun. But she was shy to go out in front of people in it until she saw what Ellie was wearing.

Ellie's skirt hung low on her ample hips and reached to her ankles. It was also coolcloth, but patterned like a field in flower, where Is's onesuit was all one shade of deep blue. Ellie's breasts were bare. Her blond hair was pulled to the side and braided so it fell over one breast. A string of black, polished river shells was braided into it. Her feet were bare. Is thought Ellie was the most beautiful woman she had ever seen.

She began to feel less conspicuous in her onesuit. It covered her breasts quite modestly and was in no way interesting to look at.

She allowed Ellie to braid her thick, black hair and tie it up in some intricate knot on top of her head, until only a few wisps fell about her ears and neck. She didn't see Ellie braid the string of glistening white pebbles into it.

They were walking toward the area where the feast would be held, when John came out of a tent. The moment he saw Is, he hurried toward her. She was unprepared for the leap of joy her heart felt. He came right up to her, clasped her arms to her sides, and looked deep into her eyes. She suddenly felt overwhelmed by everything, and for a moment she was afraid she would cry. When he pulled her against him, she didn't resist. She found she had wrapped her arms around him too. She stood, feeling his body against hers and being amazed at how her body responded. She smelled the clean male smell of him, different from the sweat and smoke smell she'd known. Everyone else might as well have ceased to exist.

When John let go of her, he took Ellie in his arms and hugged her too. Is felt confused and disappointed. It was just his way of greeting people.

He seemed to have his own direction to go. Is let Ellie lead her away.

Somewhere ahead drums were beating like a pulse. People moved around a big pit full of coals. An occasional blue flame licked upward. Meat and tubers were being roasted by various methods. People of both sexes and all ages sat gossiping while they tended their cooking.

Some young people were already dancing on the bare, hard-packed ground where the drummers played. Is was fascinated by the sound. The drum players moved their hands in sensuous and delightful ways, and Is was amazed at the variation in sound they could produce by using the heel of their hands, the flat, or the fingers. The beats interwove with one another in impossibly intricate patterns. Is couldn't imagine being so in tune with other people as to be able to make music like that with them. It must be like the magic that could happen between a horse and rider, only with other people. She had never thought about the possibility. She looked from one player to the next and thought, *They must love each other in some very special way to play together like this.*

One of the women began to sing. Sustained, mournful vowel sounds issued from her open throat, startling, and yet perfect in some way. A man's voice joined hers, working a pattern of deeper, shorter notes through her song. Enraptured by the music, Is didn't see Petre approach.

He stood with her awhile, watching her enjoy the music. He didn't speak until she noticed him.

"It's beautiful, isn't it?"

Is felt suddenly flushed and confused, as though she had been caught doing something too private to be shared.

Petre's words somehow cheapened the music. Beautiful? It was so much more than that. But Is also recognized that he was trying to be friendly. He was trying to reach out to her the way people did, through words.

"Yes." She had to clear her throat. "Yes. It is."

His smile said more than any words.

"I had hoped you would let me show you around. This must be very different from what you are used to. I would like to help you feel at home."

Is's mind whirled. Was he offering her protection? He was much more polite than the boys at the government school, or the men at the Equestrienne, but it could be the same thing. Was he claiming her? If she went with him, what was she agreeing to? She meant to confront him, but there was such an earnest hopefulness in his face . . . Is hesitated, confused. He took her eye contact for consent and smiled. The smile came up from within him, joy-filled. There was no trace of the calculating, victorious, demeaning things Is was expecting to see.

She went with him, feeling more unsure and off balance than ever. He introduced her to his friends, fielded questions whenever she didn't know how to answer, and made her feel . . . protected.

She studied the interactions between people. There were obvious couples. Yet they were different from the couples Is was used to. There was no blatant possessiveness. The men did not dominate the encounters. The women were as likely to speak to her as the men were, and that without jealousy or trying to show her up.

Not everyone was coupled. There were groups of unattached men. Is felt them looking at her, sizing her up in sexual terms, not unlike in the government school.

What surprised her were the groups of unclaimed women. In the government school they would have belonged to one man or another. Perhaps it was just more subtle here, but Is couldn't see it.

No one seemed to be making a serious challenge to

Petre's claim on her. That could only mean he was very powerful and feared. If that was the case, he must have other women, and maybe men, under his "protection." Is tried to discover who else belonged to Petre, but again she couldn't discern it.

No one seemed afraid of him. There was much humor at his expense. But Petre never seemed to take offense. Is was getting more confused by the minute. Nothing she had learned about people seemed to apply.

The Hluit wore a great variety of clothing. Most people went bare above the waist, but not all. Some had painted themselves, or wore polished stones, shells, or feathers for decoration. Others seemed not to have bothered to change from clothes they had worked in that day. There was an intermixing of everything from tanned animal hides, to woven plant fiber cloth, to the expensive, exotic Alliance coolcloth. Most of the men wore their hair as long as the women. Many of them had taken great care with their dressing and body ornaments.

Petre had covered himself more than most men his age, who seemed to delight in displaying their bodies. Is felt shy, scared, and fascinated at the same time by the nudity of the peoples' upper bodies. She was glad Petre was more covered.

She caught people looking her over when they didn't think she was noticing. Her dark skin and hair must have been exotic to them. Perhaps no one contested Petre's claim because they found her ugly. But in the government schools that wouldn't have mattered. Ugly or not, fighting over her would have been a way for someone to prove, or lose, their power. The more beautiful, or sexy, she was, the more power could be had by owning her. But even an ugly or flat-chested girl could make herself an item in the power struggle if she played the game right. The only people who hadn't been worth anything to anyone were a few kids who were too retarded, mentally or physically, to fit in, and Is. But Petre did not seem to be like those rejected ones. And

the way some of the men looked at her, Is knew she hadn't
been immediately dumped into that category either.

One of Petre's friends offered her a juice fruit to suck. It
had the bitter aftertaste of alcohol. In the government
schools, you had to be highly connected to get such a
contraband substance.

Food was set out on blankets, and everyone helped
themselves. If there was any order, or etiquette, Is couldn't
detect it. Somehow Petre was always near, unobtrusively
guiding her.

Through it all the drums continued like a heartbeat.
People began to gravitate over to the players. Is watched
them dance. Dances taught in the government schools had
intricate footwork, but people held their bodies stiffly. Here
the steps could be as simple as a shuffling of the feet, but
the body movements were fluid and gorgeous. Some people
were elegant dancers. While they hardly appeared to move,
they somehow conveyed the music through their bodies, so
gracefully Is was fascinated. Other people moved energetically, spinning around, jumping in the air, doing back bends
and splits that seemed impossible to Is.

Some couples danced together, bringing their bodies
close with sensual movements that made Is feel funny
inside. In the government school, half that amount of
touching would have brought swift punishment.

But in all their various styles, the people seemed beautiful
to Is. She was intimidated by their grace and freedom, and
even by their good spirits. She felt overwhelmingly out of
place.

She saw John once, with the woman he had kissed. He
didn't see her.

Once the cooking was done, the people built up a big fire.
Its orange glow was cast on the dancers. Blond hair turned
to burnished gold, set off by deepening, violet shadows.

"May I have the honor of dancing with you?" Petre asked,
startling Is.

"I don't know how," she stammered.

His eyebrows went up. She had surprised him, but in a second he recovered.

"There is nothing to know. You let the music come into your body and go out again."

Is shook her head, too terrified now to speak.

"Look, I will show you."

She wanted to bolt away from him.

"Look, look," he called her. "See, the music comes into my foot through the ground." His foot began to tap and then to flop about in a most comical way. Several people stopped to watch. They laughed.

Is did not want to be the center of attention. She felt more scared than ever.

"Look," Petre called to her. "It starts in my foot and goes up my leg." His leg began to bounce as if it had a life of its own. More people were stopping to watch.

"Now the other foot is getting it," Petre said, and while his right foot was bouncing and hopping most energetically, his left somehow began to twitch and give an occasional hop. People were forming a circle around them now, laughing and calling encouragement to his backward left foot.

"And the music gets into my right arm," he informed Is, while his right arm began to jerk and wave about.

"Come on, left arm," he said, and with his right hand he picked up his limp left arm and shook it, all the while dancing with his right foot and giving strange little, awkward jumps and taps with his left. Slowly, his left arm seemed to get the idea. But when he let go of it, it immediately fell limply to his side. The crowd that had gathered "Ahh"ed their disappointment.

Petre picked up his left arm again and made it dance. This time when he let it go, it danced on a moment before falling to his side. But again he picked it up, and this time it seemed to get the idea. So now he was dancing energetically with his right leg and arm and awkwardly with his left leg and arm. Is couldn't help but laugh. But under Petre's clowning, she was aware of how agile and athletic he was.

"And then the music gets into my center," he informed her and slapped his belly. Instantly he was transformed. His whole body knew how to dance. He leapt and spun, and the drums went faster and faster. Most of the dancers had stopped to watch. Some called encouragement. Some clapped their hands faster and faster with the music. Finally, throwing his arms wide, Petre gave one last magnificent spinning jump into the air, and landed, arms and legs thrown wide, in front of Is. The drums rolled to a stop and then began again, slower.

Petre stood in front of her, grinning and panting for breath. The people applauded by slapping their hands on their thighs. Petre ignored them. His eyes twinkled merrily as he watched Is.

He began to tap his right foot again very pointedly. The people were still surrounding her, watching. The pressure of their eyes made her try.

She tapped her right foot as much as Petre was doing as she could. He grinned wider and began with the left foot. She imitated the best she could. He began waving one arm. She followed suit. He added the other arm. So did she. He began to weave and dance with his body. She tried to imitate and felt awkward and stiff. People laughed and clapped, calling encouragement. She tried to jump the way Petre jumped. It was a whole lot harder than he had made it look. She tried one of his spins and nearly fell down. Hands caught her and set her back on her feet in the circle. She laughed, surprising herself. Petre baited her with all kinds of exotic jumps and spins. Is danced until she was exhausted and too out of breath to go on.

Petre stopped too, breathing hard, but grinning widely. Is had only a moment to wonder at how happy he seemed. Then, without warning, he threw his arms around her and pulled her against him. The feeling that went through her body was like an electric shock. Her heart got all out of time. Her arms and legs were instantly weak. Her mind tried to tell her about six contradictory things at once: He *was*

claiming her. No, it wasn't like that here. He expected her to
"pay" him for his protection. No, it wasn't that sort of hug.
She couldn't tell. The reaction of her own body was so
intense and unexpected. Part of her mind was trying to tell
her it was OK to do what Petre wanted. She should try to get
along better here than she had in the schools. She should do
whatever that took. But she couldn't. She knew she couldn't!

Petre released her. She tried to walk away from him, from
the dancers, everything. Her legs felt funny and she stumbled.
Petre put his arm around her waist and steadied her against
his side as she walked. She surprised herself by allowing
him to do that.

"The alcohol," he said. "It creeps up on you." He was
sweaty and he smelled strongly, but Is was fascinated by his
smell and touch.

They sat on a little rise overlooking the fire and the dark
silhouettes of the dancers moving around it. Petre didn't
touch her any more, and Is began to relax. She could feel the
beat of the drums as though it were the pulse of the
mountains. Occasional, half-formed thoughts and small
hopes chased through Is's mind, riding the beat of the
drums. She wouldn't let any of them stay.

They sat while the fire burned down to the red glow of
coals and the drums fell silent. Only a few people sat around
the fire now, their still forms dark against its shimmer-
rippling warmth.

"May I walk you home?"

Petre's words startled Is into realizing she didn't know
where "home" was. Ondre had said she could live with him
and Ellie, but Is didn't remember how to get to their tent.
She didn't think she could distinguish it from all the others,
and it was only one room. They wouldn't want her there, not
really.

"I'd like to pitch my own tent."

"Fine. I'll show you where Ondre put your things."

Is was suddenly afraid that Petre had invited himself to
spend the night with her. He insisted on carrying some of

her stuff, and showed her which one was Ellie and Ondre's tent, saying she might want to be close to them. He stayed to help her get her strange little tent up. Then he hesitated and said, "Well, good night."

"Good night." She wondered if the relief she felt showed in her voice.

"I hope you feel welcome here," he said. "I hope you like us."

She wondered if he had wanted to say, "I hope you like *me.*"

In a sudden rush of gratitude, she said, "I do," and added, "Thank you."

He laughed very softly. "Thank you," he said and walked away.

-XIV-

Is had thought she would sleep late after having been up half the night, but she woke early, strangely alert. She crawled out of her bag and stood still, testing the air for what had awakened her. There were many footprints in the dew, all going in the same direction, so she followed them.

On the top of a little rise, in an open field, she saw the people. They were all moving in unison, lined up more or less in rows, with one man leading them. They did a fast, spinning turn with arms outstretched, and stopped suddenly, then turned back the other way. Again and again. The movement was beautiful. The sun was not yet above the mountains. Fog lay in streamers on the plains below the knoll where the people exercised. The people spun and stopped, spun and stopped. Except for the swish of clothing they were silent.

Suddenly they all knelt down. The man who had been leading the movement stood in front of them. A young man walked forward, seeming to glide over the ground, fit and strong. He picked up a long stick, like a stave, from a pile at the outskirts of the exercise area and advanced menacingly on the leader, carrying the stick behind him. Suddenly he ran forward and swung with all his might.

Is's body jerked with reaction as she expected to see the leader slammed to the ground with a broken skull. Instead the stick whistled by him and the attacker flew through the air as though launched. She expected the young man to land hard and not get up. Instead he did a sort of a flip in the air,

straightened his body out parallel to the ground, and landed
all in one piece. In an instant he was on his feet again, but
the leader was now holding the stick. He held it out to the
attacker, and that man took it again and, without an instant's
hesitation, swung again. Again he went flying through the
air. This time Is knew what to expect. There was a beauty to
their movements, a timing and unity she had never seen
anywhere else except in the best riders.

After a few more throws, they went through the attack in
slow-motion. Is saw exactly how the man moved out of the
way, how he used the attacker's momentum while twisting
the stick for leverage. It made so much sense, Is wanted to
cry out with understanding. A deep excitement took her.
This was what John had used against Chest and the men in
the town, and there were as many women out there
practicing it as there were men. Maybe they would let her
learn this too. If she could, she would never have to be
afraid of a man again.

All the people who had been kneeling stood up. They
paired off, one with a stick, one without, to imitate the
movements of the teacher. Some of them were very good,
but some were not. From them Is got an idea of how hard
the movement really was. It made sense, and it should be
easy, but getting the timing right would take experience. Is
was dying to try it. With her years of riding, she thought she
would not be too bad. But she noticed that the partners
always switched roles after a few throws. She wondered if
she could learn to fall like that. In riding, falling was bad,
always to be avoided, and Is had never thought of it as
something that could be beautiful, or fun.

A young girl came walking across the field to Is. The
child smiled at her in a shy way and said good morning very
low.

"Good morning, Chandra," Is replied, hoping she had
remembered the girl's name right.

The child went from shy to beaming in an instant.

They watched the practice together. John was working

out with a stout man who looked as if he could break the stick over John's head if he ever connected. But John was having no trouble with him. He was grinning.

"He's really good," Chandra said.

"He looks good to me," Is admitted.

"He is. Is it true he can't talk?"

"He can talk," Is told her, "but only sometimes, and only if he isn't speaking to someone directly."

"Are you going to marry him?" the child asked. "I wish you would."

Is felt as if someone had kicked her. She took a moment to seem nonchalant. "I thought he was already married."

"No. He's 'sposed to marry Alene. But she's not good like you are. I wish you'd marry him."

Is tried to remain nonchalant. "What do you mean she's not good?"

The girl looked at her and away. "She's dark at the center."

Is wondered what that meant. "And I'm not?"

"No. You're beautiful."

Is almost laughed. "Who says that?"

"You are. And all the men think so too."

Is decided she'd better discount everything the girl said. She was probably just a lonely child with a good imagination. They watched awhile more in silence, as more children collected near by.

"I have to go now," Chandra said. "It's almost our turn." She ran over to the other children.

The people lined up again, kneeled, and bowed to the man who had taught. Then they began drifting away, laughing and talking together. They all seemed very happy after their workout. Is could almost see the energy sparkling in the air around them.

John and some of the other adults stayed to work with the children. Is watched John correcting the way one child was moving during the warm-up exercises. He did it all with mime. Is understood him perfectly. The child laughed at

John's rendition of the mistake he'd made. Others stopped to watch and laughed too. Is could see that the children loved John. She loved him too. All of a sudden it was easy to admit that. She wondered if Chandra were right about him not being married.

The children's practice looked different from the adults'. They did a lot of tumbling. Is watched intently and tried to learn how the falls were done. Some of the children were fearless. They would dive over each other and roll to their feet. Others were more timid, but the adults who had stayed to help were patient. Although the children were having fun, there was an undertone of discipline Is could only have called strictness. But it was not the same sort of dry, hateful strictness of the government schools. Loving strictness. She wondered how that balance was achieved.

The children didn't work with the sticks. They practiced throwing someone who had grabbed them. Is was amazed at how even the small children could throw someone bigger. It seemed to be a trick of leverage and timing rather than strength. Again she was struck by the feeling that the moves made so much sense, it was a wonder she hadn't ever thought of them. But she had never thought about defending herself at all. How could she? She would have had to fight everyone in the school. And how could she have defended herself from the teachers, like Riding Master Masley, who had so much power over her? And the berserkers? She felt certain that even the best of these people would not be able to handle a berserker.

When the class ended, Is went over to the children, intending to walk with Chandra, but John saw her and came to her immediately. He put both hands on her arms and looked deep into her eyes, as he had last night. Is thought her heart would stop. Her whole body felt strange, hot and weak. After a moment he let her go, and she walked with him back toward the camp. Other people surrounded them, talking. They asked her what she thought of what she had seen.

"It was beautiful," she said. They laughed, and she wondered if she had insulted anyone. "It looks effective," she added.

Everyone seemed to radiate energy and good spirits, and Is found herself feeling good just to be around these people. The children chattered and laughed and rough-played their way back to camp.

The talk switched from practice to breakfast, and the day's work. Breakfast was a communal affair featuring large pots of slowly bubbling cereal. Petre saw Is and came over to her. He had overslept, he said, and a lot of people kidded him for missing practice. He seemed to take the razzing good-naturedly.

"Someone has to stay here and cook," he said in defense of himself. But no one believed him.

"Cook!" they said. "Only if you've learned to do it in your sleep." And they wouldn't allow him to argue. Is watched the exchange carefully and could detect no malice in it—so unlike the government school.

After breakfast Is agreed to talk to Ellie and Ondre some more. John had disappeared, and so had Alene.

They rolled back the roof of the tent so it was basically a roofless wall encircling them. The mid-morning sun shone in. The sky was blue, and birds sang, but Is felt sudden trepidation.

They sat sipping tea together, and finally Ondre started. "I hope you understood, the feast last night was to thank you for what you've done for John, as much as it was to celebrate John's return."

Is had not understood that, any more than Ondre's people had understood that a big, public get-together was the absolute worst thing they could have done for her. When she didn't say anything, she heard Ondre sigh. She was not making whatever he wanted to say easy for him, but she was not doing it on purpose. Ellie stepped in.

"Is, we love John. We thought he was dead. We're so glad he's back, and we thank you for helping him. Nothing would make us happier than for both of you to stay here forever. But that isn't what John's going to do. It is important that you understand your options, and it is important we understand you." She looked directly into Is's eyes, and Is felt a flash of warning go through her. She made herself nod so Ellie would continue.

Ellie backed off from the intensity of what she had been trying to express. She glanced at her husband, and Ondre spoke.

"The mirror/non-mirror thing that was in John's letter . . . the Alliance claims it is an alien device, perhaps a machine, that came from another world. They did teach you there *are* other worlds?" he interrupted himself to ask.

Is nodded. When she had been in the government school, she had sometimes sneaked from her bed at night, unable to sleep, to sit by the window and look at those stars and wonder if there weren't a better world out there somewhere. It had become like a friend to her, that imagined world, a place she could escape to in her thoughts when the real world was too tough.

Ellie said, "We have never completely trusted the Alliance's explanation of the mirror. But we do not have a better one." She paused and pinned Is with her honest blue eyes. "It is important for you to realize, most of what your government has taught you about our side of the Boundary is simply not true. They don't send the berserkers against the Blueskins. They send them against the mirror."

They were both watching for her reaction. Is wished they would stop referring to it as "her" government. She was an outlaw too.

Ondre took up the tale. "The Alliance has a certain vested interest in keeping its citizens on its side of the Boundary, and therefore a certain interest in keeping them ignorant and misinformed. The Alliance doesn't want people to know anything about the mirror, or about us, or the Blueskins."

Is could see Ondre was getting wound up into real anger.

She didn't understand what he was trying to tell her. She was glad when Ellie interrupted him.

"The Alliance has worked out an 'arrangement' with the Blueskins. It doesn't prosecute them for the farmers they kill, or the goods they steal, and the Blueskins let the berserkers pass. The Alliance wants the Blueskins to attack a certain percentage of farmers every year. That way the people believe there is a real threat and that the berserkers are necessary." Ellie stopped because she could see how pale Is was getting.

"What's wrong?"

"Blueskins killed my mother and father."

Ondre slapped his thigh with a loud report and turned angrily away. No one said anything for a few minutes. Then Ellie said.

"I'm very sorry." Her voice was so filled with compassion that Is had trouble believing a woman who hardly knew her could care that much.

"She still has to know," Ondre said to his wife. His voice was gentle and without anger now.

Ellie didn't say anything, but Is had the feeling she agreed with her husband. Is did not want to be treated like a child. She tried to think of something to say that would show her toughness and let them know she wanted the truth.

"Why do they send the berserkers against the mirror?" she asked.

"The Alliance would have us believe it is their way of studying the mirror," Ondre answered her. "The mirror kills everyone who approaches it. The berserkers are designed to be unafraid of death, to fight hard, and not be killed too quickly. They are the government's eyes and ears. When they fight the mirror, the government can see and hear what happens. It's transmitted to them, as when people fast their talk." He was watching her acutely, and Is felt he was trying to simplify what he was describing down to her level. It embarrassed her to be so ignorant.

"If it kills everyone, then it will kill John." She heard

herself sounding a lot more calm and impersonal than she felt.

"He seems to think he has learned something that will make a difference," Ondre said. Is could tell Ondre didn't want his brother going anywhere near the thing.

"One of the mirror's programs, or functions, or abilities—depending on whether it's a computer, a machine, or a sentient being," Ondre went on doggedly, "has the properties of a mirror. It reflects anything that approaches it. But it isn't just a surface projection, like a mirror. It seems to somehow reflect what's inside a person's mind. We know of no one who has lived through a direct encounter with the mirror, but people sometimes live through encounters with the herd fogs, which can do similar things to a person's mind. We think the herd fogs are the mirror's appendages, like hands, with which it can reach out and manipulate things. People who have gone through experiences with the fogs are often very confused." He looked at her closely, and Is could tell he was holding back something. But her years of training in the government school had led her to accept having information withheld from her. It never occurred to her that she could simply ask and he would tell her.

"It's important to us to know about your experiences in the fog so that we can learn to understand the herd fogs better," Ellie said. "It could also be important to you. If you go with John, the more you understand, the better off you'll be."

"And if the dark bodies rescued you from the fog," Ondre put in, "that could be very important. We don't know enough about them."

"They seem to be another form of life that might not have originated on our planet, like the mirror," Ellie said. "They may have come with the mirror. Numerous people have seen them, but very few have actually heard them speaking."

"I may have imagined it," Is said.

Ondre and Ellie exchanged a look.

"In a sense, all our experiences of the herd fog and the

dark bodies, and even the mirror, are imagined," Ondre said. "None of them is exactly 'real' in the way that, say, a horse is 'real.' They exist only when our minds have some reason to make them exist."

"You may have caused the dark bodies to come into being at that moment to help you," Ellie tried to explain. "If we can find out how you did that, you may be able to call them or send them away at will."

"Why would I want to do either?" Is wanted to know.

"Because, if you go with John, you may be able to help him find the mirror, and you may help him have the right dialogue with it." Ondre's voice was serious. "John seems to think he can get the mirror to reflect something that won't kill him. He thinks it can cure what the Alliance did to him."

Ellie took Is's hands. "John desperately needs to talk again. You know he was posing as a scholar and spying on the Alliance for us. We try to keep a few spies in the government all the time so we will know if they are planning anything concerning us. For years they have just let us live here in peace, but we know there will be a time when that will change. So we keep our spies watching.

"John had a very special task. Our people have kept record of the changes the Alliance has made in the berserkers and their horses over the years. It seemed the Alliance was trying to perfect something, using the mirror like a mirror, to reflect their flaws. What we have never been able to understand is *what* they are trying to perfect. Years ago, our people thought it was the physical perfection of the fighting team of horse and rider the Alliance was after. But they have taken man and beast as far as they can in that direction, and still they send them." Ellie paused, and Ondre took up the story.

"A whole network of industry has grown up around developing and supporting the berserkers and their horses. You were part of it. You saw all the levels of training, the different Barns, the Equestrienne schools, the elaborate apprentice program. Of course not all of it is aimed at producing berserkers—there are the Breeding Barns, the Troop Barns, the Training Barns—but the berserkers and their horses are the ultimate achievement. The whole thing is too complex for the explanations the Alliance offers.

"John had worked his way up in the research branch of the Alliance dealing specifically with the berserkers. He must have learned something very important."

"All we know is, he is willing to risk facing the mirror, and the possibility of being killed, for the chance to regain his speech," Ellie said bluntly.

"He may have a better chance of succeeding if you help him," Ondre said.

Is looked away, giving herself a moment to think. She could see how much these two loved John. She wanted to help them, and she certainly wanted to help John, but she didn't know what they thought she could do, and she was afraid. Deep in her soul she didn't want to go anywhere near the mirror, or the herd fogs or dark bodies again, ever.

"There is another reason you might want to go," Ondre said. He sounded tentative. Is met his eyes, and she was suddenly more scared. "Have you thought about what you'll do when your stallion reaches maturity?" His voice was grave, his eyes compassionate.

He could only mean when Lark was old enough for his berserker. But there would be no berserker for Lark. He would never feel the man coming. He would not change the way the other horses had changed. Is had never believed it would be otherwise. But now Ondre was looking at her with such concern and sadness, he could only mean she'd been wrong.

"You didn't know?" Ellie asked compassionately.

"But his berserker won't come," Is cried out. "Lark won't change."

"He came from the Castle Stud, didn't he?" Ondre asked. "He had the brand on his forehead, didn't he?"

Is could only nod. He had arrived at her place as a leggy yearling, his coat still fuzzy like a colt's, and his tail the short flag of a baby. He had been so friendly, making up to her immediately, as if she were some long lost friend. She had rubbed his forehead where the scar was, and he had loved it because it was itchy with new healing.

"He's about seven or eight now, isn't he?" Ondre asked.

"Seven," Is confirmed.

Ellie spoke to Ondre. "He's too old. We've never successfully removed the chip from a horse older than two."

"It gets too integrated into their brain," Ondre explained. "It controls the chemical output of the pituitary and other systems. Among other things, it tells his body when to make the hormones of fear, or anger, or aggressiveness. So far it had only regulated his hormones for maximum growth and development. He is as strong and fast and smart as his biochemical makeup, and his breeding, and your training, can make him. But when the chip determines that he is fully developed, it will switch its message. It will make him as aggressive and fearless as it is possible for a horse to be.

"Each chip has a frequency all its own. It is set to resonate with the chip implanted in the berserker they were preparing for that particular horse. That is why the horse and the berserker do not fight each other. Their brains recognize each other."

"Even if his berserker doesn't come," Ellie continued, "Lark will become too aggressive to handle. His training, and his love for you, will not be able to override the hormones his system will be putting out. I'm sorry."

Is did not want to believe them, but she had seen too many of her beloved stallions change. There would be no way to control Lark when that happened to him. She grasped at the small hope that had mentioned earlier.

"But if I go with John, that could make a difference?"

Now Ondre came over and put his arm around his wife and took one of Is's hands. "We don't know," he said. "From John's message, he seems to believe he has found a new way to approach the mirror. There may be some very

sophisticated answers to a lot of things about the mind
there."

"But I don't know how to help," Is said.

"Maybe you do," Ellie said. "You just don't know how to
access that information."

"It's like riding," Ondre tried to explain. "It is really your
body that knows how to ride. You can't possibly use your
conscious mind to instruct your body to move with a horse,
any more than you can consciously instruct your body to
walk. The motor skills are too complex. You have to let your
body-brain do the work, not your thought-brain. This sort of
knowledge is the same. It's too complex for your thought-
brain, your conscious mind. But the information is somewhere in you. You may be able to access it through your
body-brain, or some other way we don't fully understand.
But we have ways of bringing those experiences up to the
conscious level, and then we will know, if you will let us
try."

Is wasn't sure she had understood everything they'd told
her, but she liked Ondre and his people, and wanted to
belong here. In her experience, one had to earn every
privilege. To live here would be a privilege she was ready to
try to earn.

"What do I have to do?"

"Just listen to my voice," Ondre said. "Do what I tell you.
I want to get your conscious mind to relax so I can talk to
another part of your mind."

Is had her doubts, but she agreed. Ondre had her sit in a
comfortable position, then he began talking to her, telling
her to relax her face, her neck, her arms . . .

His voice was like a caress on her skin. Muscles she
hadn't been aware of holding tight suddenly relaxed. Her
whole body seemed to sigh, and something inside her mind
let go. She was aware of Ondre's voice manipulating her
body. She could feel it touching her in long, stroking
motions, in a way no man had ever touched her with his
hands. She could feel her body responding, letting go of

everything—tension, fear, desire. In some distant part of herself she was amazed. Ondre was the first man since her father who didn't threaten her.

She was watching like that, from a great distance it seemed, when Ondre said, "You are back on the hillside with the fog. What do you see?"

Instantly, Is was surrounded by the thickly shrouded trees. She was alone. Lark was gone. John and his mare were gone.

The breeze was doing battle with the fog. She could see that so clearly it didn't occur to her to question it. She was trying to get to a little clear place so the breeze would have an advantage. Her arm hurt, and she could barely turn her head. Walking was strangely difficult. John was riding out of the fog on Lark. He grinned his relief when he saw her. He opened his mouth and was going to speak, just as ordinarily as anyone ever spoke. But the voice Is heard was Ondre's.

"What are you seeing inside the fog?" And instantly she was back inside the fog. John and Lark were gone. The voice became more insistent.

"It is important you tell us what you are seeing."

Is wanted to answer that voice, but other voices were saying something else, very fast, on many tracks at once.

"Can you hear me?" the voice out of the fog asked. "Tell me what you are hearing?"

Is tried, she really tried, to repeat what she was hearing.

The next thing she knew Ondre was gripping her shoulders. "Wake up. You are safe now. Wake up." She seemed to remember that he had been saying that for a long time.

She stared about her frantically. The fog was gone. She was inside the tent wall. The sun shone through the open roof. Insects buzzed. She tried to move, but there was a weight on her legs. Ellie.

Ellie's face was red with exertion. Her hair was tousled and her pupils were big. She moved off Is's legs. Ondre was

still gripping her arms so hard they hurt. She wanted to tell
him to stop, but her throat was dry and sore.

Ondre moved back from her. Ellie brought her some
water. No one said anything. Is tried to remember what had
happened. The other two looked as shaken as she felt.

Ondre started to say something. His voice cracked, and he
had to clear it. "I'm sorry. I didn't know . . ."

Ellie made a harsh noise to interrupt him.

"Are you all right?" she asked Is.

"Yes. What happened?"

"I asked you to do something you weren't able to do,
when you were in a state of mind in which you had to try,"
Ondre said.

"Oh." Is felt better. If that's all that had happened . . .
She was used to being in the position of having to try to do
something that seemed impossible—training the young
horses, dealing with the berserkers. "Did you learn what you
wanted to learn?"

Ondre shook his head. "No, but you might have."

Is tried to remember what she was supposed to have
learned—something that might help John survive his encounter with the mirror. "I don't think so. We better try
again."

Ondre drew in his breath, surprised. Ellie's eyes got even
bigger.

"Not on your life," Ellie said heatedly.

"You're very brave to want to try again," Ondre explained. "But you could be hurt. We won't do it."

"Not brave," Is said. "It wasn't anything to me."

Ondre shook his head. "If information was given to you,
it was given in a way you cannot repeat."

Is was swept with disappointment. She would be no help
to John, or his people, or Lark.

"What's wrong?" Ellie said.

"I wanted to help."

"You already have," Ellie exclaimed. "You brought John
back to us. You saved his life."

"And you brought us you," Ondre said. "Don't you realize? Some of the things you've experienced! The way the Blueskins treated you! Seeing the dark bodies. Hearing them! And the house, the house where you met the old man, Amil? It doesn't exist. But where you saw that house is the ruin of an old chimney. There used to be a house there. But now there is no such house, and no such person living there."

"Stop, Ondre. You're scaring her," Ellie interrupted.

Is felt the hair standing up on her arms. "What?" she asked weakly, and they had to repeat that there was no house, and no old man living there. There was only a ruin, as if a house had been there a long time ago.

"But John saw it too," Is objected. "And you have the note Amil wrote."

"Yes, we have the note," Ondre said solemnly. "And we have sent scouts to see if they can find the house. Maybe someone moved in there and rebuilt. But it would have to have been very recently."

"How can that be?" Is asked, trying to keep a feeling of mounting horror at bay. The cabin she had seen had been old and well worn, as lived in as an old shoe.

"For the same reason the Blueskins have a legend about you. Well, about a girl who roams the mountains on a war-horse the color of the earth. In fact they believe he is made out of the ground, and the girl's hair is the color of shadow, and her skin dark like the soil. That is how they disappear, those two. They go back into the ground and shadow from which they were made. But it is very strong medicine to see them, and even stronger medicine to capture them, although it is impossible to detain them for long."

Is shook her head. She couldn't begin to get the words together to refute Ondre. He saw her expression and laughed.

"Hard to understand, huh? Hard to explain." His eyes met hers searchingly. "Have you ever looked into two mirrors at an angle to each other? Your reflection repeats itself into infinity. It is a property of mirrors."

Ellie took her hand. "Enough," she told Ondre.

"No, Ellie, she needs to know."

"But it's only your *theory,* Ondre."

"Theory!" Ondre laughed, and there was a little bit of his brother's hysterical quality to the sound. "It's not even that," he said. "It's a bunch of things that don't make sense, all lumped together. How could the Blueskins have an *old* legend about you? How could an old man and his cabin be there when you go there, but we know it only as a ruin? The only thing I can think is that the mirror is involved. We know it makes hallucinations. Could it be somehow throwing partial reflections of you back in time?"

"But I've never been near it!" Is cried out.

Ondre and Ellie exchanged a look. They waited for her to understand.

"If I go with John," Is started hesitantly, "the mirror is going to get my reflection . . . and . . . but it already has it, and I haven't gone there yet. Can it do things all backwards in order like that?"

"Yes," Ondre answered her. "That seems to be part of what drives a lot of people crazy in the herd fogs. Things get out of order. Some people don't ever recover."

"Lark was lost in the fog," Is said thoughtfully. "But then John was riding him. And John spoke to me." She met Ondre's eyes. "Am I crazy? Did it drive me crazy?"

"No." He met her eyes steadily until she looked away.

"If the herd fog can do that, what will the mirror be like?" Her voice sounded small and timid even to her own ears.

"It will be even more confusing and frightening," Ondre answered her honestly.

"Ond . . ." Ellie reproved him.

"No," he said to her, "Is needs to know everything any one of us knows, or thinks, or guesses about the mirror. She might be the one to tie all this together."

"But Amil wasn't a reflection," Is objected. "We ate food

he cooked, and the note he wrote is real. You saw it. You held it in your hand."

"Is," Ellie said in a calming voice. "We don't *have* the answers, we *need* them."

Suddenly Is could see that they were desperate for her help. It was not just that they wanted to help John, whom they loved. They needed something from him, and from her. She sat back, stunned. She had never been needed like this before. She was suddenly frightened in a way she had never been frightened before.

During her hesitation, Ellie spoke to Ondre. "You should tell her about the troopers too. It's her right to know."

Is froze.

"They were here twice," Ondre said. "The first time must have been just shortly after you disappeared with their stallion last fall. They were just looking around, just wondering if we'd seen you. They only wanted to recover the horse. Seemed he was something special they wanted for their breeding program. No mention of killing him off with a berserker. Would we let them know if we saw you? They were friendly and polite, and ever so casual." He gave a crooked little grin. "This, you realize, after having not made contact with our people, in our homeland, for," he glanced at Ellie for confirmation, "fifty years."

"At least," Ellie agreed. "It was much too casual. We were very suspicious. But we had not seen you then. We couldn't tell them anything but that. We didn't immediately notice that your description matched one of the Blueskins' legends. We wouldn't have bothered to mention it anyway. They can talk to the Blueskins for themselves."

"They brought a whole troop when they came back in the spring," Ondre continued. "They weren't quite so polite. They seemed absolutely certain the horse was still alive. They were sure the only way you could have made it through the winter was if you'd come here. They demanded we turn the horse over to them. They demanded the right to search our herds, which of course they don't have, and we denied it to them on principle. They reminded us the horse was near maturity. They tried to make us believe they would know if we killed him, and they said they would be back with his berserker. Supposedly, either to call the horse out of our herds, or to wreck our village." He gave Is the crooked grin again. "Or both."

Is felt as if she had been kicked. "You should have told me immediately. I'll go right away." If she concentrated on the fear and the urgency, she wouldn't have to feel the pain and disappointment.

"That's not necessary," Ellie said. "It will not matter what you do—go or stay. The Alliance believes what it will, and we will not let them search our herds whether you are here or not. That is a larger issue. The Blueskins, also, have their own reasoning, and will act on it whether you approve or not. Each group is autonomous. You are not responsible for our actions. You are responsible only to yourself, and those you have included within that self."

Is met Ellie's eyes to see if she really believed that. Ellie's eyes didn't waver.

"If all people lived that way," Ondre said, "each one taking responsibility for his or her own self, and allowing all others to take responsibility for themselves, we would have true freedom."

He believed that too.

Is had never had the luxury to consider freedom in the sense that they meant it. She had been trying too hard not to get noticed, not to get hurt. Even when she'd been a trainer at the Border Station, although she had lived alone and made all her own decisions concerning the horses' training, she had not been free. She had trained those horses to be taken by the berserkers and killed. When she had run away, she had had no one to answer to, and yet she had not been free, not in the sense she thought Ellie and Ondre were talking about. Freedom to make real decisions, not decisions based on fear. Freedom *from* fear. Freedom from the coercion of a corrupt government. Responsible only to "yourself, and those you have included within that self."

They would have her believe she could decide to run away, or to go with John, or to stay here. For a moment she could see that they were really extending that freedom to her. But she could not accept it. In her mind there was very little choice. She had never meant for anyone else to become involved in the consequences of her decision to steal the stallion. She could not just stay and see how many people got killed over her.

She would go with John. She did not really believe she would be any help with the mirror, but there was a small chance it would not kill him. What he had learned could be important to his people. There was the even smaller chance he would be able to help Lark. Is found she didn't believe that either, but it was the only chance Lark had. And John . . . John, who wanted to have a proper dialogue with the mirror. John, who couldn't speak. What if he tried, and the mirror cast his insane, hysterical laughter back at him?

She did not want to be a part of any of this. She wanted to train horses—deal with things that were "real" the way horses were "real"—but she could not stay here now.

-XV-

Is was filled with urgency to leave, but no one else seemed to share her feeling. Ondre thought John needed time with his people, to heal as much as he could, before facing the mirror.

Ellie tried to reassure Is that the Alliance troopers could not surprise them. The Hluit had put out extra scouts, plus everyone seemed to think the Blueskins would not only report troop movement, but interfere with it.

Is objected, but she was told, again, that the Hluit could not control the Blueskins. They could not even be sure what the Blueskins would do. Is began to realize that the relationship between the two peoples was more complex and subtle than she could hope to understand quickly.

Meanwhile, Petre had become her almost constant companion. He loved to talk, and his ceaseless chatter was a great source of information.

Petre took her out to see the herd they had given Lark.

Boys and girls of ten to fifteen years stayed with the breeding herds and kept them separated. For the young people it was training in independence, as they were completely responsible for the horses. They rode trusted geldings the stallions would tolerate.

These people revered their horses in a much more natural way than the way the Alliance treated theirs. Even the youngest children seemed to know how to ride. They learned to care for the needs of their horses when they were learning to take care of their own needs. Is had seen small children lugging manure away from the camp, and toddlers tagging along to help spread it where the grass would reclaim it for nourishment. It was part of life, like dressing oneself, or taking care of one's own hygiene.

The days began to take on a routine. First thing in the morning nearly everyone would turn out for martial arts practice. Petre had formally invited Is to practice, but everyone taught her. First she had to learn to fall so she wouldn't be hurt when someone threw her; then she had to learn how to make the movements work so she could throw someone no matter how big or strong they were, or no matter how fast they attacked. At least that was the theory. In practice everyone moved very slowly and carefully with her. She understood that it was important to do things correctly from the very beginning. As in learning to ride, it would be harder to break bad habits than to develop the right habits to start with.

After practice, and breakfast, came the daily chores. At this time of year the people were busy harvesting crops they had grown in outlying plots. At breakfast someone would stand up and say something like "The roots are ready to harvest in High Plot." Or, "The harnuts are ripe in Blue Forest." The people seemed to be free to decide which jobs to assign themselves to, and as far as Is could tell, all the work was getting done. It was so different from the government school, where everyone was assigned to tasks and proctors stood over the students to make sure they kept working. Since Is had been unwilling to do the things that would have kept her in the proctors' good graces, she had had to do a lot of the work, and she was considered stupid for getting herself into that position.

But here the attitude was different. People talked and kidded one another. The only competitiveness Is could discern was a friendly try at being the one to get the most work done. As in the martial arts class, anyone who was near her was willing to teach her a more efficient way to shell harnuts or dig bigroots.

Is was unable to relax and accept this. She kept waiting for the other shoe to drop. Sometimes the tension of just being around so many people was too much for her, so in the evenings, when the work was done and people were resting, gossiping, and just being together, Is would slip off by herself.

No one ever said anything to her about it, or followed her, or tried to prevent her from going, but she knew people noticed, especially Petre. He seemed to have appointed himself her special guardian. Ever since that first night at the feast, when he had helped her face the people, he seemed always, unobtrusively, to be at her elbow.

The day the Big Rain began, all harvesting came to a stop. The people constructed a huge communal tent and sat around drinking tea and talking, smoking and canning things, or catching up on their rest.

Is was unaware of how it began, but sometime during the day the talk had gone from idle conversation to something more structured. Ondre was speaking, and his words had become simple, his sentences cadenced, as though he were reciting something. The people had fallen silent, listening to Ondre with rapt attention, and something else — satisfaction. They were like people who were thirsty and had found a well. Something very powerful was happening here, without fanfare, without introduction, and all the people were participating in it deeply, except Is.

Slowly, she realized that Ondre was reciting the history of the Hluit.

". . . We were scholars, of the Privileged class, highest in the hierarchy, but we were dissatisfied. We presented our ideas and were rebuffed. We moved to outlying villages and they brought us back. We petitioned for changes, and went unheard.

"Then Hluit came to be governor of the Grand Council. He proposed an experiment. 'Let them have their own land. Let them try to make a different society.' The ones who said man's nature must be controlled said we would fail. We would end up with a worse government than the Alliance. Hluit said, 'Let them try. If they fail, it is no difference to us because they will be beyond the Boundary. And if they succeed, we will learn from them.'

"We became the Hluit. We are an experiment.

"Our forebearers numbered one hundred and eighty. We honor them all. Among them was William Demanse, the great philosopher who set the tone of our government; Annette Aneet, who brought us the science of ecology; Lis Mistome, the great mathematician; Bihl Ahmanhet and Ondre Dreel, who brought us knowledge of medicine . . ." The list went on and on.

Is could not believe anyone could memorize so much. But Ondre must have been getting it right, because everyone was watching, and some were nodding slowly to themselves. Some were mouthing the sentences silently along with him. Even the children seemed to know it.

Ondre began to catalog the differences between the Hluit and the Alliance.

"We did not build houses. We did not rape the land. We did not set one person above another. We did not withhold knowledge of any sort from any person." As the list went on, Is began to recognize the things she had only sensed as "wrongness" in the government school.

These people had made a study of what was wrong in the Alliance, and had tried to change those things. They had purposefully formed their society to be as different from the Alliance as possible.

"To say, '*This* will be the way,'" Ondre went on, "is only a first step. People must have a road to walk. The road must have a map. Intention was the beginning. The map was the second step. But the map is not the road. Each person walks the real road. Sweat, blood, tears, laughter, frustration, joy—these are the real road. Horsemanship and martial arts are the map. Love is the destination."

Is didn't hear the rest. *Love is the destination.* Not control. Not power over someone else.

She had seen the women taking an equal part in the Hluit
society. She thought of the fearlessness of the children. She
thought of the bridle-less horses. The Hluit would not even
coerce their horses!

Even their martial arts could only be used effectively in
self-defense. The success of the throws depended on the
aggression of the attacker. Is mostly missed the rest of
Ondre's recitation as she thought her own thoughts. A whole
new world of thoughts and questions opened for her. She
was surprised at herself, now, that she had never thought to
ask Petre about his people's history. The government school
had taught her well. Don't ask questions. No, something
even deeper than that—don't *want* to know.

That was the biggest wrong the Alliance perpetrated
against their people, not just the withholding of knowledge,
but their attempt to kill the desire to learn.

Set above those uneducated, unawakened masses were
the privileged few—the scholars. They had all the knowledge, the books, and the resources with which to learn. For
the first time Is really wanted to know, not just what the
scholars knew, but what it was that the Alliance did not want
the people to know. Suddenly she understood why the Hluit
had spies, and why John's need to tell the people what he
had learned was so urgent that he would risk his life to do
it. Why his brother, who loved him, would let him take that
risk.

She couldn't listen to any more. She had to think about
what she had already understood. She was sitting on the
edge of the crowd, so it was easy enough to slip out from
under the tent which had no walls.

The rain was like ice water. She pulled her coat up around
her neck and began to walk. A few steps away she made the
mistake of looking back, and met Petre's eyes. No one else
had noticed. Everyone's attention was focused on Ondre.

Is began to walk again. Quickly, against the chill of the
rain. For the first time she wished Petre would follow her.
She wished she could talk to him as easily as he talked to

her. She would tell him all the things that were happening inside her head. She would tell him about all the changes; as though the ground she was standing on were shaking; as though her heart were filled with sky one moment, and heavy stone the next; as though her brain were exploding like the sun—and the only thing she had to hold on to was something from the government school, dark and heavy and bitter. But Petre didn't follow.

Eventually Is sat with her back against a tree, cold and damp, and watched the rain, and felt it finding its way into her clothing, and thought about how much she wanted to tell someone what was happening to her, and how much more John must want to tell his people something much more important.

In the end Is convinced herself she was glad Petre hadn't followed her, because she didn't know what would have happened. She didn't trust herself right now. And there was no point in finding out more, because she was going with John to try to help John do something that *was* important.

The next day Is rode out with a group to dig roots from one of the people's many widely scattered plots. They were near Lark's herd, so when the work was done, Is and Petre made a detour to see Lark.

They had given him a herd of six mares. While the kids who were in charge of the herd chatted with Petre, Is visited Lark. It was good to have his soft, brown nose snuffling over her hands and arms. It was good to see his big, intelligent eyes, and the familiar way he twitched his ears, to smell him, and have the big, reassuring bulk of him next to her.

Inevitably Is thought of what Ondre and Ellie had said about Lark going crazy. Her fingers ran through Lark's mane, absently untangling it. If she rode him to the mirror, would it trigger him as the coming of his berserker would? Would it kill him? If she left him here, the Hluit would have to kill him. If the Alliance got him back, they would send him against the mirror and that would kill him. If she rode him . . . was there really some chance the mirror wouldn't kill John? Was there a chance it would heal him, and he would heal Lark? It seemed an impossibly small hope, but it was the only one Lark had.

Back at camp the mood was energetic and festive. The people were getting ready for the feast of the Splitting of the Ways.

Each year, when the harvests were in, and the good summer grazing was depleted, the Hluit split into smaller groups and traveled slowly outward, letting the horses graze in outlying places where they had not eaten all summer. While the horses ate some of the grass, the people would cut most of it for hay. Later in winter, when all the grass was gone, they would retrace their steps, moving from haystack to haystack, as needed, until they all came together again when the spring grass was full.

The feast for the Splitting of the Ways was similar to the feast they'd had in celebration of John's return. But it was more elaborate because the people had more time to prepare. The final harvests had been brought in, and whatever couldn't be preserved must be eaten.

Is dreaded the coming festivity. She had become somewhat comfortable with the people in the structured activities of martial arts practice and daily work. But standing around talking, and just the thought of dancing, still made her very tense. She spoke with Ellie, and got herself assigned to herd duty so that someone who wanted to be at the festivities could be there instead of her. Lying back on the hillside, looking at the stars, and listening to the distant beat of the drums, Is was content.

Eventually Petre found her. He had brought a picnic of roasted meat, honeyed bigroots, a variety of spiced, baked breads, and some of his people's excellent mead.

Is found herself glad for his company, but she felt that he would probably rather be at the feast. She thanked him for bringing the food, which she really did appreciate, but then she said, "You should be there, dancing."

"Oh," he shrugged it off, "it's not so much fun without you." He said it easily, lightly, but it worried Is.

"Sometimes I just need to be alone," she blurted out of the silence.

Petre had been leaning back on his elbows, his legs sprawled out toward their small camp fire, relaxed. Her words surprised him. He sat up and looked at her closely, trying to understand what she really meant. Is was suddenly afraid he would decide she meant she wanted to be alone now. Or that she didn't like him and didn't want him around at all. That wasn't true. She'd be terrified to face the community without him. So she said, "I don't mean you. I like you." Then she was even more flustered. She could feel him watching her in the stretching silence.

"I am glad you like me," he finally said. His voice had a deep graveness to it that didn't sound like Petre.

Afraid she had hurt him, Is met his eyes. For the first time she saw not the brotherly, joking, good-natured person who had seemed so friendly but had kept his discreet distance; she saw the sudden hope Petre felt, and his need, and instantly she was frightened.

He reached out and touched the side of her face, and she couldn't move. She knew very well what he was asking, but she didn't know how to respond. She wanted to deny his feelings for her, and her attraction to him.

His fingertips stroked her hair, so lightly, and she still couldn't move, fascinated by what his touch was doing to her. When he leaned near her, she knew he was asking permission to kiss her, but she didn't know how to stop him, when she really did want to feel more of the way his touch was making her feel.

His lips were almost touching hers. She could taste his breath in her mouth. Then his lips touched hers, and they were more moist and soft, not at all the hard and needy things of the boys at the school who had tried to force themselves on her, and her body was filled with heat and exquisite, almost painful rushes of pleasure.

Suddenly he pulled away from her, and in the next instant he was on his feet. Is's body jerked with reaction, and she heard her own breath pant harshly a few times before she controlled it.

"I'm sorry." Petre's voice was husky, in a tone Is had never expected to hear him use. "I'm way out of line. I'm sorry." He faced her, looking confused, and scared, and very sorry.

But Is was fighting her own battle with fear and confusion and shame. In the government school such behavior would have been punished. But she was not afraid of that here. She had seen how easily the Hluit touched one another and exchanged hugs and kisses.

In the school a kiss would have been for any reason except that that person cared about her. Sexual advances were all wrapped up in issues of power, ownership, and runaway need—games that Is would not play. There Is would not have cared if she hurt anyone who tried to kiss her.

But this was different. What Petre wanted was more subtle, more complicated, and much more frightening, now that Is had a moment to realize it.

Petre was still looking at her. For once he didn't seem to have anything to say. Is felt more vulnerable sitting down, so she stood up. Petre tried to give her an encouraging little smile. It didn't quite work.

"Are you all right?" he asked her.

She nodded. He seemed more like the familiar, brotherly Petre now, and the fear and shame Is felt had taken care of her other bodily reactions.

"Will you forgive me?"

His question surprised her. "I . . . wanted it too."

He was looking at her very closely, but when she began to feel too uncomfortable, he looked away.

"I don't know how it is where you come from, but for me, it wouldn't be what I wanted if we just . . ." A vague hand motion said what he meant.

"I think you are in love with John, and I know John loves you. I wouldn't do anything to hurt him. Or you. I . . ." He tried a little grin. "I was . . ." The shrug of his shoulders expressed the way he had been helpless, the way Is had been helpless too. "I apologize," he said.

Is couldn't speak. She didn't know why Petre thought she loved John. She never spoke about John. As for John loving her, he *couldn't* have told Petre that. But Is couldn't ignore the hope she felt, even as she was telling herself it was all false.

"I'd uh . . . I'd better go back," Petre said. He started to collect the things he had brought for their picnic, and Is saw the hurt in him then, and finally she understood. He had fallen in love with her.

She went to him and put her hand on his arm so he would stop what he was doing. But when he looked at her, she didn't know what to say. Eventually she said, "Thank you." They seemed the only words that half fit.

He cocked an eyebrow. "For what?" he asked her, and since she thought the question was real, she gave him a real answer.

"For being such a good friend. For looking out for me when it wasn't in your best interests. For showing me things. For *talking* to me. For, I don't know, for being you."

The smile he gave her was real, and the spring was back in his step as he finished packing up his horse. When he was ready to go, he hesitated.

"Can will still . . . be friends?"

"Yes." Is felt relieved. She had been worrying about facing the camp without Petre's guidance, and she would have felt terribly alone if he had withdrawn his friendship.

-XVI-

Is rode Lark ahead of the creaking wagons. John rode on her right, and Ondre drove the first wagon. A young couple drove the second wagon, and the others of their group followed behind, herding the extra horses.

The Splitting of the Ways had begun. Is occasionally looked back. The plains were covered with similar parties heading out in all the directions of the compass.

Is had taken it for granted that Petre would come with her group, but it was not so.

"I thought I'd best not," he'd said when she confronted him. He would only look at her in quick glances. She hadn't known what to say.

"I'm sorry."

He'd given her a little grin that looked sad. "You take care of yourself." He was trying to make their parting seem like something easy. But Is was not just going to winter with the rest of her group, she and John were going on into the mountains to look for the mirror. She might not ever come back, but if doing it this way was easier for Petre, she owed him that much.

"Sure. I'll do that." She didn't say, "I'll miss you." And certainly not "I'll be frightened having to deal with the people without you." She hoped it would be easier in this group. There were only eighteen people, and soon it would just be John and her.

But when she had turned and walked away, Petre called after her.

"Is?" Then, from the safety of four strides away, he said, "I love you."

She hadn't known what to say. He was like the brother she had never had. He was the friend she didn't know how to have. But if she said she loved him, she would not be saying what he would think she was saying. She didn't want to hurt him, and she didn't want to mislead him. They might never see each other again, and she wanted desperately to say the right thing. But, in the end, she hadn't said anything at all. Now that bothered her.

She tried to let the quiet creaking of the wagons soothe her. The solitude of the mountains drew her. It was better this way. She would leave the people, and all the complicated social interactions she was no good at, behind.

She would go with John. It was really important to him to return to his people, healed, and able to help them. So she would try to do everything she could to protect him, even at the risk of her own life. With that vow made, she felt something shift inside her, as though her whole future had changed. And suddenly she felt good about herself, and strong in a way she had never felt before.

For the first few days, while she and John traveled with the group, there was much work to do. There was hay to cut, turn for drying, or stack for winter caches. The work was hard, and in the evenings everyone sat around the camp fire talking, or just staring, until they rolled out their sleeping bags and slept.

Alene had not come with them. People said she and John had broken up. Is wondered if that were true.

In their group there was a young couple who were deeply in love but not yet married. They would live the winter together before they decided whether to marry or not. Then they would need at least one couple, and one elder, to stand up for them before the clan would accept their marriage. The girl, Bonice, explained all this to Is. They had come with Ondre and Ellie's group because theirs was one of the most envied marriages. The couple hoped to learn from them, and, it seemed to Is, they thought if Ondre and Ellie gave their approval, it would guarantee the success of their own marriage.

Is asked Bonice what they would do if they didn't get that approval.

"We'll go on living with each other as long as we want."

"No one cares?"

Bonice gave her a funny look. "Of course they care."

Is was struggling with her upbringing in the government schools, where sex was a tool to advance oneself, a weapon to hold over others, or a means of winning favor with someone you feared or whose protection you needed. Love was something uncontrollable that sometimes happened and had to be hidden from all adults or they would surely separate the couple completely. Students caught at sex, or suspected of being in love, were punished equally severely. That didn't stop any of it; it just forced it underground and gave it even more power.

Is had never imagined a society in which a sexual relationship between two young people would be openly tolerated by adults. She was often present when Bonice discussed her relationship with Ellie, and there didn't seem to be anything Bonice couldn't talk about. The couple practiced contraception with lady's root and a careful accounting of the days of the month.

One of the other people in the group was an old lady. She had family of her own, but she had opted to come with Ondre's group for some reason Is didn't understand and was too inhibited to ask about. The woman was too old to be much help at anything except taking care of a baby that belonged to one of the other married couples. Surely she would be a burden to the group. Is watched carefully, but she could detect no animosity toward the old woman for her helplessness.

There was also a teenaged girl, Ahl, who had a crush on Ondre. Is worried about it. It was obvious to her, so it must be apparent to Ellie and Ondre. Ellie treated the girl as

though she were fully adult and her equal in every way.
Ondre treated her with a beautiful balance of love and
discipline that amazed Is. She sometimes compared his
response to the way Riding Master Masley would have
acted. To have had that kind of power over a young girl's
emotions would have brought out the worst in him. He
would have been either taking advantage of her, or blatantly
and hurtfully rejecting her. Is found herself loving Ondre for
the way he was behaving. Why couldn't she have been
brought up by people like these?

She watched John most carefully, but as discreetly as
possible. She did not want people to think she was like Ahl,
with a crush on John. She didn't want to bother him, and
most certainly didn't want him treating her the way Ondre
treated Ahl. She wasn't sure what she did want.

She missed Petre a lot. She thought about how he had said
good-bye and worried all sorts of interpretations into it. In
the end she was disgusted with herself. Why should she let
him make her uncomfortable like this? He probably was
with someone else, having a good time, sleeping with her.
And if not, he was part of his people. He had all of them to
choose from, and someday there would be someone for him
to marry. There was no reason for him to have come with
her.

The ground began to get steeper and the grass less thick.
The wagons turned aside, but Ondre accompanied Is and
John another two days. Is had once asked Ondre why he
wasn't coming all the way with them.

"The mirror isn't exactly a solid 'thing' in a solid
location. Each person takes his or her own path to find it. If
I tried to come with you, I might keep you from finding it.
Or, at the very least, I would change the complexion of what
you did find.

"It's hard to explain. The two of you belong together in
some way on this. I think you were given some information
John needs. Hopefully, when the time comes, it will fit in
somehow."

Is doubted she had any such information, and she hated to see Ondre place a false trust in her. She had tried to tell Ondre that several times. On their last night together, she tried to tell him again.

"Ondre, I don't know anything. I can't help John. I wish I could, but I can't. You're sending him on with some sort of false hope. I don't know anything."

"I'm not *sending* him," Ondre said softly. He was sitting cross-legged by the fire, his boots lying beside him. "And as for 'false hope,'" he glanced at his brother, "if I were in his shoes, I'd probably have to go too. And if he were in mine, he'd understand how much I don't want him to go."

John met Ondre's words with a look of desperate pleading.

"It's OK," Ondre said quickly. "I'm not trying to stop you. I just want you to know, I love you."

John's answer was to clasp hands with his brother, and a moment later they moved together and embraced. There were tears in John's eyes when he faced Is, and that made her less ashamed of her own tears. When she looked into his eyes, she seemed to be falling forever and ever, into somewhere very beautiful, very important. How could there be a place inside another person's eyes like this? She couldn't tell if the feeling of love that was generated in her was something John was feeling for her, or only something precious within him he let her glimpse.

As always he released her without making any further move that would confirm what he was feeling for her. She looked down, feeling confused and embarrassed.

"Please, try to have faith in yourself." Ondre's voice was so kind, Is couldn't resist it. She met his eyes even though he would see her tears.

In the morning she was crying again as they packed up their camp. Ondre didn't say anything, but he took her in his arms for a long time. Then he touched his brother's hand, just that—one small touch, no words. They were that much

at peace with each other's love. Then Ondre mounted his
mare and headed back the way they had come.

Is watched his back and knew she had been entrusted
with an enormous gift, Ondre's love for his brother.

They rode the morning in silence. Sometimes Is's tears
ran freely, sometimes they cleared. She didn't realize John
was crying too until they stopped for lunch and she rode up
beside him. He touched her hand, and she was quick to
return his grip.

The night was colder than it had been on the plains. They
huddled close to their small fire. Is wondered if John felt as
lonely as she did. She wished he would touch her.

In the morning John was gone.

Is had never heard a thing. Lark was tied, likely to keep
him from following. It seemed strange to Is that he had not
whinnied a farewell to the mare. Is felt totally adrift. Why
would John leave? There was no sign of anything having
taken him against his will. In fact there were no signs at all.
His sleeping bag was gone from its place next to hers. All of
his equipment was gone. She could find no tracks to tell her
which direction he had chosen. It was unnervingly as though
he had never been there at all.

Lark wasn't behaving right either. He was not anxious to
be off after the mare the way he had been when he'd been
left before.

Is had a vague, disquieting feeling, as if she had been here
before and knew what to do. But she could not bring it into
focus.

Instead of concentrating, she found herself sitting and
staring blankly. The air was crisp and still, too cold for
insects. The bird sounds began slowly. A meadowlark trilled
distantly. After a while it was time to rise.

Her feet were asleep, and she walked around a bit to
restart the circulation. She found herself packing up the
camp. Well, OK, she couldn't stay there. She should
probably go back to the meadow before the people left it,
and tell Ondre what had happened.

But when she thought of Ondre, she knew she wouldn't do that. She would try to find John. When she had Lark tacked, she headed out in the general direction they'd been going last night. Lark picked his way leisurely. He gave no sign of knowing which direction the mare had gone, or caring to find her.

Their direction took them down into a deep cut. It didn't seem odd to run into fog down there, but Lark snorted and hesitated entering it. They moved along to the soft clop of his hooves on the gravelly ground and the rhythmic wuffling of his nostrils, betraying his tension with every step.

A crow called harshly, once, twice, and the third time it sounded too distant for it to have flown that far that quickly. A horse and rider appeared out of the fog, twenty meters to her left.

Lark hadn't seen them yet. Is turned him in their direction, but he still didn't see them. By now Is was certain of who they were. The mare's finely chiseled head was turned toward her and Lark, ears pricked. The man was wrapped in his coat, looking away from them.

Lark continued to edge along, snorting to himself, while Is waited for him to see the mare. John turned and saw her, raising his hand in greeting. Is kept waiting for Lark to raise his head, pause in surprise, whinny—anything.

He never showed any signs of seeing the mare. John was looking in her direction, but he seemed to be focused on a spot a distance behind her. The mare also seemed intent on something beyond Is. She did not act as though a horse she was friends with had come to stand right in front of her. Is's skin began to crawl.

But John was undeniably real. "Hello," Is said. But of course he didn't respond.

"Why did you leave?" she said anyway.

He seemed to be listening intently, looking at something distant, right where she was.

She started to twist around in the saddle to look behind her, to see what had his attention.

"No. Don't!"

The desperation in his command, as much as the fact that he had spoken, spun Is back around.

"You can speak?" she stammered. He ignored that.

"You have to come back," he said in a perfectly normal voice. And while Is groped with the implication that *she* had been the one to leave, not him, he said, "There is only one path. You must make the horse follow that path."

In confusion Is started to glance around for the path.

"No!"

The sudden distance of John's voice startled Is into looking at him again. The mare was bearing him away at a rapid pace, but Lark didn't react—and there was something wrong with how the mare was moving, not in any gait Is recognized, as though she were floating, or sliding, not trotting. She almost missed John's words.

"Take the left turns. All of them, except the third one . . ." His voice faded, and a crow cried over his last words, obliterating them.

"Wait!" But it was too late.

Is sat a moment and tried to collect herself. She could sleep, or blink, or look aside, or a crow would call, and the whole world would be different.

She looked around at the meadow they had been traveling through. There was no path, only a little gravelly rut that was more of a spring runoff than a trail.

When they came to a fork, she guided Lark left.

The third time the trail forked, Is went right. Why not? She had no other clue as to what she should do.

She didn't sleep well that night. She kept feeling that someone was nearby. She'd catch herself thinking John was in camp, just down at the river or something, and have to correct herself.

The morning was crisp and cold, no fog, and Is hit the trail early. It wasn't long before she saw smoke, one thin strand of white rising straight into a sky so blue and so distant it didn't look real. The trail seemed to be leading her to the camp fire, so she stayed with it. Lark picked up the pace on his own, and Is began to hope they would find John and the mare.

The man sat at the fire with his back to her, but Is would never have mistaken him for John. He was slumped forward, sleeping. But even in that position Is could see the width of his shoulders and the height he would have if he stood up. Her heart wanted to stop. The bright morning threatened to go dark. She fought to see through the sudden darkness. He could only be a very large man. Her eyes raced around the camp, searching for clues. No tent. No packs. Traveling very light.

She spotted the horse grazing downhill of the camp. War-horse. There was no mistaking his massive hindquarters.

At that instant Lark whinnied.

The horse's head came up. He turned on ponderous legs the size of tree trunks. His bridle hung from the saddle he wore, as though the berserker had stopped here only for a short rest.

Is glanced at the man, but he had not moved.

The horse came toward them. He lifted his knees and hocks high. His huge feet flattened the shrubby, bushlike covering that grew on the rocky soil. He carried his head high. His massive neck rose out of a chest as wide as a small building. His nostrils flared and his ears were pricked as he tried to make out the nature of what he was approaching. He was taller than Lark and a lot heavier—a mature, fully trained war-horse. Is's heart rushed. He was gorgeous, and deadly.

But he wasn't behaving right. He raised and ducked his head as though trying to focus on something he was unsure of. Instead of displaying the aggressive posturing Is had expected, he stopped uncertainly, as though he were having trouble seeing Lark and her.

Lark wasn't acting right either. He stood with his head high and ears pricked, but he did not seem to be seeing another horse. He showed no signs of challenge or intimidation.

The other horse gave a loud, trumpeting blast through his nostrils. The berserker came out of his doze and onto his feet with impossible speed. Lark never reacted to the abrupt movement. It was as though he couldn't see the man at all.

Standing, the man was well over seven feet tall and as massive as his war-horse. His biceps bulged as he gripped a knife that had appeared in his hand. He was looking where his horse was looking, but he did not seem to be able to see either Is or Lark.

Is began to back Lark down the trail. The other horse snorted, arched his neck, and trotted forward a few steps. Is was on the verge of turning Lark to make a run for it when the berserker spoke, and his horse halted on the spot.

Is pivoted Lark on his hindquarters and began to walk him quickly away. She watched over her shoulder as the berserker reached his horse and began to put the bridle on, then she pressed Lark with her calves and sent him into a trot. The other horse whinnied once, but it was not a challenge, more of a "where are you?" sort of query.

When they had gone a little ways, Is turned Lark off the trail and up among the trees. In a few minutes she heard the war-horse's hooves crunching the gravel as he trotted by below. She gave them a few minutes, then dropped down to the trail and continued in the direction she had been going. She did not know if the berserker would turn around. She didn't know which way he had been traveling before she found him. When she got to his camp fire, she'd stop and look for hoofprints from the other direction.

They rounded the curve at a trot. There was no sign of the berserker's fire. Is didn't think he had taken the time to put it out. Anyway there should still have been signs of it. There was nothing. Maybe the next bend?

Nothing.

She slowed Lark to a walk. No sense risking his stepping on a rock and laming himself when there was no one chasing them. They were as likely to run into the berserker ahead of them again as they were to have him overtake them from behind.

Until Is thought that thought, she'd been calm. Now she began to shake, not because she didn't know where the berserker was, but because she didn't know *when* he was.

He could have been as long ago as Amil's cabin. But Amil had seen them, and the berserker hadn't. Although his horse had sensed Lark, neither horse had seen the other well. Is was sure of that. Did that mean the berserker was from longer ago than Amil's cabin, which even the oldest of John's people knew only as a ruin?

She acknowledged then what she had been hiding from herself about John. They were separated, not by distance, but by time. Somewhere—some*when*—had he awakened and found her gone? But when she had seen him again, or some image of him, he had spoken. Did that mean he had found/would find the mirror and be cured? Is was suddenly lighthearted. If she never caught up to John again, she could at least believe he had been successful.

That thought sustained her for several hours.

-XVII-

Is was jarred out of her thoughts by the loud, trumpeted challenge of a horse. She had heard that sound too many times not to recognize it for what it was—a berserker's horse. The echoes rolled around the valley, confusing the direction of the sound. Lark snapped to a halt, his head up. His ears flicked this way and that uncertainly.

The whinny came again while they were both standing, undecided. Lark's head came around to the right, and he set off in that direction. For a moment Is was going to stop him. She didn't want to be anywhere near a berserker or his fully trained horse, and she didn't want such a horse seeing Lark. But there was something else at work in her mind too. What if the berserker had found John? What if he had found the mirror? She would learn nothing wandering around in the fog. If she was too timid to go investigate, she should probably go back to Ondre's people and admit her defeat. They might want to send someone else.

She let Lark have his head, but when the meadow funneled them into a ravine, Is pulled Lark back from the entrance and made him go along the ridge top instead. She didn't want to get trapped in a narrow space with a berserker. From up here they could look down on him, and he wouldn't be able to get at them quickly.

She spotted the berserker and stopped Lark. All she could see was horse and rider in a bare spot in the ravine, but both of them had their attention riveted on the empty air in front of them. The horse was in his most aggressive posture, neck arched, nostrils flared, stepping high as he advanced on the empty air. The berserker had drawn his long saber. He looked ready to strike. That was all Is could see. She wondered what Lark was picking up with his keener senses.

Lark's head was up and his ears pricked, but he did not seem aggressively inclined or frightened. He was merely interested. Is was glad he hadn't whinnied.

Suddenly the berserker's horse reared, slashing out with his front hooves, and plunged forward, exactly like a horse fighting another horse. The berserker slashed to the left with his saber. Slashed again. Is couldn't see what they were fighting, but they were definitely fighting something. The horse plunged, wheeled, kicked, wheeled again. The rider struck first to his left, then to his right, parried, stabbed, slashed.

The hair on Is's arms stood up. She had never seen a war-horse in full action or a berserker. The horse was magnificent. There was a beauty to it, but there was also something in her that responded positively to the violence, surprising her.

For several minutes the horse lunged, struck, and kicked with all his might, while the rider was equally busy. Then the horse began to tire. His dark bay coat was stained black with sweat. There was white foam between his hind legs. The whites of his eyes showed. The red lining of his nose was visible as his nostrils stretched wide with his exertions. The man was becoming tired too. His strikes had less power in them, his parries sometimes collapsing in the face of a force Is couldn't see. Then he would call on the horse to wheel him away and attack again from a new angle.

The horse reared, lifting his rider clear of some blow Is couldn't see. His hindquarters gave way, and he collapsed to a sitting position. In an instant he had righted himself. The rider drove his spurs into the horse's ribs. The horse lunged frantically against the unseen force. The rider swung with his saber and dropped it as though he had hit something so hard he could not hold onto it. Is expected to hear the clang of metal. All she heard was the harsh breathing of horse and rider.

The rider wheeled the horse away and drew a shorter blade. Is saw him dig his spurs into the horse again. The horse leapt forward, but now his movements were desperate and ill-coordinated. She saw the rider's exaggerated aids with bit and spurs to make the horse rear. Before, the signals between the two had been invisible, as though they saw and reacted to the same thing with one accord.

Where the horse's movements had drawn an awe from Is because of their beauty, now she felt an awe for the gallantry of the animal. Where the violence had illicited a response in her gut, now it drew a sharp pity. Where it had been answered by an unfocused anger, now that anger was focused against the rider who was going to push his horse to its death.

The horse reared and lost control again, going down on his hindquarters and this time over onto his side. The rider jumped clear. Ignoring his horse's struggle to rise, the berserker attacked the invisible foe on foot. He had lost his blade in the horse's fall, and now he attacked with his hands and feet.

Is had enough training in Hluit self-defense to appreciate the skill the berserker showed in his attacks. Meanwhile the horse got to his feet. His sides heaved and his nostrils expanded with each breath. Is expected him to stand, head low, legs wide, and try to recover. Instead he attacked, charging, and viciously biting the air to the left of the berserker.

A cold shiver shook Is's body. Horses didn't behave like that!

A stallion would fight another stallion, but when beaten, he would retreat. But the war-horses were crazy. Whatever had been turned on in their brains could not be turned off. She had been feeling sorry for the horse, thinking she should somehow try to rescue it. Now she saw the proof of all her years of training in the Berserker's Barn and the Last

Station: you could not handle a berserker's horse after it had connected to its berserker.

The horse fell, and thrashed on the ground, struggling to rise. It was terrible to see the massive animal like that. Whatever force the berserker battled, it had moved away from the dying horse. Is didn't want to watch the horse die. She felt a deep sorrow for the animal. It had not wanted to be a berserker's horse. It had been made this way by people, and Is was as guilty as anyone. In her mind's eye that horse was all the horses she had ever trained and sent to their deaths. In her heart she knew that horse was also Lark. There was no way to save him from his fate.

To keep from watching the horse, she watched the man fight. She cold not let herself get lost in grief and guilt. She had to stay focused on the danger here and now. The man had grown so tired he could barely lift his arm to deliver another blow. Kicks were out of the question for him now. His technique had vanished. He was a drunken street brawler, staggering, striking wildly without focus and without force. He fell more and more often and took longer to get up, but he could no more quit than the horse could have.

Is locked all emotion away in cold storage. She watched the berserker dispassionately, and she began to see something. Whatever he was fighting never struck him. When he fell, it was from his own exhaustion.

She had seen him counter blows, and seen his arm give under the impact of those blows sometimes as he tired. But he had not been cut. He was not bleeding anywhere.

Is could only conclude that he wasn't fighting anything. He was struggling up off the ground again, looking around for his adversary. Now he saw it. But the adversary didn't take advantage of him. It could have knocked him flat. *She* could have. Why didn't it? Was it exhausted too? Was it hurt? Or was it nonexistent?

The instant she thought that, a berserker appeared in front of her, up on the ledge, fully armed, rested, mounted, and his horse was as fresh as he. Fear raced through Is before she could control it. She started to wheel Lark to run away.

Lark didn't respond right. That broke through to her. If Lark had seen the berserker and his horse, he should have either gotten aggressive or scared. At least he would have been attentive. Instead he was still looking at the man and horse down in the ravine.

The berserker in front of her advanced threateningly, saber drawn. His horse arched its neck, snorting its challenge with every breath. Lark didn't even look at it.

Is forced herself to sit still. The berserker's horse reared and came forward on its hind legs. Its front hooves trashed the air. In an instant it would crash into Lark, sending both of them sprawling into the ravine. Is forced herself not to move.

At the instant it should have hit her, a strange tingling sensation rushed over her skin and the image disappeared. A moment later Lark shook himself like a dog, wagging his ears, as though he too had felt something.

Is looked into the ravine again. The horse lay flat out on his side now. His hind legs were still kicking, but feebly. She looked away from him, keeping her emotions in deep freeze.

The berserker was down too. As she watched, he rolled onto his side and looked up at her. He raised a hand toward her, obviously at great effort.

"Help me."

She could barely hear him. Her skin crawled. She would never have expected to hear a berserker plead like that.

"Help me." It had to be a trap. He sagged back onto the ground, his sides heaving as though breathing were an effort.

For a moment Is was moved by pity. Then suddenly all the fear Is had ever known broke loose of the control she had slapped on it. She could not go near that man!

Immediately the berserker appeared at her side, unmounted. He reached to pull her from Lark. She felt the heat of his hands on her thigh as he grabbed her. He would drag her from the horse and rape her. She could smell him and hear the grunting sound he made as he breathed, excited, and violent. She swung at his head with all her might, nearly throwing herself from the saddle and startling the hell out of Lark. Until that moment she had sort of forgotten Lark. But now he spooked and snorted, rearranging his legs to balance if his rider was going to do such crazy, unexpected things.

In spite of her fear, Is realized Lark did not see, feel, smell, or hear the berserker who was still at her side, still ready to pull her from his back. Although Lark wasn't a fully trained war-horse, he would respond to anyone suddenly appearing at his side, exuding bad intentions like this.

Is forced herself to sit still. The berserker grabbed for her, grinning wickedly. For a moment her mind supplied scenes that were intermixed and inseparable from the memories of watching her mother being raped and killed. It took every bit of her willpower to not move. As the berserker's hand touched her, he disappeared.

Is breathed a shaky sigh of relief and stroked Lark's neck. Twice Lark had saved her from believing in the illusions that had seemed so real to her.

She looked into the ravine again. The horse had stopped kicking, but his hind legs stuck stiffly out from his body, vibrating with quick little jerks. As a fully trained, fully augmented, mature, switched-on war-horse, he had seen what his rider had seen: an enemy, probably another berserker mounted on another war-horse. Feeding on each other's emotions, connected to a degree Is's unaugmented senses could not reach, they had not had the cognitive powers to realize that what they were fighting wasn't real.

She wondered if the horse could feel or think anything now. Maybe he was already dead. The twitching of his legs could be some leftover reflex that would die away in a few minutes too.

Her eyes went to the man. He had gotten turned onto his side, and Is could see his lips move: "Help me," too soft to hear now. A strange fear took her, not of him exactly, but of his death.

A strangling sound, practically at Lark's feet, brought her back. John lay there convulsing and vomiting. All the fear she had felt when she had first rescued him came back instantly, tangled with all the love she felt for him now. She picked up the reins, closed her calves against Lark's sides, and guided him to step on John.

Lark went without hesitation. He never even picked his foot high, just set it right in the middle of John's chest. The vision vanished as the others had.

Now Is was curious. Purposefully she thought about something nice, her memory of how John had looked that first time he had opened his eyes and seen her—a look full of joy, and rapture, and love—and how she had felt.

Mistake! Instantly she was so lonely and bereaved she could hardly stand it. The pain racked her body. Her mouth twisted in a silent scream. She slid from the saddle and clung to Lark's neck. There was no image for her to make him step on this time. She had to handle this one on her own.

Ignoring the emotion was impossible. Turning it off, like a water faucet, didn't work. Covering it with other thought— impossible. *Balance,* she thought, *balance it with something else.* Without conscious choice she found herself thinking about the people's martial arts.

"Never meet an attack head-on," they had told her. "Do not take the attacker's force into yourself. Turn with it, deflect it around you, return it to the attacker."

The overpowering emotions were gone, replaced by a small sense of triumph. *Careful,* Is cautioned herself. *The goal is not to vanquish the enemy. Even if you "win" such an encounter, it is only temporary.* She heard Ondre's voice instructing everyone in one of the classes. *You have done nothing to diminish the overall aggression, or the need to place one person over another, or the need to win or to lose.* His words had seemed so esoteric. Is had just wanted to know how to move, where to place her foot or her arm, how to turn her body, to throw someone who was attacking her. She had waited through Ondre's lectures, impatient for practice to begin. But now there was no one to throw, possibly no one to beat, no one to place herself above or below, to win or to lose to.

No more visions and no more exaggerated emotions came. She had not given her attacker anything to work with. Good.

She looked at the berserker again. He was still watching her, but he had stopped begging. She turned Lark and rode back to the entrance to the ravine. To the berserker, it must have seemed that she was riding away.

When they came into sight again, the horse was still, no longer twitching. Lark snorted distrustfully and sidled by it. The berserker had collapsed onto his face. Is wondered if he were dead. It took a lot of willpower for her to get off Lark. It took more to kneel down by the man. Surely she did not fear his death. He meant nothing to her. And surely she did not fear he could hurt her. He was too spent for that. But still Is was afraid.

Suddenly the man leapt up. He wasn't hurt at all.

No! No! Is cried in her mind. *He's nearly dead!* Desperately she tried to make that the reality she saw. At that moment Lark snorted and pulled back. Is could not take her eyes from the berserker, but she heard Lark gallop away. He had seen this. This was real!

She was desperate enough to think that even though her self-defense wasn't very good yet, she'd try. Maybe there was some small chance she'd defend herself. She threw out all doubt, all thought, and waited.

The berserker seemed to sense the change in her from easy victim to composed, prepared defender. He hesitated. Is heard a sound she shouldn't have heard, the slurpy sound of a horse opening his mouth to graze. She laughed. If she turned around, she was going to see Lark right behind her, trying to pick the few sparse bits of grass that grew nearby.

The image of the menacing berserker vanished. Is knelt and touched the man's neck, trying to find his pulse. It was quick and fluttery. His skin felt clammy. With considerable effort she rolled him onto his back. His eyelids fluttered, but only white showed behind them.

Shock, she thought. What was wrong with him? Exhaustion? He didn't have a cut anywhere. Could a person die of exhaustion? Maybe his heart was damaged. But as long as he was alive, he'd be susceptible to hypothermia, pneumonia, and dehydration. Those things Is understood.

She got her jacket from Lark's saddle and put it over the man's chest. He didn't look very comfortable lying on his back. She brought over other pieces of her clothing and pillowed his head.

What if he lived? she asked herself. Would he still be crazy? Was she doing him any favor, helping him?

But if she walked away, would it be because she feared him and didn't want him to recover? Or would it be because she had decided that that was the best thing for him?

She sat back on her heels and looked at him. He was the nightmare she had had when she was treating John, come true.

If she made a decision, there was no way to know what motivated it—fear or logic. There was no way to know what was best to do.

She found herself just sitting, staring at nothing, thinking nothing. After a while she stood and stretched. It would be cold when night came on. She should have a fire. She began to look for firewood and realized that the decision had been made, for now.

While Is collected kindling, she looked for grazing for Lark. After they had brought the wood back to "camp," Is untacked Lark and took him up the ravine, to a place with some grass. He could graze there all night while she sat with the dying man. But for a few minutes Is just stood with Lark, watching him attack the grass hungrily. She was afraid to leave him. She was afraid of losing him. Her logical mind told her there wasn't much chance of that. The ravine ended not much farther ahead. Lark wouldn't climb up its steep sides. If he went looking for more grass, he'd have to come back by her camp. The ravine was narrow there, and she'd see him by the light of the fire. But another part of her mind told her that that wasn't the only way to lose him. She had awakened from what had seemed like a night's sleep, and John had been gone. She wondered if she could lose Lark the same way, maybe even without sleeping. She didn't know what she would do without him. She loved him, and once again he was the only companion she had. He was also her transportation. And how would she tell real from unreal without the horse to guide her?

She was becoming angry and frustrated and scared. How could she make the right decision when she didn't know the rules? She didn't know *if* Lark could disappear. She didn't know *if* the man could recover.

Just in time Is recognized what was happening. She calmed herself before her emotions could be used against her again . . . With sudden clarity she realized that the issue wasn't about making a right decision. It wasn't about whether Lark or the man was more important. It wasn't even about what would give her the best chance to survive. It was about something more important, more subtle, harder to define. It was about what was "right." And it was about being brave enough to do what was right.

She left Lark and went back to the camp. It was easy while she could occupy her mind with building the fire. When she checked on the man, he seemed to be having trouble breathing. She thought he would be better off sitting up more. She could see how she could use her saddle and sleeping bag to prop him up.

He was awfully heavy. There was no gentle, or graceful, way to do what she had to do. His skin felt cold and clammy, as if he were already dead. It took an awful lot of nerve for her to touch him. To grab hold of him and pull and push as she had to to get him situated was almost too much to ask of herself.

Finally he looked more comfortable and his breathing sounded less labored, and Is was glad she'd made the effort.

She took a long time heating some water and making a soup of the provisions Ondre had sent with her.

Then it was time to wait. Wait for the man to die, or recover enough to give her trouble. Wait for some sort of renewed attack from whatever had attacked her before. Wait for morning. Wait to find out if Lark had disappeared. Wait to become too afraid to go on.

She slipped into the non-waiting mode she used when she hunted, and sat a long time in non-thought, in touch with the night and its many small presences. That worked until the man began to snore.

It wasn't any ordinary sort of snoring. It was an unbelievably loud rattling, punctuated by snorts, gasps, and sudden seconds of unnerving silence.

Is tried to reposition him so he could breathe better. His body was even colder than before. She couldn't think of any way to make him warmer. It was not a very cold night. The fire was putting out good heat. He was insulated from the ground by her sleeping bag and Lark's saddle.

She was sure he was dying. Well, that should be a relief really, and she could feel good about herself for having tried to help him. She tried to sit and non-think again, but it was impossible with all the noise the man was making.

She became aware of a new sound within the snoring, sort of like a breeze in the bushes. She'd better cover him more, she thought, if there was a breeze. She was staring at the fire when she thought that, and she didn't move right away. It took her a moment to sort out what was wrong. The flames were going straight up, as they had all night. There was no breeze. There weren't any bushes nearby either, she remembered. Then she knew where she had heard that sound before.

She turned slowly to look at the berserker. He was lying

just as he had been before. She watched the flickering flames make the shadows dance in the background and let her eyes see anything they wanted to see.

The dark man shapes were all around the berserker, talking in that quick *shush-shush*ing way that sounded like breeze. They were in constant motion, as though the heat from the fire buffeted them.

One man was sitting on the berserker's chest. He seemed more stable than the others. Is thought he was sitting cross-legged, then she realized that she couldn't see his legs because they were somehow inside the berserker's body. The other man shapes moved about constantly. They seemed to be caressing the berserker all over.

Is wasn't afraid. After a very long time the man stopped breathing. The night was suddenly very quiet. Is could no longer see the dark bodies.

-XVIII-

Is had slipped into her comfortable state of non-thought, non-emotion, where anything was possible, when she heard the horse coming. She looked up from the coals and was startled to realize that it was close enough to dawn for her to see shapes away from the fire. The rider's silhouette was very familiar.

John and his mare, Celeste. Is stood up and moved around the fire toward them. John looked at her, at the dark hump the dead horse made, and at the dead man propped up by the fire—equally, and without reaction or recognition.

"John," she called. "It's me."

John glanced at her and away again. His mare was looking intently down the ravine. No doubt she could hear Lark down there. John seemed to take his cue from that. He headed that way. They were going to pass right by.

Is stepped in front of the mare, and Celeste stopped and put her head out for Is to scratch. Only then did John believe Is was real. He grinned, leapt from the mare's back, and grabbed her in a bear hug. She found herself laughing, trying to hug him as hard as he hugged her, trying not to let him crack her ribs.

"It's so good to see you," she said. She thought he would say something in return. The last time she had seen him, he could talk perfectly. But he could barely see her then, and she couldn't have touched him at all. Now he was obviously very glad to see her, but he didn't speak.

"What's wrong?" she asked him. "Can't you talk?"

He shook his head, puzzled that she would think he could.

"The last time I saw you you could talk," she told him.

He shook his head, more mystified. He didn't remember it. It hadn't happened to him yet. Or else it had only been a reflection of him, sent to her by whatever had sent the illusion that had killed the berserker. Why? To lead her here? She saw John's eyes go to the dead horse and the dead man.

"They're real," she told him.

The mare whinnied, and a moment later they heard the hoofbeats of a trotting horse as Lark approached. Is's heart jumped for joy. She had to restrain herself from running to the horse and hugging him. She and John stood back and watched the horses greeting each other. To Is it seemed they were giving each other a very thorough investigation. It reminded her of the way a dog sniffed its owner to learn where the owner had been and what he or she had been doing. She wondered what the horses were learning. Did running into illusions, as they both obviously had, leave some sort of odor?

Is went over to the coals and dug some breakfast mix out of her food pack. Seeing what she was doing, John picked up the water can and headed for the canteen on the mare's saddle. As he passed the dead man, he stopped and looked at him a long time.

The man's eyes had come open. They stared lifelessly into the lightening gray sky. His mouth hung slack, and a string of spittle had run from one corner and dried on his face. He looked unloved and uncared for. He had been used and discarded. Is felt slightly ashamed of herself. She should have taken better care of him. John's face registered a deep sorrow, and Is thought he would look that way if he were looking at a child who had died without having had a chance to live. Tears flooded her vision. She had never expected to feel such compassion for a berserker.

While breakfast heated, Is told John about everything she had seen and felt. She told him how what she had learned of his people's art seemed to help control the illusions. He nodded frequently, as though agreeing with the conclusions she had drawn. Sometimes he gave her hand a squeeze of agreement and encouragement and, she thought, praise, until she told him about the dark bodies.

"I think they took what life the berserker had left," she said. "Maybe I should have tried to chase them away. I guess they killed him." She stopped because John caught her hand in his, shaking his head. He desperately wanted to explain something. He began to shake. A moment later he dropped his eyes away and took his hands back. Is could see what he was doing, drawing into himself, building walls, regaining control. She had seen this enough to know he had to do it. Otherwise, in a minute, she would hear his high, hysterical laughter. She never wanted to hear that again. But, illogically, suddenly she couldn't let him go either. She reached out and touched his arm.

"I love you." If she was surprised at her own words, John was more so. His eyes sprang to hers. The emotions of joy, hope, pain, and doubt that ran through them left Is whirling. Then he put his arms around her and drew her against him.

Shudders ran through his body as he began to sob, silently, in her arms. It was not anything like the wild, hysterical sob-laughing she had heard from him before. She held him for a long, gentle time, until he stopped.

She wasn't hungry, but she ate because John ate, and because it postponed whatever they had to do next. She felt light, and joyful in a way she had only had small glimpses of before. Saying three simple words had released her in some way. How much more would being able to talk release John?

Is could have stayed at that fire with him forever—even with the bizarre company of a dead man and a dead horse. But by late morning John was ready to go. He helped her retrieve her saddle and bedroll from under the berserker. A few late flies had found him. They buzzed out of his mouth as John rolled him on his side to allow Is to get her things. Flies buzzed up from the dead horse too as they rode by. There wasn't anything worth doing for either of them. Carrion eaters were the next step in the chain.

They rode in silence, and Is let John lead, wherever they were going.

Suddenly Celeste halted. John was staring intently at something Is couldn't see, and neither horse was responding to it.

"I can't see it," she told John.

He turned and gave her a small, wan smile. If it were meant to reassure her, it didn't work. He dismounted and signaled her to stay where she was as he walked forward.

He stopped and bowed the way his people bowed to one another before they practiced their martial arts together, the way he had bowed to Amil. Is waited for something to happen. After a while John knelt down on the ground. He sat for a long time as though in meditation.

Is got off Lark and let him go graze with the mare. She sat down, intending to keep her eyes on John in case he needed her help.

She woke, not quite sure where she was or why. Then she remembered and sat up quickly. She couldn't believe she had fallen asleep. She wondered if some trick had been played on her mind. There was no sign of John or the horses, or the meadow. In front of her stood a large, shiny building. In all other directions all she could see was thick fog.

Is started to walk toward the building, and almost immediately she was inside it. She didn't think she had taken enough steps to get there. She hadn't opened any doors, and hadn't noticed it move toward her.

There didn't seem to be anything in this building, but it wasn't an empty shell either. It was filled with a glistening, foggy stuff, maybe as the fog outside would look if it were somehow compacted and backlit. Whatever this stuff was it felt denser than fog too. It wasn't so much like walking through a substance, like water, as it was like moving through an electrical current. But it wasn't that either.

Is gave up trying to figure it out when she saw John. He didn't see her. It was as though he were in another room or something. Only there weren't any walls to section this thing off into rooms.

He was kneeling the way he had been when she last saw him, and he was talking. Is couldn't quite make out what he was saying. She could hear his pitch get higher, then lower, and his volume get louder, then softer. She had the eerie feeling that someone was tuning him as they might tune a musical instrument.

Even though she had the distinct impression she would not be able to do it, she began to walk toward him. He was only a few steps away. He remained at that distance as she walked.

A berserker and his horse reared suddenly in front of her. She flinched back, but they were not attacking her. As the berserker in the ravine had been, they were fighting something Is couldn't see. She had never seen a video image or a hologram. She recognized what she was seeing as a memory. It was not her memory, so she concluded it was the building's memory. That changed her thinking about the building. It had seemed to be a structure. Now she wondered if it were a living thing, this mirror/non-mirror. A mirror reflects things—perhaps it held the reflection of everything it had ever seen.

She continued to walk and passed more berserkers and more horses. They were all fighting something. They were as three-dimensional as life. She could hear them, and smell them. They were more than reflections. *How could there be that much room in here?* Then she thought, *How much room is in a memory anyway?*

Some of the berserkers were from the distant past. She recognized their costumes and saddlery from what she had been taught about the history of her profession. The weapons the berserkers carried had always been the same. But the berserkers and their horses had gotten bigger, more powerful, and better trained as they progressed.

This made Is realize how much research and development had gone into improving the berserkers and their horses. She wondered why nothing had gone into improving their weapons and answered herself: *Because they were never fighting against anything.*

Distracted by her thoughts, she blundered into one of the

images. The tingling sensation she had felt before shot through her. All the hair on her body stood on end, but the slashing sword did not cut her. In fact, berserker and horse dissolved into a much more complex and confusing image. Part of it was similar to the words and letters and numbers that had been so off-limits to her; part of it was intense feeling. A strange curiosity swept Is. As though from a different perspective, she experienced the desire to learn what made these animals work. A wonder, like the wonder she had had the first time she saw a real horse, engulfed her. She felt all the childlike awe she had had then, but there was something far more sophisticated too. At her command were ways to experience these animals most thoroughly.

Is brought her/the mirror's abilities to bear on exploring the thing that interested her most: the augmented psychic connection between horse and rider . . . Suddenly she was engulfed in a white flash of *loud* light. The sound rattled her brain in her skull. It didn't occur to her to question how a light could be loud. It didn't hurt, exactly, and she wasn't afraid until later, because at that moment there wasn't *room* to be afraid.

For a long while—or perhaps nanoseconds—her mind worked completely differently from how she'd ever used it before. Thinking seemed a totally different process.

Then the light/noise became too much for her small brain to hold. She felt it go crashing down her spinal cord and out into every nerve in her body. That *did* hurt, as each nerve lit up with the screaming light.

If her skull had been a cage, her skin was absolutely no barrier to the light/noise. It flowed out every nerve ending, right through the pores of her skin, and was gone. She was left behind, physically and mentally shaken, gasping from relieved pain, and clutching, frantically, at the fading wisps of white-hot understanding.

The best her ordinary mind could cling to was that there was something like a fast station which had been shrunk down to fit inside the berserker's head, and was somehow powered by the death process itself. The horse's energy, and its death agony, added to the strength of the transmission. But it was the rider's mind that went back and was received by someone the mirror thought of as the Silent Watcher.

There was more, much more, but Is couldn't take any more. If she didn't stop and organize what she already had, something was going to snap and she'd forget everything.

She tried to move away, and her body reeled drunkenly, as though it were under the physical impact of the blows her mind had taken. She staggered, falling to her knees, and somehow falling through the floor of what had appeared to be a solid building set solidly on the solid ground. When she looked around, the "building" was sitting on the meadow, apparently the same distance from her as it had been when she had started to walk toward it before.

A moan made her look in the other direction.

John!

He was lying only feet away from her, huddled into himself, moaning as though he were in deep pain.

She scuttled to him on all fours.

"John! John!" He didn't seem to be aware of her. He looked right through her and began to talk as he had been talking in the "building." Only now it was a quick, dull monotone, all in one pitch, all at one volume. Is shook him, trying to stop him, trying to make him see her.

His eyes seemed to look a little more at her instead of beyond her. She couldn't be sure. He kept talking. She had wanted so badly to hear him talk, and now all she wanted was for him to stop. She was getting hysterical.

She found herself screaming at him, shaking him by the shoulders . . . and caught herself. The monologue had stopped. He was looking *at* her.

Her nerves had had all they could take. Suddenly she was the one who was going to pieces. He pulled her against him and held her, hard.

When she had herself together, she sat back from him and he looked at her with sane, gentle eyes. Is would have liked to have just left it like that. She didn't need to hear him speak ever again if it was going to be that awful monotone, but she felt forced to know.

"Can you talk? Normally?"

"I . . . think." His voice was hoarse. He had to clear his throat. But the grin that spread across his face was gorgeous. Is was ready to celebrate with him. Instead his mood had already changed.

"Is," he said and caught her hands. "I've got so much to tell you. You must understand. You have to make Ondre understand." His eyes bored into hers, pleading, demanding.

But all Is understood was that if she was the one who had to make Ondre understand, then John wasn't going back to his people. He was going to go inside the mirror again.

She felt her fear, as hot as the light that had crashed through her nerves, as sharp as a knife, ripping her open, bowels to heart. The mirror would kill him. She was certain of it, and she knew with the certainty of her pain that she could not stop him.

He began talking rapidly, urgently.

"The mirror is not an alien. It's not a natural phenom- enon. It's not any of the things my people thought. The Alliance made it. It's an experiment. It's a computer . . . a thinking machine.

"But it's more than just a com— a machine. It doesn't just do, or think, the things it has been, programmed, trained, to think; it can teach itself new things, and new ways to think." He watched to see if she would understand. The government school would never have taught her about computers.

"I felt how it thinks," she said, and told him about her experience. He watched her, deep excitement in his eyes, energy, like electricity, springing from him.

"Why did the Alliance make it?" she asked him. "And if they made it, why are they sending the berserkers against it?"

"They created it especially to kill berserkers, which they created just to be killed by the mirror. That is the berserker's whole purpose, to be killed by the mirror. But it doesn't just kill them, Is. It downloads . . . it keeps . . . them in holo im . . . you saw, complete images. Sound, sight, smell, emotion. And it can project them.

"Interactive holo images of complete downloaded personalities," he said to himself.

The words might have been a language Is had never heard before, but her experiences had given her their meaning.

"It keeps them alive after they've been killed."

John looked at her and his pupils expanded. "Yes! What else could command so much of the Alliance's attention, so many resources, such secrecy, for so long? They are trying to create life after death. They want to live forever."

Is felt the truth of it. The highest of the high government officials wanted to live forever, and of course they would keep that for only a select few. They would rule forever. No good would come of it.

"I have to go back in there," John said. "We have to know how far they've succeeded."

Is rebelled. "It will kill you," she practically screamed at him. "What good will it do you to know? You'll be dead."

He met her eyes, but didn't refute what she'd said. He believed it would kill him.

"It will not matter," he said about his own death. "You can tell Ondre what I've learned."

Fear come up from places Is hadn't known were inside her.

"I don't understand half of what you're saying," she protested. "I won't be able to explain it right."

"There is a way," John said, and then he changed it to "I think there is a way. If you come into the mirror with me, I think I can forge a link between us—" Is didn't let him finish.

"I *was* in there with you," she cried. "You were totally unaware of me, and I couldn't reach you."

"I was fixing the linkages in my mind. I was busy. And I was not totally unaware of you."

"You were fixing yourself? The mirror wasn't doing that to you?"

"No. I don't think it realized we were there. It is sort of

'blind' to physical manifestations—us, you and me, and our horses—unless we respond to its probes—its holo manifestations. It couldn't 'see' either of us because we responded in ways outside its experience—its programming. Like you can't see the pictures in written words because you have not been trained, programmed, to read."

"But you said it trains itself."

"Yes," John answered slowly. "It may train itself to see me. Or it may not. But meanwhile it is also a machine. I used some of the 'machine-like' aspects of it to repair what had been done to my mind, and it ignored me like a building ignores a rat wandering around in the basement."

Is had had the same impression. She was ignored as she walked through the mirror's memory/thoughts.

"Could you make it 'fix' Lark?" She saw John's eyes change.

"I don't know. That's really a different sort of fixing. Lark has a chip, a physical thing, in his brain. I can't remove it. I might be able to tell it never to turn on . . ." His voice faded into nothing. His eyes came back from looking at something Is couldn't see.

"Is, I think it's more likely I'd kill Lark than help him." He met her eyes until she lowered them. He began to talk again, believing that he owed her more explanation.

"In my mind, they used a . . . light, to damage very select areas. I couldn't repair that physical damage, but I could bypass it. It was a matter of reestablishing pathways that used to be there, only putting them in different places. Like making new roads around obstructions." His eyes questioned if she understood. "I was fairly confident because it is my own mind. But the horse's mind is so different. I'd be lost in there. And what if he panicked inside the mirror? The mirror would notice *that*. It would do to him what it's done to the other horses." John shook his head. "Is, I'm sorry. I don't think I can do it." He met her eyes. "I'm afraid to try. I'm afraid of ruining the chance we do have."

Is saw the deep pain in John's eyes.

"I know how much he means to you. I'm sorry."

"I understand." One horse, who had been bred and trained and destined to die from the beginning, weighed against the need to find out what the Alliance was really up to and warn Ondre, Ellie, Petre, and all the Hluit.

"When your people know what is happening, what good will it do them? Can they stop it?" They were a few hundred nomads against the Alliance, and all its troops and technology.

John looked away. "Sometime, Is, sometime. Some way. In the meanwhile, they need all the pieces, all the information, and then, when the right time comes, and the right things happen, they'll be ready, they'll act."

And you'll be dead, she thought, her eyes clouding with sudden tears.

"Will you help me?" he pressed her. "It has to be me, Is. I know enough of the language they programmed this computer with that I can probe it. I need to know, Is. My people need to know."

She could understand the need for knowledge. She had always wanted to learn more than was allowed her. But she was afraid, and she did not want to lose John.

"I don't know how to help you."

"If you come inside the mirror with me, I think I can forge a link between us—that's another 'tool' function the mirror has. That's how it makes the holo images interactive. If I open that link from my side, I think you will be able to respond. I think you'll be able to hear my thoughts. Then you'll come back outside the mirror, and you'll 'hear' the things I learn. As I go deeper into its programming, the more dangerous it will become. Sooner, or later, it will notice me. At that point, I may be able to have a dialogue with it, or I may not. I think the chance it will kill me is greater than the chance I'll survive. But you'll be outside. You'll be safe, and you can take everything I've learned back to Ondre."

"Will it . . . download . . . you, like the berserkers?"

"Possibly."

"Then you won't really be dead?"

"I don't know. Those images are not really 'alive' either."

"You could be trapped like that. You want that?"

John shook his head. "I don't know enough. I would say if I'm trapped like that, I am dead."

Is could tell he hadn't said everything. She waited for him to continue, and finally he said, "Remember the dark bodies?"

"Yes?" Something flipped over inside Is. "What are they?"

"I think they are what's left of the berserkers after the mirror disassembles them. The mirror doesn't download everything into the holo images. There's something left over, the spiritual part of the man, I guess."

"So the mirror hasn't succeeded. It hasn't created life after death for the Alliance."

John hesitated before he replied. "I would say it has not completely succeeded. Yet. I need to know more, Is. How do the dark bodies get created? They're like ghosts. Real ghosts. All people who die don't have ghosts. At least not ones we can see and hear. What's really going on here? How much is the mirror's doing? And how much does the Alliance know? They don't know anything about the dark bodies. Could the mirror be hiding the dark bodies from them?"

Is remembered the night the dark bodies had come and surrounded John, caressing him. "They communicated with you?"

"Yes. Not well. And there was danger. They have little of what you might call life energy. They exist in sort of a dream state, physically as well as mentally. To get enough energy together to communicate, they must draw on the life forces of a living person."

"They could kill that way?"

"Not with malice. There is none of that sort of emotion in them. That takes too much energy. But yes, I think they could kill someone. I'm quite sure of it."

"Like the dog?" Is suddenly wanted to know. "He looked dead the whole time you were with the dark bodies. But he wasn't really . . ." She trailed off in confusion.

John gave a little laugh. "That dog is very interesting. You know, I never did see him."

Is was shocked. She had never questioned the dog's reality. He had seemed just like any other dog to her. She remembered trying to chase him back to Amil's cabin. He had dodged around Lark until Lark had understood the game and pinned his ears and gone after the dog as a horse will go after a cow.

"Lark saw it," she said to defend herself.

"I don't doubt you," John said. Then he was quiet for a long time, until Is asked him what he was thinking.

He gave a little embarrassed laugh. "Crazy stuff," he said and wanted to stop. But when he saw that Is really wanted to know, he continued. "Ondre would have told you that Amil and his cabin don't exist in our lifetimes. But when you and I went there, we could both see them, but when the dog followed us, only you could see it. And Lark," he added, giving his head a confused shake.

"I thought the dark bodies killed it," Is said. "It looked dead. But afterward, it seemed fine again." John was watching her so oddly, she couldn't stand it. "Tell me what it means."

"I don't know what it means, but I will tell you my wildest guess because it could be important." Then he hesitated so long Is thought he'd changed his mind. "One of the dark bodies that night wasn't a berserker."

"The dog?"

"I'm not sure. It didn't seem as . . . as alien as I would imagine a dog would seem. It was more like someone familiar, but not an old friend. I couldn't animate it enough to tell more about it. It would have killed me to give more. Evidently it nearly did kill the dog."

"John?" Is's voice sounded hoarse, as though she had been screaming, not just feeling as she should. "You are not making sense."

He looked at her and away again. "I think Amil rode in that dog somehow. To follow us. I think he left the dog's body to join the dark bodies, and then went back into the dog to follow us again. I don't have a shred of proof," he added.

"But you think Amil could do that? Become like a ghost, project himself into the dog, and get out of it again?"

"I don't know. Put that way, it sounds too fantastic. I only know what I felt."

Is took a moment to organize her thoughts. "If Amil did those things . . . and he wasn't created by the Alliance the way the mirror was, and besides, he lived before it was invented . . . If he could do all the things he did with the dog, then you should ask him for answers, not go back inside the mirror."

"Maybe," John said pensively, "and maybe I'm totally wrong."

Is jumped on his hesitation. "You should wait. We should go back to see Amil before you go into the mirror."

John was silent a long time, thinking it over while Is held her mental breath. Then he shook his head.

"Amil might have some answers. We *might* even be able to find him again. But I can't take the time now. I have to do this *now*. I have the right knowledge. I understand this computer better than anyone. I suffered to get here, and now is the time. Do you understand?"

Reluctantly Is nodded. This was too important for lies. "Yes." Her voice was thick. She understood about right timing. It was part of the chain, like death; it came when it would.

"Is," he said suddenly, soft-voiced, "I never wanted to use you this way. I wish I could do this alone. But I can't. I would have chosen someone else, even Ondre, over you. You've been hurt enough. But," he hesitated, wanting desperately to explain so she would understand, "it might be because of that that you have to be the one. I've seen you do things no one else can do. The ruin was a cabin when you were there, the Blueskins have a legend about you, you heard the dark bodies, you withstood the mirror's attacks." He spread his hands wide to show the enormity of the things she had done. "You've been *inside* the mirror. I know of exactly one other person who ever got inside the mirror and lived to tell about it." He gave her a crooked little smile. "Me." Then, serious, he said, "And, we're connected, aren't we, you and I, somehow? This link might work between us, when it might not work with someone else."

Is could only nod. The lump in her throat was too big.

"I love you," he said simply. "I love you." Then he drew her against him and held her, and after a very long while, he said softly, "I wish this could have been different."

Is nodded. She was crying inside, not because she was sad, but because she was happy, which didn't make any sense at all. But she understood John, and that gave her joy. More than life itself, John wanted to know about the mirror. Is could understand not caring about living. Many times in her life she had wished to be dead. If the mirror killed her—she was willing to risk that. But she didn't have much to lose. John did. He had his people and their love, and Ondre's love. If she had had such things, she was not sure she would have been able to give them up. She did not even want to give John up, and they had not had anything but a very strange and mixed-up friendship. It was one thing to desire knowledge. It was another for John to be willing to lose everything he had. Is did not think she had that sort of courage, but she would help John, because he did have it.

There wasn't any more need for talk. John stood up and took her hand, and they walked into the mirror.

It looked the same. There was the same silvery-gray fog that wasn't fog, that tingled her skin. But Is thought they had entered a different "room," this time. There were no berserker memories to see here, and it felt different. The tingling wasn't just on her skin; it was somehow inside her mind. She felt as if she wanted to scratch but didn't know where she itched. It was intensely unpleasant. She began to feel very irritated. She wanted to pull away from John. She wanted to leave this stupid place. It was hard to remember why she was supposed to stay. She had to focus her attention on John. But she was in some sort of mind-set where emotions were just an irritation.

In an instant all that changed. She was swept by one emotion after another—rage, terror, love, sorrow—complete with their physical manifestations in her body. Fortunately each one only lasted a moment. She did not have time to act on any of them.

Suddenly she was calm, suspended somehow with no emotion and no thought. Radiant. Silent. Cessation of all.

That lasted an amount of time that was neither long nor short.

The other presence swept her with an embrace, so loving, so radiant, so filled with joy it was indescribable. Is lost herself in that union.

. . . *This is of me,* it tried to instruct her, and she could hear/feel how there was something other-than-self. *That is of the mirror,* and she could see/taste how that was so. *This is how to access memory,* it told her, and she was flooded with sight, sound, smell, sensation. *This is how to sort your memories from mine,* it instructed her, but she was having fun being John. This was how it felt to be a boy, having boy problems. This was how it felt to be loved by a family, to have real friends, teachers who loved you—to have love and support everywhere.

It was a long time before she reined herself in. By then she'd run through all John's most intimate, most embarrassing, most tender moments. He hadn't made a move to stop her.

Is knew how it was to be a boy becoming a man, a man with a woman, and without one. She knew his worst disasters, his secret fears, his hopes, and the things that shamed him.

Now she was ashamed of herself. She had had no right to take all that. She wouldn't want him running through her memories that way. She wanted to withdraw.

He showed her how to do that too.

From the distance of the encapsulated, other-excluding self Is formed around herself, she extended a tentative touch. Yes, he was still there. She formed an apology. He accepted it, she thought. It was hard to tell. Everything was getting very distant.

Something pushed against her. She pushed it away, increasing the walls around her encapsuled self. Sharp pain shot through her. Blinding light. Searing heat. No oxygen. *This is how to let me reach you.* It was gone.

She clung to her shattered walls, shaken, frightened, violated. Nothing else happened, but she was afraid of the power John had shown he had over her. She had always hated the power men had over women. Because he was stronger, because he *could* rape, she had to fear him. After a lengthless period of time, after she got done being angry at him—at all men—she got angry at herself. It was her fear that gave men power over her. If she took away that fear, she took away that power.

How could she not fear the kind of violation she had just been through?

How could she not fear rape?

She worked on these things a long time. Mental understanding was a start, but only a start. She could not erase the fear with it. Action was needed.

She used the information John had thrust into her to open her shield. Yes, he was still there. She could bridge across to him.

He was full of apology. *I was going to lose you. You wouldn't have known how to get back out of there. I'm sorry. I should have taught you the bridge before the wall. I really didn't know how much I'd hurt you. I felt I had to do it. I'm sorry . . . sorry . . . sorry . . .*

She withdrew and he didn't try to follow. OK, that had been very brave of her, she thought, cynical of herself. She could reach out and withdraw. Very brave. So why was she still afraid? Because that wasn't good enough. Is knew what she was going to have to do.

She reached out a little tentatively and touched him. His quick joy and continued apology reached her. She gave him a little bit of a push, akin to saying, "Shut up," startling him.

When she had his attention, she began disassembling the wall, opening the link wide.

You don't have to. She could feel him trying to hold back. He wasn't able to. He came flowing into her, into all her most intimate moments, her fears, her embarrassments, her hopes, her woman-ness.

The memories washed through them—sight, sound, smell, and pain. Her mother's blood was as vivid as Riding Master Masley's touch. She laid it all bare, and she was defenseless and very, very sorry. John would see how twisted, and frightened, and truly ugly she was. She could never be someone as beautiful, confident, loved, or loving as any one of his people. He would abhor her.

He was saying something, saying it over and over again. It didn't have any words. It didn't need any words. It meant he cared for her. It meant he forgave her the things she hadn't forgiven herself. It meant he deeply appreciated her allowing him to do this. He understood her fear, and the courage it had taken to let him see her this way. He cherished her beauty.

Beauty? she asked.

Yes, her uniqueness. Her intricateness. Her difference. She accepted that because that was the way she welcomed/ loved him.

His joy sparked hers. They were together in their intimacy a long time.

We must go on now, he finally said.

Yes. It wasn't really possible for either one of them to be sad. They rearranged the linkage until it was more distant and more formal, more like speech. But what they had shared was inside both of them.

How do I go? she asked him, and suddenly she was falling. She landed on the meadow. There was no fog, no mirror. Both horses grazed nearby.

John!

Wait. Please.

-XIX-

Is rode Lark, and the mare followed behind. She'd put John's saddle and all of his equipment on the mare. His people never wasted anything.

The meadow where she had last seen Ondre's group was empty, hay stacked neatly. The horse droppings were old and cold.

The wagon tracks were easy to follow. At the edge of the bowl, Is spotted three scouts. They stood with their horses silhouetted against the skyline so she would see them. She let Lark move toward them at his own pace. Only two scouts came down to ride with her. They could see John's empty saddle. They didn't say anything. Is left it like that.

The next day Ondre met her. His mare looked as if he had ridden all night, but he didn't question her. He just rode up and dismounted. After a moment Is dismounted too, and he hugged her. He didn't say a word. When he let go of her, he stroked Celeste's face, and Is saw the tears in his eyes as he remounted his own horse.

Is remembered the first time she had seen Ondre, galloping to meet his brother, and how they had hugged and laughed, and the teasing that had started almost immediately. For the first time in what seemed a very long time she thought of Petre.

The people came out of the camp to watch them approach. This time no one ran from the crowd to welcome John. No children cantered out on reluctant brood mares. Is watched as though this were happening to someone else,

cataloging the similarities and differences. Even Lark seemed
to feel the difference. Although he arched his neck and
whinnied a few times, he did not prance and rear. He was
tired and underfed. Is stroked his neck, promising him good
care now.

Ellie appeared at her side when she dismounted. "I'm so
sorry," she said feelingly. Is let Ellie hug her. Other people
touched her, saying gentle things to her.

"Can we talk now?" she asked Ellie.

"Wouldn't you rather rest first?"

Is shook her head. Rest? Rest was not something that
applied to her anymore. There was sleep with its dreams and
pain, and painful awakenings. There had been hours of
sitting, doing nothing, staring at nothing, and not caring, but
not rest. There had been hours of sitting in the saddle,
hypnotized by the horse's steady rhythm, thinking nothing,
but not rest.

She heard Ellie speak to other people around them. She
watched Ondre give the horses to a young man, who led
them away to care for them. John's mare would be Ondre's
now. Is felt an unexpected tug of pain, but it was gone in an
instant. She slipped Lark's saddle off and let him follow the
mares. She let Ellie lead her. She drank the water Ellie gave
her. She looked at the people who spoke to her. She tried to
see them; she tried to respond. She couldn't remember their
names. They didn't seem real. *She* did not seem real.

. . . The people were seated, waiting for her to speak.

Is told them about finding the mirror. She told them how
she and John had gone inside it and John had used it to fix
his speech. She told them what he had wanted to tell them:
The mirror was made by the Alliance, and for the express
purpose of killing the berserkers.

"What he didn't know was why. What purpose the whole
thing had. The knowledge was off-limits to him as a
research scholar. He was just supposed to do what he was
told. There were people, higher up, who knew what it was
all for.

"John got caught trying to find out more. The Alliance probably didn't realize he was a spy from the Hluit. They did what they usually do to people who want to know too much, making it so he couldn't tell anyone anything he did learn. He said it was a refined version of cutting out a person's tongue. They can do it without ruining the person's mind. In some cases the person can keep right on working for them; they haven't ruined their 'tool.' " Is listened to her own expressionless voice and felt none of the anger and horror she knew other people were feeling.

"They didn't try to kill John until he tried to escape. He would never have eaten the poisoned trail rations if he had stayed there and continued to do his job. It was sort of a trial and execution all wrapped up in one."

She found Ondre's face in the group. What his brother had been through should have been enough. John had shown enough courage in getting into the Alliance and spying on them. He had suffered enough. He did not have to go to the mirror. No one would have blamed him. No one would even have known. But that had not been enough for John. Even after he had repaired the linkage in his brain, and could have returned to his people and told them what he knew, he had needed to give more.

"John wanted to learn more," she told Ondre. "He was in the position to learn the most, the fastest. He thought it was very important for all of you. He knew there was a good chance the mirror would kill him. But he knew I would report everything to you." She could have refused. She could have run away from him. She could have saved his life. Ondre must know that.

But there had been the other thing, the way John had made her feel. He had done what he had done out of a feeling of incredible love and gratitude. It was right. It was more important than his life. In the end, he was not afraid. His life was joyously given because of his love for his people, his appreciation for what the Hluit had made of their society, and his need to protect that.

While Is had been with him, she had been caught up in his feeling of optimism and gratitude. She had experienced love and joy and generosity the way John did. She had understood the rightness of his actions.

Now it was all gone, changed to pain. Even her memory of that feeling no longer made sense.

She had stopped talking. People were waiting.

"I'm sorry." Her lips moved. There was no sound in the words.

Ondre came across the circle to her. He took her hands. She could not respond even enough to look away from his eyes.

"You did the right thing for John. I know him. He needed to do what he did. You gave him a great gift by understanding and helping him."

That was how it had seemed.

"You did a great thing for all of us, Is. Forgive yourself." That was Ellie. Is had seen how much she also loved John, and she loved John's brother even more. Ondre's pain was her pain.

"Aren't you . . . doesn't it . . . ?" Is asked them.

"Hurt? Yes," Ondre said. "Many things in life hurt. But you can stand them. You can always stand them, if you . . . if you stay *true* in your heart."

Is looked away from them then. She could not let them see that there was nothing left in her heart except pain. Pain and confusion. She didn't have their confidence. She didn't have their broad base of love, or their belief system. They had given her a glimpse of all those things, but they were not "hers." She had seen something bigger and more wonderful than she had ever understood love to be, and now it was gone. Gone with John. Gone from her heart, locked away from her. She would deliver the rest of John's message, then she would go. She could not stay among the Hluit with her false heart; and she could not stay because the Alliance now *knew* she and Lark were alive. The berserker she had helped had seen her and Lark. He would have fasted that back to the Alliance at his death. She listened to her voice resume its story.

She told how she and John had gone into the mirror a second time and John had forged the link with her. All she said of that incredible link was that it worked. She could talk to John while he was inside the mirror and she was outside.

He'd gotten really clever at accessing its memories, and Is tried to explain about walking through its memories. You could see them, and then you could get inside them too.

John had done that five or six days. Is didn't tell them about the nights, when they lay together in that link, making love. She didn't try to explain how there had been no room for anything but joy in that link even though the end was so near.

She listened to her own voice telling the people about downloaded berserkers, about interactive holograms, about death agonies powering fast transmissions to the Alliance. She was vaguely amazed that she understood the language she was using.

She explained how the mirror disassembled the berserkers and reassembled them, and how the Alliance sent continually more complex berserkers.

"The mirror does not think of itself as killing the berserkers; it thinks of preserving them. That is what the Alliance wants it to do . . . but not just preserve someone after they're dead; they want it to actually keep them in some living, changing form." She let them think a moment about that. "A few of the very highest people in the Alliance are trying to create eternal life for themselves.

"The Alliance keeps track of the mirror's progress by what the berserkers fast back to them. The mirror thinks of the Alliance as the Silent Watcher. It wasn't troubled by being watched. It wasn't in its program to fear, or distrust, or really to question anything about itself or its program.

"But it's a special kind of computer. It can learn, and it can teach itself to learn. It had to be set up that way because it has to learn to do something its makers don't know how to do. They can't teach it. It has to teach itself. They could only give it the program, the *desire,* to learn this thing.

"That was all fine, until it happened to kill a Hluit. It 'preserved' that man too. In his mind it found more complex things than in any berserker's mind. It found things it wasn't ready to understand. From the Hluit's distrust of the Alliance, it learned distrust. From that man's fear of death—which none of the berserkers had—it learned something about death. Before that, it had killed without malice, or anger, or any understanding of what it was doing. It was obeying its program, without questions.

"But the Hluit had many questions in his mind. From his questions, the mirror learned to question the motivation of the Silent Watcher.

"Because the mirror is capable of teaching itself to learn, and it is not under anyone's guidance when it learns, it draws its own conclusions. Amazingly quickly it put together the concepts of placing one self above another, of winning and losing, of lying, of hiding, of war. And of what death means.

"John wasn't able to determine what it really 'thinks' about the Alliance, but we know that it is now hiding its best work from them. It has completed what the Alliance programmed it to do, but the Alliance doesn't know. We think it understands that the Alliance can 'kill' it, turn it off. We think it's trying to preserve itself by pretending it hasn't completed its program.

"The Alliance believes all the mirror can do is download berserkers and store them as interactive holos. That isn't good enough. That isn't really life after death. They want the mirror to take the next step and learn how to capture the living, changing personality. So the Alliance keeps feeding it more complex berserkers in hopes it will create something more suitable for their ambitions of life after death.

"Meanwhile, the mirror *has* created what the Alliance wanted."

"The dark bodies," Ondre said.

"Yes."

Ellie breathed a curse.

"They're alive. They are the real persons, not just up to the moment they died, but after too. But the mirror cannot bring them inside itself because it fears the Alliance will be able to find out about them. So it leaves them outside, and unpowered. They have no energy except other people's agony."

"So they could speak to John, because of the pain he was in, not being able to tell us what he had learned. And you could hear them, because, because of what the Alliance has put you through."

"Yes."

Ondre met her eyes for a long moment. "Did it make John into a dark body?"

"Not that I . . . could find. He was in the mirror, he had just finished transmitting some knowledge to me, then, there was a flash. Like . . . I'm not sure if it was bright or loud. It . . . After it, there was . . . my brain . . . was different. I can remember these things, to tell them to you, because, because I was . . . told, programmed, to do it. But before, I remember that I could taste memory, and smell sight, and touch. . . ." She stopped because she couldn't tell them how she had touched John.

. . . Ellie was touching her. Outside, distant, incompletely.

"That's enough for now, Is. You need food and sleep." Ellie's body had told her body to stand up. It told her body to walk. Is watched the interaction, incurious, and distant.

Only a few mouthfuls of food would go down. The rest was impossible beyond even Ellie's control of her body. The tea was bitter, and it made Is sleep. Her voice told one last thing.

"The Alliance knows I'm here. A berserker saw me before he died. He spoke to me. I touched him. He saw Lark."

-XX-

Is woke to heavy pain, like a thick blanket pressing her down, warming her through and through. There was no place in her that it didn't reach. She opened her eyes inside of a tent. She should get up . . . but she was unable to find the energy.

She didn't notice Petre until he spoke.

"Hello."

She didn't even try to use her voice. She couldn't respond to him.

He began to talk. He told her all kinds of things she should have wanted to know: A special regrouping had been called. A full council would meet. There would be discussions. All the people would hear John's story. They would decide what to do.

When she turned her head away, he fell silent. After a while he said, "I just wanted you to know I'm sorry. I'll do anything I can."

"Thank you." She had to try twice to get sound into the words. Because it was polite. Because it wasn't Petre's fault. He'd always been good to her. He just didn't know, didn't understand anything.

She heard him get up. "I'll go now."

She lay awhile, relieved of his presence, alone with the aloneness that had become the only presence she could tolerate. But she was not done. People would have questions. She would answer everything she could. Then she would leave. She didn't think about where she would go.

Her body would take her back to the mirror. She wouldn't
take Lark. It didn't matter how she got herself killed. The
people could have Lark for the spring breeding. Then they'd
have to kill him. Or maybe they'd give him back to the
Alliance. That might save a lot of lives. Maybe she'd ask
them to do that. Petre would loan her a horse if she asked
him, but she wouldn't. She'd take one of Ondre's. He'd
understand, and a canny, old brood mare would be able to
find her way back to the people once Is was dead.

She got up and went out. People were stacking hay. For
a moment it was as though nothing had changed for them.
They had not understood the enormity of what John had
given them. Their lives were no different. For a moment Is
was furious at all of them. Then, as suddenly as it had come,
the emotion was gone, swallowed by the colorless void in
which she now lived.

Ellie came over and tried to get her to eat some breakfast,
but Is could not swallow anything, so Ellie began to talk.

Men from the Alliance had come again while Is had been
in the mountains with John. The Blueskins had been
blocking the troopers, as the Hluit had suspected they might,
but this contingent was of scholars and ambassadors. The
Blueskins had let them through.

"They were very polite, this time, no threats at all. They
wanted to talk to you. That's all. They said. They offered
you amnesty. All crimes forgiven. Work with horses. Early
retirement. Or stay here. Whatever you want."

"And Lark?"

"Lark goes with them."

When Is didn't respond, Ellie continued. "It's hard to
believe the Alliance would go to *this* much trouble over one
war-horse, Is?" The last word turned it into a question, but
Is could not seem to get herself to speak.

"We are forced to certain conclusions," Ellie continued.
"There must be something *very* special about this horse, or
about his berserker."

"No." Is found her voice abruptly. "It's not the berserker."

Then, realizing how harshly she'd spoken to Ellie, she tried to soften it with more explanation. "If it was the berserker, they could recalibrate another horse's chip for him. That's happened before. Not every horse that goes into training makes it. Some of them get injured, or go lame, or just don't turn out right. It doesn't happen very often because the government has put so much effort into the breeding program, and all the young horses are screened before they're sent to the trainers, but it has happened occasionally."

"So it *is* Lark," Ellie said heavily. Ondre, and Petre, and everyone else who was nearby had come over to listen.

"Is," Ondre spoke to her gently, "you've handled warhorses most of your life. How is Lark different from the others?"

Is tried to focus herself and think. The bond she had with Lark was deeper than with any horse before, but it wasn't, in essence, different. Lark had been easier to train than most, but again, not essentially different. He was smart, willing, and cooperative, but she could say that about a lot of horses. He was certainly the gentlest stallion she'd ever handled.

"I think . . ." And her tongue stopped at the incredible words she had been about to say. "I think," she started again, stubbornly, "Lark doesn't just take his rider over distance; sometimes he took me over time." Said, they were just words on the air. She heard Ondre release his breath.

"The Blueskin's legend, and when you heard John talk, could have been images the mirror projected, but not Amil's cabin. Amil's cabin was the piece that never fit."

"But John and his mare went there too," Is found herself objecting weakly.

"Uh-huh." Ondre drew out the sound. He had no answer for that. "But that wasn't the only time something of that nature happened, Is. Remember, before you met John, when you saw the Blueskins and started the landslide running away, but they never heard you. They never came to investigate. And the time you saw the government riders talking to Blueskins, and you rode by them right out in the open, because you somehow knew they couldn't see you." He had become very intense.

There had been another time too. Although Is had not realized it then. The time she had run away from John, and Lark had stumbled, but instead of falling they were suddenly standing in a meadow. She remembered how she had noticed that the grass was spring green. No one had found her there all day. But when she slept, the Blueskins had come, and she remembered how she had noticed, as they walked out of the valley, how the grass swished with the dry sound of late summer. She had not thought anything about it then, but she had *noticed*. She came out of her own thoughts in time to hear Ondre say, "I'm afraid the Alliance may know a good deal more than John supposed. How else could they have created a horse like Lark? His ability to move through time is similar to the mirror's ability to throw images back in time, and perhaps forward, for all we know."

"Yes," a woman, whose name Is had forgotten, spoke. "The disorienting effects of the herd fogs also seem related. And whether the Alliance has learned to manipulate these things from the mirror, or whether it taught the mirror, it doesn't matter. They both know now."

"So it might not be enough to just shut the mirror off," Petre said, and Is was left whirling. She had not even tried to put any of this together. But the other people seemed unsurprised. They must have talked all night. They were way ahead of her.

"Even if that were possible, no," Ondre confirmed. "It would not stop the Alliance. They can build another one."

"And it isn't even necessary to have a computer involved, if Amil could follow John and Is across time in the body of a dog," Ellie put in.

Everyone was silent a moment considering the impossibility of Ellie's words. Finally the woman who had spoken before said, "It is hard to accept without more knowledge. It would be necessary to return to Amil's."

Is felt that the suggestion was aimed at her, but not one person even glanced at her to see how she was taking it. She was free to do, or not do, what she chose. She did not want choices. She did not want life. She missed most of the discussion, and only heard someone say, "We can't do anything until we've had a full council meeting, anyway."

"Yes, unlike the Alliance, we must consider not only the consequences of our actions, but the morality of them. Do we have the right to interfere? It is not science and knowledge that is harmful, it is the fact that the Alliance has no morality, no ethical guidelines to help them decide what to do with their discoveries. Even the eternal life they are after is not necessarily 'bad.'"

"But they will put it to bad uses, you can be assured," someone else added. And while the people talked, Petre leaned over to Is and spoke softly.

"They will discuss it forever, and they will decide they must have more information first. That is what always happens."

His tone expressed an indulgent sort of impatience. He believed in government by the council enough that he would not go against its decision, and yet he thought they were too slow and too cautious. Is wondered what he thought the Hluit should do.

"Some will say it is not our business how the Alliance governs their own people," Petre explained. "Others will want us to look to our own future, saying we may find some way to use our knowledge to pressure the Alliance to recognize us as a sovereign people and force them to negotiate a truce with us. We have been looking for just such a leverage point, and this could be it.

"Others will want to go further than threatening the Alliance, saying that any truce the Alliance makes, it will break whenever it suits them. They will want to use whatever we learn to tear down the Alliance government.

And others will take the opposite side, and not want to do anything, believing we can just go on forever depending on the good graces of the Alliance for our continued existence.

"But the one thing they will agree on is that we need more information."

Is had never thought about the Hluit having a chance against the Alliance. Her own problems had centered around Lark. Turning him over to the Alliance seemed like a worse and worse idea. Whatever use they intended for him, Is doubted it would be any good for anyone except a few high officials. Leaving him with the Hluit would mean people would get killed over him. Is didn't doubt that the Alliance wanted him back badly enough to kill all the Hluit if they had to. She was stuck with one answer: take him with her. But he'd find his way back here when she was dead. That meant she had to stay alive, and that meant she shouldn't go back to the mirror seeking death.

Questions crowded her mind. Would Lark still berserk when he was older? Maybe that was not built into him. Maybe he had never been intended to face the mirror. Could he be trained to get control of his time-traveling ability? What triggered it? Could he be trained to use it on some signal from her? Or was it something only his specially developed berserker could control? What were its limitations? Would Lark use it someday and disappear from her life? Could Lark's ability somehow help the Hluit?

She had no answers, but more and more Amil's cabin seemed like the place to find them. Is walked away from the others to think. She had not wanted options. She wanted to go back to the mirror and get herself killed. She did not want to be a hologram, or a dark body. She wanted to be plain and simply, truly dead.

Then she wouldn't have to worry if there was some remnant of John left somewhere. She wouldn't have to worry about what happened to Lark, or to John's people.

She knew that was a wrong and selfish way to think. It was the antithesis of what John had felt and done. She was letting him down, and letting her parents down again—worse than she'd ever let them down in the government school—letting Ondre, and Ellie, and all the Hluit down, letting Lark down. But going on with this pain, looking for answers, trying to help the Hluit, was too much to ask of herself. She tried to make herself want to do the right thing. But all she wanted was death.

By the time Is had faced that decision, it was too late in the day to leave without arousing suspicion. She did not want anyone following her to stop her. Walking among John's family was like treason. Accepting more hospitality from them was impossible. She pitched her own tent and refused food, and the drug that had made her sleep the night before.

When it was dark, she went inside her tent long enough to make everyone think she had gone to bed, but she could not sleep. After a while she came back out to sit under the sky, feeling the land all around her. She was not afraid of her decision to die, and yet she could not be alone with herself, cut off from the land this night. Her thoughts drifted idly . . . the bad times she had endured, the good times that always got snatched away from her . . . but she did not feel sorry for herself. At least she had had those good times. She had met the Hluit. She had had that incredible link with John. She had had wonderful horses. It was only that now there was too much pain and she was too small to hold it all, and too much a product of the government schools to do what was right.

She didn't hear Petre come up. She didn't have time to send him away before he was already sitting beside her. She was thinking what to say to get rid of him, without arousing suspicion, when he spoke.

"Is, don't let yourself down."

She didn't allow herself to know what he meant. "Oh, I'm not going to let anyone down," she lied to him.

"Oh," he said. "You are not about to ride out of here as

soon as you can see the mountains. You are not going to go get yourself killed."

They weren't even questions. They were her plan exactly, and he had no right to know them. Suddenly lying was too false for her even in her mood.

"It's none of your business."

"No, of course not. A person I care more about than anyone in the world is about to make a very bad mistake. Of course it's none of my business."

All the lies Is had been planning disappeared. "Petre, don't. I'm not John. I can't do this. I'm not like your people. I'm an Alliance thing. I'm broken. I'm dirty. I just want out."

"Then why does it bother you?"

"It doesn't."

"Don't lie, Is. This might be the last conversation we ever have."

"OK," she agreed to the rule. "I can't do what your people want. I can't go back to Amil's. I don't have the strength. I don't love enough to do it for love. It was all John's love before. All of it. Now that he's gone, it's gone. I don't have any of my own. No love. No strength. No courage." He'd asked for honesty, and damn him, she'd give it to him.

"So, I ask again, why does it bother you so much?"

"Because I know I should feel these things, and I don't."

"But you will again. You need to give yourself time."

"Sure, and watch your people get slaughtered."

"They won't get slaughtered."

"Good, then I don't have to worry about it."

"No, you don't have to worry about it when you're dead. You don't have to give us anything, Is. You're the only one who might be able to ride Lark back to Amil's place. But you don't have to do that, because you don't love us. You have chosen not to owe us anything."

"That's right," she said. "I am choosing my own freedom. I am being responsible only for myself. I do not choose to

be responsible for your people." She spouted Hluit philoso-
phy back at him. Let him answer that one.

But Petre didn't argue with her. He said, "It is not for the
people that you have to do this. You have to do it for
yourself. You owe yourself, not us."

That made no sense. "I owe myself what?" she asked
angrily, and heard how her voice sounded like a petulant
child's.

"You owe yourself the chance to prove to yourself you
are a good person. You can give from love. You are not 'an
Alliance thing.' You're tougher than that, Is. You aren't
going to let those Alliance bastards beat you in the end, are
you?"

"What do you mean?" Some small part of her wanted to
hear this.

"You always fought them. Even when you couldn't do it
openly. Even when you were all alone. You don't have to be
alone now."

She saw what he was going to say. He would come with
her to Amil's.

"No. Petre, I don't want you with me."

"Honesty?"

"Damn you. I can't love you. I don't. I never will. Never."

"I'm not asking for your love. I'm only asking you to do
the right thing, for yourself. And I'm offering to go with
you, just to be your companion, just to help you in whatever
ways I can."

She couldn't ask that of Petre, especially not Petre.

"It *can't* be worth it to you."

"Let me decide what's of what worth to me. I just spent
three terrible weeks because I decided that having your
company couldn't possibly be as important as having a
sexual relationship. Because I decided that wasting my life
on some strange woman who was in love with someone else
couldn't be as important as finding a woman among my own
people who wanted me. Is, I've already tried giving you up.

I don't want to make that mistake again. If I can be nothing more than your companion, that is what I will be."

He was pleading with her, raw, open, and totally vulnerable, and Is felt stunned. She had never expected to see Petre this way. He had always been controlled, always gallant, always putting her needs first. But here he was stripped of all control, exposing what he really felt. She could only imagine the suffering that had driven him to this desperation.

"Petre." She was surprised at how gentle her voice sounded. "I *can't* give you anything."

"I know." She heard him swallow. "I have something to give you."

"No. I can't accept it."

"You can't accept it because you don't understand what it is. You can't accept it because you don't understand that you can't reject it. It is already given. You have no control of that. You never did."

His words brought all her arguments up short. *You don't understand what it is.* She closed her eyes against the sudden pain. She was ready to accept the truth of what he said; she did not understand what he was offering her.

"I don't know. . . ." The other decision was so much easier. So much safer. *You're tougher than that, Is.* "I can't promise anything."

"I know. Just do this and don't worry about me."

"I don't even know if I can find Amil's cabin again. I don't know how to make Lark do that."

"We can try."

She thought about it. The other option, death, would always be there. If this didn't work . . . If she tried, and couldn't . . . It was a coward's way to think, but she needed to know that that out was there. To suffer this much for other people, to allow herself to be loved, to risk caring—all was terrifying to her. She couldn't take more pain. She couldn't trust. She didn't owe anyone anything. But there was a place in her heart that knew none of that was the issue. The issue was what was right. Running away, when she was in the best position to help, was wrong.

Petre had been sitting silently beside her. She supposed he was waiting for her to say something. "OK, I'll try to find Amil's," she told him.

"May I come with you?"

It was his decision. *If people would be responsible for themselves and let others be responsible for their selves . . .* He was in charge of himself. She had no more right to forbid than to allow.

"If that is what you want to do."

He stood up. "Thank you." It was almost a whisper, inappropriate words because there were none appropriate. She heard him walk away.

He was waiting for her when she came out of her tent in the morning. He came up out of the mist, leading John's mare, saddled, and packed, and ready to go. Is's heart wanted to stop. No, this would be too much pain. She should never have agreed to this.

Celeste came forward and sniffed her hand. Her delicate ears were pricked, her deep, intelligent eyes looked into Is's. She raised her head and touched Is's cheek daintily with her soft nose. Petre stood back, watching. Is raised her eyes to him. This was the right choice.